stay with me

ROMANCE
BEN

JULES
BENNETT

ZEBRA BOOKS
KENSINGTON PUBLISHING CORP.
http://www.kensingtonbooks.com

ZEBRA BOOKS are published by

Kensington Publishing Corp.
119 West 40th Street
New York, NY 10018

All Kensington titles, imprints, and distributed lines are available at special quantity discounts for bulk purchases for sales promotion, premiums, fund-raising, educational, or institutional use.

Special book excerpts or customized printings can also be created to fit specific needs. For details, write or phone the office of the Kensington Sales Manager: Attn.: Sales Department. Kensington Publishing Corp., 119 West 40th Street, New York, NY 10018. Phone: 1-800-221-2647.

Zebra and the Z logo Reg. U.S. Pat. & TM Off.

First Printing: April 2018
ISBN-13: 978-1-4201-4496-3
ISBN-10: 1-4201-4496-0

eISBN-13: 978-1-4201-4497-0
eISBN-10: 1-4201-4497-9

10 9 8 7 6 5 4 3 2 1

Printed in the United States of America

Chapter One

Get it, get out, get the job done.

The mantra Olivia Daniels lived by had taken her from small-town girl to kick-ass city woman—stepping over men on her way to the top. So many from this tiny suburb of Savannah said she couldn't, wouldn't make it when she set out at eighteen to start her adult life in a big city. She'd intended to prove them all wrong and she was one promotion away from having all her goals met.

Olivia had certainly never planned to return to Haven, Georgia, ever again . . . yet here she stood at the very same place that held so much of her past.

Glancing around the open airfield, Olivia squinted behind her sunglasses at the bright morning sun. The hangars, if that's what people called the old rusted metal heaps, sat next to another building that was just as run-down. The main building had mostly been wasted space, save for the small room her father had used as his office.

With no paved lot and barely a functional sidewalk connecting the main building to the first hangar, it was clear this place could use a fresh start—or a wrecking ball. Gutters dangled precariously, the office roof looked as if it were made of sandpaper versus shingles, and the windows were so grimy it was unlikely anyone had seen in or out of them in the past decade.

The only positive thing Olivia could say is the "landscaping" didn't look as mistreated—if wildflowers counted as landscaping. There were tulips and daffodils popping up as far as the eye could see, which was pretty far considering this dump was in the middle of godforsaken nowhere.

So what if Haven was her hometown? She wasn't one to look at the world through rose-colored glasses—and even if she were, she doubted that they could help this heap.

A twinge of guilt coursed through her at her initial thoughts since leaving so long ago. This had been her father's life. Literally. He spent every single day at this airport, leaving Olivia and her mother mostly alone. He claimed it was for the income, but they hadn't had much, so she always figured he'd just rather avoid his family.

Olivia couldn't afford to get nostalgic and from her first impressions, nothing here was going to change her mind. She was going to make this quick and painless, make this business deal and get back to Atlanta before anyone knew she was even in town.

She was used to getting what she wanted, not because she fell into it, but because she busted her butt and worked hard to prove she deserved it. Right now, she was laying eyes on her next acquisition, if one could call it that. Too bad someone else currently owned the other half.

Get in, get out, get the job done.

Olivia repeated the reminder—she wasn't leaving today until she got the deed in full.

Pulling in a deep breath, Olivia straightened her pale pink suit jacket and headed toward the office. When she reached the back door, she rehearsed her speech once more.

Confidence and preparation were key to any good negotiation. Olivia learned early on that the only thing that beat tenacity was being prepared to face your nemesis.

"Livie Daniels."

She came to a dead stop. Who the hell called her Livie anymore? So much for that mental pep talk she'd just given herself. She wasn't ready to be thrown into the past with the simple drop of a name she had so long ago altered. Livie no longer existed . . . not even in Haven.

Shielding her eyes from the sun, Olivia put her hand over her forehead and turned toward the hangars. And just like that, nostalgia hit her as her past sauntered toward her outfitted with broad shoulders, a greasy T-shirt, equally greasy jeans, and a crooked smile.

Jackson Morgan.

Holy . . .

Where had all those muscles come from? He'd been thirteen and hanging around the airport with her father when she'd left. A gangly teen with an awkward overbite.

He was neither gangly nor overbiting now.

Breathe, Olivia. He's just a man. Offer the money and get out.

"Olivia," she stated when he was within just a few feet.

He tipped his head. "Pardon?"

Those eyes were just as striking blue as she recalled. A lock of coal black hair hung down on his forehead. The rest of his thick hair seemed just as unruly. Totally the opposite of anything she'd ever considered her type since she left Haven and had her heart broken by a country boy.

So the tingling in her belly had to be from hunger, that's all. She refused to get her feathers ruffled over an attractive man. She also refused to allow anymore hick-like sayings to creep into her head.

"Nobody calls me Livie anymore."

Jackson shrugged. "I didn't get the memo, text, or however you communicate with those city folks—to me you're Livie. But none of that changes the question. What do you want? I assume you're here to see me, considering I'm the only one around."

She stared, trying to find some semblance of the quiet, awkwardly thin boy she'd last seen when she lived here. "You look quite a bit different than I remembered."

"Military," he replied, as if that one word summed up everything.

Angling her body so the sun was at her back, she dropped her hand to her side. "Is there somewhere we can go to get out of this heat and discuss the property?"

"Oh, there's nothing to discuss unless you want to help fix faulty air controls on a Cessna Skyhawk."

"Not without my socket wrench."

The sarcasm flooded out of her before she could stop herself. Damn him for baiting her.

Olivia was not going to explode. Pasting on a practiced smile, she crossed her arms over her chest. The sooner she could resolve this situation, the sooner she could get back to Atlanta and climb that last rung of the ladder at her firm . . . which was a whole other issue she didn't have the mental capacity for right now.

"You know full well why I'm here, so let's not play games." When he said nothing, she went on. "I'd like to talk to you about selling this property, Jackson."

"Jax." He took another step forward, then another until he stood close. Too close. "Nobody calls me Jackson anymore."

Obviously, they were not getting off on the right foot if he was already throwing her words back in her face.

"Anyway," she trudged on, trying to ignore those soul-piercing eyes. "I'm sure you're aware—"

He swiped a fingertip down her cheek.

"Wh-what are you doing?" she jerked backward, but ended up teetering in her heels.

In an instant, Jackson—or whatever he wanted to be

called—snaked an arm around her waist and caught her . . . his hand landing on her ass.

Olivia's breath caught in her throat as his hand remained firmly on her backside. Flattening her palms on his taut chest, she extracted herself.

"Get your hands off me."

His abrupt release had her stumbling back a few steps, finally catching her balance. Infuriating man.

"What were you doing?" she demanded.

"You had something on your cheek." He propped his hands on his narrow waist and appeared to be biting back a smile. "What were you saying?"

If he thought mocking her was going to get him anywhere, he was dead wrong. The city had been good to her but it had been hard—she'd worked with men who thought they could best her simply because she was a woman. She learned early on to never back away from a challenge.

"With acreage this size, the land is worth more if we can tear down these buildings and sell the empty space."

Jackson shifted his stance, his eyes holding her in place. "Are you that detached from everything outside your perfect world?"

"Excuse me?" How dare he talk to her like a child? And after he'd manhandled her with those filthy hands no less.

"You heard me. You can't just drive your fancy car in here, expect me to bow to your wishes, and be on your merry way."

Okay, so this wasn't going like she'd hoped. Why was Jackson treating her like a spoiled princess? She was fully prepared to make him an impressive offer—and he wasn't even open for a discussion. Who didn't like money?

"Listen, I understand your livelihood is wrapped up in this place." Appealing to his softer side should pay off—

if he even had one. "But, in the end, this would be the best scenario for you and for Haven."

One dark brow lifted. "And I'm sure you're not getting anything out of this?"

"Money, of course." But beyond that, Olivia wanted closure on this town once and for all.

"This is my life," he countered. "If you want to make money off this land, then I suggest you come up with some miracle on how to revamp the airport, because we sure as hell could use it. I want this place to live up to its full potential like it used to be. The concrete is all cracked, the buildings need new roofing, I won't even get into the plumbing issues in the office area."

Olivia opened her mouth, but closed it when Jackson turned on his booted heel and walked away. Really? Did he think he'd just ended this conversation? She was not leaving here without a firm resolution to her issue.

And just like that, the walls came down. Olivia could play hardball all she wanted, but at the end of the day Jackson had something she desperately needed. Not just for financial gains, but for her to keep her sanity. Otherwise, she might just crumble, something she swore she wouldn't do when her past came back to haunt her in the form of this half ownership fiasco.

Olivia marched right into the open hangar where she'd seen Jackson disappear. Nobody walked away from her—ever. That was a life lesson she learned long ago and made her into the business shark she was today.

Blinking against the sudden change from bright sunshine to a darker space, she glanced around the near-empty area. One plane sat near the closed bay door. She recognized the plane . . . she'd learned to fly in that Cessna.

Pulling in a deep breath, she forced herself to focus, but the door to the cockpit was open as Jackson leaned inside.

She was not looking at his butt in those worn jeans. She refused. But, damn it, that's all she could focus on and he . . . well, now he was just fighting dirty.

Smoothing a hand down her pencil skirt, Olivia prepared for battle.

Jax gritted his teeth as he checked the panel once again. He didn't have the time or the patience for some city slicker who thought she could come in and take charge . . . no matter what their past entailed.

Clearly, Olivia—"don't call me Livie"—wanted to keep a personal detachment. Fine, he could play her game. But he wasn't about to let her just sell this place out from under him. He had too much to lose if the airport was taken from him.

After she'd hightailed it out of town in her little sporty car and a whip of her short blond hair, Jax truly didn't think he'd ever see her again. Unfortunately, life happened and she was back for the first time since she'd been eighteen . . . with a more expensive flashy car and much longer hair in a paler shade of blond.

That punch of lust to his gut wasn't going to be a problem. There was no way he'd be persuaded by another beautiful woman ever again—he'd learned that lesson the hard way.

Just because she came strutting in claiming she now owned half, that meant nothing as far as he was concerned. Obviously, she was ignoring how this partnership came to be.

Livie Daniels was all business wrapped in a perfect, curvy package. That pink suit was a nice touch . . . if he found city chicks to his liking. Jax was rather amused at how she thought she could talk down to him like he had no idea what she was doing.

That whole "better for you and the town" speech had been a nice touch, but he'd been a senior airman in the United States Air Force. She'd have to do better than that if she was going to try to get on his good side.

"Excuse me."

Of course she'd followed him. Someone like Livie didn't like being told no. Well, she better get used to it because he wasn't selling his half. Ever. No amount of money could compete with loyalty and family—and Paul Daniels had been like a father to Jax.

Not only had he told her no, he'd ignored her, so that probably didn't make her happy either. Too damn bad. He didn't have time to cater to a pampered princess . . . no matter how sexy she looked in that suit wrapped over her curvaceous body. She was still trouble in stilettos and he had other things that needed his immediate attention.

Slowly Jax eased out of the cockpit, reached up and curled his hands around the wing, staring at her across the way. It was all he could do not to smile at the streak of grease across her cheek.

She hadn't had a thing on her when he'd swiped earlier, but he'd been in a mood and couldn't resist the petty maneuver of messing her up. He'd seen that bright red Beemer pull onto the grassy lot, had taken one look at her face, and known the prodigal daughter had returned.

The thirteen-year-old boy inside him didn't have to remind him how he'd had a silly crush on someone five years older than him, how he'd always felt awkward when she looked his way or flashed a smile. He was well beyond that kid now—and had the life lessons to know better than to get sidetracked.

Livie Daniels in all her perfection and class was an instant reminder of the last time he'd let lust guide his judgment. Never going down that path again.

She returned his stare as she crossed her arms over her

chest. Okay, time to draw this little meeting to a close. As much as he enjoyed the scenery, they were not going to come to an agreement right now . . . maybe never. And as long as he never agreed to sell, then she was at his mercy.

"I realize you don't want to be tied to this place," he started. "Believe me, I don't want you here either. But we both own an equal amount, so you're going to have to get along with me."

Her mouth dropped open on a gasp. "Excuse me? I'm buying you out. We don't have to get along or even be friends."

When she threw out an impressive number for his half, Jax raised a brow and whistled. He immediately thought of what he could do with that much cash, but instantly pushed pipe dreams aside. Selling his soul came at no price. He was proud of this life he'd created. Carrying on a legacy started by a man who meant everything to Jax was worth more than any amount of money offered.

Now more than ever, Jax knew life wasn't about cash. He had a daughter to look out for and to pass on the lessons he'd been taught—lessons in loyalty and love were priceless.

"Nice, but no thanks."

"You're being ridiculous," she scolded, as if her words would hurt him. He was immune at this point in his life.

"And you're not getting my half, so suck it up, Princess."

He moved around to the other side of the cockpit and opened the door. If he couldn't get this air vent working again, he was going to have to reschedule tomorrow's flight—and he couldn't exactly reschedule when the elderly couple needed to get to their granddaughter's wedding in Sarasota.

He had to pick up his daughter from preschool in a couple of hours and he really wanted to take her to the park and a movie, but he wouldn't be able to if he didn't get this work done. He couldn't exactly work when his unwanted guest wouldn't leave him alone to think.

He should've let her just fall on her ass earlier.

Heels clicked across the floor and he knew this fight was far from over. Whatever. He could handle her . . . he just didn't want to.

This place was more than just an airport. Jax had sought refuge here during the most pivotal point in his life. It was in these very walls that he found his passion in flying, which led him to become a pilot in the Air Force. So what if the place had seen better days? Maybe Livie needed to learn that the important things in life had nothing to do with how fresh the coat of paint on the walls was. It was because of this well-loved airport that he was able to return home to his daughter and provide a stable life for her.

He had some colossal mess-ups in his past, but finally he was getting things right. His bank account may not be padded, but that didn't mean near as much as integrity and being a good dad. Jax realized that Livie saw him as nothing more than a grease monkey, but that was her problem. He was long past caring what people thought of him.

There was only one female he cared about these days.

"You want more money? Is that it?"

Exhausted with this line of questioning, Jax turned from the plane, stopping short when she'd closed the gap and stood only a few feet in front of him. He'd be damned if that streak on her face didn't diminish her beauty. She most likely had men falling at her stiletto-covered feet, offering to do anything she wished. She'd be smart to learn he wasn't going to be one of those men simply because she had a pretty face and killer curves.

Jax's parents had passed when he'd been ten, and Jax

had to live with his grandfather. The man did the best he could, but he was older and tired, with his own set of health issues. So Jax had started hanging around the airport, taking a love to the skies . . . much like the late owner Livie still hadn't mentioned.

Propping his hands on his hips, Jax leveled his gaze.

"Someone like you won't get that I'm not able to be bought." He didn't care that her cheeks tinged with pink or that the muscle in her jaw ticked. He was pretty pissed himself. "Money has absolutely nothing to do with why I'm not selling my half."

Livie rolled her eyes. "Please. Everything comes down to money."

Wasn't that a sad statement? From her tone, he could tell she fully believed such nonsense. The girl he remembered didn't feel that way. Livie had raised money for a local animal shelter when she'd been a freshman in high school. She'd formed a group and had taken up an insane amount of donations. Even then she'd had the telling signs of a businesswoman and a leader. He wasn't much liking the detached woman she'd grown into.

"Loyalty and tradition have nothing to do with my finances and both of those are what makes up this airport. You know there's more to all of this than just a business transaction."

When she narrowed her eyes, he didn't back down. She may not have wanted to address the full picture, but he wasn't going to let her hide behind the proverbial elephant in the room.

"Well, you'd know it if you'd ever been home in the last sixteen years."

Her lips thinned and those eyes turned to slits. Yeah, he'd hit a nerve. Welcome to the club. She'd hit one as well barging into his airport and assuming she'd be welcome.

"I can see you're not in the mood to discuss business."

Uncrossing her arms, she straightened that already perfectly shaped jacket and hip-hugging skirt. The years had done her an unfair amount of favors. Who knew the woman could get more attractive?

"I am determined to sell this land, Jackson. You can't be so stubborn just because I'm the one making the offer. It's a good deal."

The image of his little girl running through the open hangar, her arms wide, her excitement when she took her first plane ride, the fact that this was his home . . . absolutely priceless. Piper had planted the bulbs last spring, hoping to see them blossom this year, and they had. His daughter had a hand in this place as heavy as his own. In the grand scheme of things, money was just paper . . . kind of like his marriage certificate.

Slowly, Jax narrowed the gap between them. She tipped her head up to meet his eyes, but she didn't back up. Damn if Livie wasn't holding her ground. On any other occasion he'd appreciate her tenacity and strength, but not when her sole goal was to dismantle his life. And it was a bit difficult to take her seriously when she had that streak on her cheek.

When he took one more step, Livie reached up and held on to the wing, her eyes widened.

That's right. She was about to learn who truly held the upper hand on this fifty percent partnership from hell.

"Your offer and your big-city thinking have no place in Haven. You knew that when you left years ago. I may not look like much to you, but believe it or not, I'm more than a plane mechanic." He focused on his words and not her sweet floral scent. "And there are real people in this town. People who rely on me and my services, services your father started and hoped to pass down to you one day, but you left."

She pulled in a sharp breath. That's right. He was going there.

"I doubt my father would want you to turn down such a generous amount," she countered with a tip of her chin.

Jax couldn't help but laugh. "If you'd been around at all, you'd know Paul busted his ass to keep this place going. This is more than an airport—it's a legacy."

She pursed her pale pink glossy lips. "So, what do you propose then? You want me to just walk away and pretend I don't own half? Just let you keep going on as if nothing happened?"

Even if she did just that, something major had happened. Paul was gone. Selling this place would seem like he was severing that bond.

Did Olivia even have a clue as to what all her father had done? Did she care? Did she know his reasoning for letting her go so many years ago?

"Think about the lives you'd be impacting." Reaching up, he gripped the smooth edge of the wing, mimicking her stance.

Livie dropped her hand, tilted her chin up, and offered a smile. "We need to come to an agreement that works for both of us."

"Doubtful that can happen when we want two separate things."

Livie's smile hit him with a punch of lust to the gut. Damn it. He had to keep dodging these blows. "Then we'll just have to get creative."

Images popped into his mind of how creative he could be . . . but he didn't think her line of thinking matched his. She was trying to get him off course and if he wasn't careful, she'd succeed.

"You should know," she went on, "I never lose."

She spun on her heel and marched away. He didn't even bother telling her she was wasting her efforts fighting because he'd come out on top. How could he say anything when his gaze was fixed on the sway of her hips . . . and the imprint of his greasy handprint on her ass?

Chapter Two

Infuriating, frustrating man. Clearly, he wanted this place just as much as she did, but there was no way she was backing down. They had opposite goals and there was no way to get what they both wanted.

Olivia could've easily handled him if he'd been the boy she once knew. The quiet, mysterious teen with curious eyes, and a desperate need for an orthodontist. But now he had that whole nobility thing going with his military background and he was just as determined to fight as she was. He was definitely not the same person . . . then again, neither was she.

The man she'd verbally sparred with had a strong desire to hold on to his life, but all that did was force her into a past she wanted nothing to do with. She wouldn't let anyone pull her back in. Not Jackson, not the memory of her late father.

Olivia cringed as she walked in the back door of her childhood home. She was used to working with men wearing Italian-cut suits, not holey jeans and tees that stretched across impressively broad shoulders. And since when did airplane grease smell sexy?

She'd temporarily been thrown off her game, that's

all—not to mention she hadn't expected him to be so passionate about such a run-down place. The money she'd offered had been more than what he deserved for half . . . which only meant he had deeper ties than she'd ever considered.

Okay, so she needed to refocus and go back in for the kill. At least now she knew what she was up against. A formidable opponent is something she valued in her job—it made her sharper, made the win that much sweeter. However, with her father's airport, she wanted in and out.

In the sixteen years she'd been gone, her father had reached out to her several times. She hadn't ignored him, but she hadn't once taken him up on his invitation to return. Once she'd gotten out of the small town and into the city, she knew she'd never come back. The narrow way of life didn't appeal to her anymore.

And it didn't appeal to her now.

"I don't like that look on your face."

Olivia didn't even attempt a smile for her best friend. Melanie didn't need things sugarcoated. They all knew full well exactly what was at stake, what this buyout meant to Olivia.

Thankfully, Olivia's two best friends had come with her for support. As strong as Olivia thought she was, there was no way she could handle all of this on her own. Besides, Melanie and Jade had their own demons they were running from, so getting out of Atlanta for a while was a smart move.

Melanie leaned against the center island, her smoothie bottle in hand. From the looks of the green contents, she was back on her cleanse. Her vow to stay on top of her weight was a personal battle—stemming from an extremely arrogant, controlling jerk who'd emotionally crushed Melanie. And the jerk was still causing problems, which was just another reason why Melanie came to Haven with Olivia.

"Speaking of face, you have something on yours." Melanie tapped on her own cheek to indicate the area to Olivia.

Confused, Olivia blinked. "My face?"

"It's black."

Olivia resisted the urge to scream as she swiped with her palm. She knew exactly what her friend referred to now. Sure enough, grease.

"That bastard," she muttered.

Melanie wrinkled her nose. "I take it things didn't go as planned."

Olivia sat her bag on the worn laminate island and blew out a sigh. Where did she begin? The fact that Jackson looked nothing like she remembered, or the fact that her emotions nearly choked her when she arrived?

"He refused my offer, but I'm not giving up." She took a seat on the wooden barstool and reached for the yellow hand towel on the island. Wiping Jackson's childish prank off her hand, she added, "He's going to be tough to crack, but I will win this fight. I have to."

The back door opened and closed. Olivia glanced over her shoulder to see Jade dabbing her palms over her sweaty forehead and cheeks. "Oh, good. You're both here."

Jade McCoy was the only person Olivia knew who could go on a run and still look like a damn supermodel on the other side. With her fitted, matching workout gear, her bright red hair in a top knot that she managed to make look stylish, Jade could have just jumped off the cover of *Shape*.

She and Olivia had become instant friends when they bonded over their patent leather pink flats in the third grade. They'd met Melanie only a few years ago at a marathon. Melanie had stumbled and hurt her ankle just a quarter mile shy of the finish line. Jade and Olivia had each taken an arm and helped her limp across to finish. It was only after they learned why that marathon had been so important for Melanie, and their friendship had been formed.

Olivia stared at her friend. "He turned down the money."

And that really put a damper on her short-term plans, but Olivia never lost a battle and she wasn't done with Jackson—not by a long shot. A minor setback, that's all. His stubborn stance would keep her here in Haven longer than she'd intended. Now that he knew she was here, and what she wanted, she would give them both a bit to think on this, and she'd go back. They weren't done negotiating . . . hell, they hadn't even started negotiating. He'd closed the door in her face.

Still, Olivia was confident she would come out on top. This airport had to be fully in her name before she left. How could she go back to Atlanta a failure? How could she go back to work when it was literally her job to buy and sell companies if she couldn't even get this simple task done?

Olivia had a job to get back to, a partnership to earn in the company she'd practically shed blood, sweat, and tears for. She'd be damned if that partnership would go to her coworker, and nemesis, Steve Parsons. So, she'd have to make Jackson see the money was better than the memories. There was no other option.

"I'm sure he has reasons for turning you down." Jade headed to the fridge, grabbed a water, and uncapped it. She turned to lean against the counter opposite the island. "Like maybe his daughter."

Olivia stilled. A daughter? That definitely did not come

up in conversation. How the hell could she fight properly when she wasn't fully aware what she was up against?

Why did life have to keep smacking her in the face? Just when she thought she was on target, something happened to push her back down.

"You okay?" Melanie asked in that soft, delicate tone of hers.

Olivia smiled. "Of course. This changes nothing."

Okay, that was a lie, but if she acted weak or scared, she'd never get this job done.

"How did you find out?" Olivia asked Jade.

Smoothing a stray, sweaty strand off her forehead, Jade took a long drink before answering. "I was jogging down my old street and Mrs. Kinard was outside. She stopped me and started talking. As much as I don't want to be in this town either, I couldn't be rude to my old neighbor. Besides, I never can turn down gossip."

Olivia raised her brows and made a circular motion with her hand.

"Right, so anyway, she mentioned your father, then she mentioned Jax and the airport. I'd all but tuned her out until I heard her mention Piper and how much the four-year-old loved spending time with her dad at the airport."

Okay. This was . . . okay. Everything would be fine so long as she didn't dwell on the fact Jackson's and Piper's lives somewhat paralleled Olivia's and her father's when she'd been a toddler. She'd always been her father's side-kick and had wanted to be a pilot. Somewhere along the road to freedom and adulthood, something changed and she honestly couldn't even pinpoint when that occurred.

Olivia could deal with a daughter. Surely, Jax wanted to do what was best for his family, she totally understood that. So, why not take the money? This bit of information was a game-changer. Olivia would have to appeal to him as a parent, which may be difficult considering she knew nothing of that topic.

"Maybe you should leave the airport as is," Melanie suggested. She held up her hands to her friends and went on. "Hear me out. What does it hurt if you own half? Let him continue to run it and you can just pretend things are the same as before."

Olivia shook her head. "Because things aren't the same. I want out of this and he will just have to see things from my point of view."

"So how did you leave things?" Jade asked. "Since you didn't know about his daughter, you guys clearly didn't get too personal. Did he tell you why he didn't want to sell his half?"

Olivia flattened her hands on the scarred island. The place really needed an overhaul—it was just as neglected as the airport and office.

Once upon a time, these kitchens walls were a beautiful Tiffany blue with white cabinets. Her mother always had fresh flowers on the counter, pink usually. Cheery tea towels would hang over the oven handle. The entire house now seemed so depressing, a shell of what it used to be. With the white walls, white appliances, tan linoleum, beige countertops. It was all so dated. Clearly, her father hadn't wanted to keep the reminders of a time when they'd all lived here, because every single room had been repainted, pictures changed out.

Unfortunately, while she was here, she was going to have to go through and get out the personal stuff. Furniture, curtains, cosmetic items could be sold with the house. But there were boxes to go through, memories to face.

And one more thing to pull her back into the past she'd give anything to avoid.

"He mentioned tradition and loyalty. I get that, I really do, but not when it comes at a cost to my sanity. I actually managed to get the last word in," Olivia stated, proud to claim that minor victory. "He's wrapped up in the nostalgia. Nothing I haven't handled before. Most people who are in a bind have a rough time cutting that last tie."

Like me. But she could do this. Where once she could have been construed as a nostalgic sap, now she was an accountant working closely with an HR department in a respected, prime position. The present, not the past, was what mattered.

Jade clutched her water bottle and smiled. "Good thing you're holding the scissors."

"And the checkbook," Olivia stated with confidence. Maybe once he saw a check made out to him, with a few zeroes, he'd change his tune. "I'm going back and I'll keep going until he gives in. This may take more time than I anticipated, but I'm determined to be done once and for all."

"Are you sure?" Melanie asked. "I hate to play the devil's advocate here, but—"

"Please, you've never had an evil bone in your body," Jade pointed out.

Melanie shrugged with a slight smile. "Still, if this place bothers you so much, just leave. Let Jax go on with his life and you go back to yours. You have that partnership to work on back in Atlanta anyway."

"I do," Olivia agreed. "But I have to figure out this partnership first."

Why didn't her father just leave the entire airport to Jackson? Then Olivia wouldn't be here, taking time away from other projects she needed to focus on—like the career move she'd worked the past decade to maintain. If she were just doing her regular job, and not vying for the top spot, she could technically work from anywhere.

But she didn't want to work from Haven. This may have been her childhood home, but she'd left here long ago and never looked back. Why did she have to be pulled back in?

When she and her mother had left, they'd sworn to never return. Olivia didn't want to be so hard about it, but . . .

No. She couldn't travel down that lane of memories, not when she was desperately just trying to get out and keep this a business arrangement.

She glanced to Jade and Melanie, who stared back at her as if they were afraid she was going to crack or have a meltdown at any moment. Pity looks, or the sympathy hugs, were a surefire way to get her to break.

Another wave of emotions swept through her as she thought of how amazing these girls were. Not that she expected anything less than for them to band around her and offer support.

After her father's death, they'd all come to Haven to the cute women-only spa, Bella Vous. Jade had booked the trip because they all needed to get away from Atlanta and just unwind. What better way than a spa? They'd all heard the buzz over the new resort run by three brothers in honor of their late sister. How poetic and amazing was that? There was no way Olivia and her friends were going to be left out.

Just after the trip Olivia learned of the will, Jade's career literally blew up in her face, and Melanie was embarking on her own journey after her hellacious marriage came to an end. So here they were with no clear path, but they were always a team. If they were going to succeed or fail, they were doing it together.

"We need a ladies' night. Is there a bar in this town?"

Melanie took one last drink of her smoothie. "I mean, I saw one, but it was . . ."

Olivia laughed at Melanie's shudder. "Yeah. Taps is the only bar. It's not terrible if you want a neat whiskey or beer."

"I never trust a place that doesn't have a wine collection. And I don't mean the box variety."

Olivia laughed. She could always count on Jade to have her own "crisis" during someone else's. Still, they deserved some bonding time.

"We'll just do a girls' night in. I need a manicure in the worst way and there's nowhere around here I'll go."

"Good thing I packed the necessities," Jade replied. "Melanie, you do the liquor run."

Melanie held up her empty shaker. "Wait, is there even a store that sells the supplies we need?"

Olivia rolled her eyes. "I would think. Surely the town isn't made up of complete savages."

"I'm not so sure." Jade came to the other side of the island, holding her bottle, and resting her palm on the counter. "During my jog I saw a man watering his lawn in only plaid boxers, a woman in curlers and a hideous floral robe standing on the curb getting her mail, and I won't even get into the man who was standing in his doorway wearing nothing but what the good Lord gave him. He had the balls to actually wave at me. Pun intended. But in my too-long chat with Mrs. Kinard, I did learn that our favorite teacher's husband passed just yesterday. I thought we should send flowers or . . . I don't know, bake a casserole."

"Flowers," Olivia muttered. "We're not baking any-thing and getting too cozy with the neighbors. We won't be here that long."

Olivia didn't want to hear anymore. She didn't want to know what was going on in this town or who the people were. All she wanted was to get this deal in motion so she could get out.

"Remind me not to take that same path when I go tomorrow," Melanie said as she sat her bottle in the sink. "I'd rather not have Mr. Balls waving at me."

Olivia came to her feet. "Well, as fun as discussing balls has been, I need to get to work cleaning out the closets. I'll never sell this place with all the boxes and knickknacks."

She shoved her hair back from her face, wondering if she should go on a jog herself. She'd been so anxious to talk to Jackson, she'd skipped her morning workout so she could take extra time and care on her appearance. It was like he didn't even care about her new killer suit. She could definitely use the release and time alone to clear her head and work on another game plan.

Piper. His daughter. Was the mother in the picture? Not that his personal life was her concern, but damn it, she deserved to know. Because of her father's will, now Jax was her concern. She would've been perfectly fine not receiving anything.

Olivia had just gotten to the doorway leading into the living room when her friends burst into laughter.

She jerked around. "What?"

"Did you leave out something about your visit with Mr. Morgan?" Jade asked, her smile wide, her eyes sparkling with something that frightened Olivia.

"No, why."

Melanie picked up her phone from the counter. "Turn back around."

Confused, Olivia put her back to the kitchen once again, and once again her friends' laughter filled the space.

"What?" Olivia asked, throwing her arms in the air and facing them. "What is so funny?"

Melanie flipped her phone around and showed Olivia the picture. A picture of Olivia's ass.

A picture of Olivia's ass with a greasy handprint right where Jackson had tried to catch her . . . after he'd put a grease mark on her face.

Fury bubbled through her. "I'm going to kill him."

"Well, that would be one way to get your half of the airport, but orange isn't your color."

Olivia glared at Jade. "Not funny."

"So, you only *thought* you got the last word in because I'd say—"

Holding up a hand, Olivia cut Melanie off. "I know. Damn it, I know. He got the one up on me. But I'm not done."

"Do you want me to send you this picture?" she asked, causing Jade to laugh even harder. "In case you wanted to update your profile on any of your social media outlets."

"You two are a riot," Olivia stated dryly. "I'm going to change and I'm going back to the airport. Jackson Morgan will not make me look like a fool."

"I think he already—"

Olivia marched off, ignoring Jade stating the obvious. Her friends at least attempted to snicker quietly, but Olivia couldn't worry about that now. She had more pressing matters and a brand-new suit Jackson had to dry-clean.

"Livie Daniels. Is that you?"

Again with the name. Did people get a nickname and then never part from it? Why couldn't she have been dubbed "O Great One" or "Her Highness"? If she were to go back and pick her nickname in school, she definitely wouldn't have let "Livie" pass.

Olivia clutched the shopping bag she carried . . . a bag with her soiled suit. It took every bit of Olivia's willpower not to explode on the young woman leaving the airport hangar, but all she had done was call Olivia by the annoying name.

No, Olivia would rather save her frustration for Jackson.

Not recognizing the blonde headed her way, Olivia pasted on a smile that was as fake as this lady's nails. Did people actually still do acrylics?

"I'm sorry, I don't recall your name."

The lady with dark blond hair, which was actually a pretty shade, waved a hand in the air. "It's okay. I was a couple of years behind you in school. You wouldn't know me." The woman held out her hand. "I'm April Collins."

Olivia ran the name through her head, vaguely placing the woman who stood before her. "Of course I remember you now," Olivia lied as she shook her hand. "How wonderful to see you again."

"I'm sorry about your dad." April pulled her hand back and shielded her eyes against the late afternoon sun. "I know words don't change anything, but he sure will be missed around here."

Forcing her smile to remain in place, Olivia nodded. Just another person her father had left an impression on. Another reason she didn't want to stick around too long. All of these people would be coming forward, wanting to express their condolences, and Olivia truly didn't have the mental capacity to cope. Years of an absentee father hurt, but knowing he hadn't fought for her and remained here catering to everyone else was absolutely crushing.

Well, he'd e-mailed randomly. Maybe twice a year and called on Christmas and her birthday. He never asked why she left, but he always asked her to come back. Why? She never fully grasped why he wanted her to return unless he only wanted someone to take over his precious airport. But he had Jax for that, didn't he?

It had been easier to settle into her new life and push away her old . . . her father included.

Olivia couldn't get into all of that with April, so she just replied with a simple, "Thank you."

"I'm glad Jax is keeping the place running. He's got as much determination as your dad did," April went on. "Maybe more since Piper is still so young. She absolutely loves coming here and she told me in class today that her dream is to be an air force pilot like her daddy."

The guilt punch to the gut impacted her more than she would've liked. She had to push personal feelings aside. If she wanted this deal to be done in her favor, she had to keep her eye on the prize . . . and the prize was getting out of here as soon as possible with the full deed to the airport and her sanity intact.

"Piper is quite the tomboy." April went on as if they were old friends reuniting for a chitchat. "All she talks about during school is planes and how her daddy lets her help with repairs. She's got a passion for flying, that's for sure." April laughed. "I'm sorry, I shouldn't keep you."

"Oh, it's no bother."

Surprisingly, she meant that. Small-town ramblings were how anyone found out anything going on. Jade's run was proof enough.

The fact that Jackson had a daughter may have tilted the stakes just a bit, but Olivia couldn't let it deter her from seeking what she wanted . . . what she needed for closure.

"I need to get going," April said, pulling Olivia from her thoughts. "It was good to see you again."

Offering a nod and a smile, Olivia waited until April got in her car and started to pull out of the grassy lot. With bag in hand, Olivia headed toward the closed hangar door.

Besides the inevitable partnership chat, Olivia wanted to know what he planned to do about her suit. Her *new* suit.

As soon as she pushed the door open, she wasn't sure what she expected to find. The same lonely plane she'd seen earlier, the same sexy man who grated on her last nerve and stood in the way of her closure. Definitely those, but she hadn't anticipated that same sexy man dancing around the same damn plane.

Dancing around with his daughter. The little girl squealed as he twirled from one end of the hangar to the other, her blond pigtails bouncing with each step. Jackson's arms extended out, and his little girl lay across the top in plank position as a human airplane. As Jackson ran back to the other end, she let out another high-pitched noise somewhere between a laugh and a scream.

Olivia remained in the doorway, hand clutched on the doorknob as she took in the sight. Memories she'd wanted to suppress had slammed her right in the heart and there was no stopping the flood of emotions. She blinked against the tears, instantly taken back to her childhood when she and her father would do that very thing . . . in front of that exact plane.

For the first time since being so hell-bent on removing this place from her life, there was an unwelcome tug on her heart. What did she do with that emotion? She hadn't counted on feeling anything other than elation as she skipped back out of Haven with the property solely in her name.

Once upon a time she'd wanted a family, children. She'd given up on those dreams—or so she thought—to have a lucrative career. Yet watching memories being made right before her eyes was more than her biological clock could handle.

Damn it. She thought for sure that thing stopped ticking.

She didn't want these emotions and the doubts. There was a plan in place and she was going to see it through.

The bag slipped from her hand, banging against the concrete. Jackson froze, turned with his daughter in his arms, and met her gaze across the hangar.

Olivia pulled in a breath, blinked against the unwanted tears filling her eyes. This was not what she came for. A stroll down the lane of memories could not be part of this business deal.

The sooner she could get him on her side, the sooner she could say good riddance forever.

Chapter Three

Jax knew instantly that they weren't alone anymore, but he wasn't going to stop playing with his daughter simply because the princess had returned. Piper's squeals had him spinning and running faster. She had an adventurous spirit just like her father. His spunky daughter may have been the exact image of her mother, but thankfully she didn't have the personality.

"Daddy," Piper giggled. "You have a visitor."

Yeah, he knew, but he didn't like this visitor. He slowed down and slowly put Piper on her feet. One of her ponytails was lopsided, but he was pretty proud he'd mastered this little-girl style. Those tiny rubber bands he had to use in her hair were damn hard to maneuver with hands his size.

Piper raced across the hangar toward Olivia. Jax opted to stand back to see what she wanted. No doubt she thought they'd pick up where they left off in conversation earlier.

He had to bite back a smile when he realized she'd changed. Now she wore a pair of white cropped pants and a fitted red tank. She still had on a pair of damn heels. Did she always have to silently scream money?

"My name is Piper," his daughter greeted because she'd never met a stranger. "I'm four. You're really pretty. Did you need Daddy to fly you somewhere?"

Olivia met his gaze from across the open space. When she quirked her brow, he merely smiled.

"No." Olivia looked back down to Piper and squatted down to get on her level. "I'm actually here to give him this sack."

"Like a present?" Piper exclaimed.

"Exactly like a present," she stated, holding her hand out. "I'm Olivia and you are pretty, too. My age isn't important."

"Does that mean you're old?" Piper asked. "Because you don't look old. Can I guess your age?"

Oh, this was always a fun game. Jax waited to see what number she'd come up with. He never knew what she'd say . . . the joys of parenthood. Sometimes she guessed him to be fifteen and others she pegged him as eighty-eight.

"Well . . ." Olivia stood back up and shot a worried glance to him.

"I say nineteen."

Olivia's wide smile did that whole twisty thing to his gut again. He liked it better when she was grouchy and frowning.

"I'm quite flattered, but I'm a little older."

Piper shrugged and turned, threw her arms wide, and ran back toward Jax. "Go open the sack so I can see your surprise," she told him as she ran right into his leg.

He scooped her up and tossed her over his shoulder, causing an instant scream. "Daddy," she squealed.

Easing her down just a bit, he kept hold of her against

his side as he headed toward Olivia and the mysterious sack . . . though he had a pretty good idea as to what she had in there, especially since she had changed.

"You didn't have to bring me a peace offering."

Olivia's bright eyes narrowed into slits. "This is your dry cleaning. My new suit apparently has a stain on the a—"

"Yes, I believe I saw that when you left earlier." Jax smiled as he darted a glance to his daughter, then back to Olivia. "I'm sure it was already there when you arrived."

"Oh, I think you know exactly how it got there."

"Can I go get some juice in the office?" Piper asked.

Jax sat her on her feet and she darted off out of the hangar to the adjoining office where he kept snacks and drinks. They seemed to be here more often than home, so he liked to keep things stocked. He even had a pull-out sofa because before Piper had started preschool, she'd be here most days and would take naps. Only when he was flying did he pay for a sitter.

Now that Piper was in all-day preschool, his schedule was a bit freer, but he missed her. He wasn't used to being without his knee-high sidekick. They were a team. Where he went, she went. Even some flights he'd taken her on when the passengers didn't mind and seating allowed. She loved the sky as much as he did, maybe more because she only knew the fun side of this job. The hard work hadn't come into her life yet, but as she got older, he'd teach her the mechanics, the technical things so she was independent.

Not to mention he wanted her to know that sacrifice was all part of the job. But, when you were doing what you loved, then even the most trying things didn't feel like work.

"She's adorable," Olivia stated once they were alone. "She must take after her mother."

Jax knew her comment was meant to be a jab, but she'd

hit a nerve. "Beyond her looks, she's nothing like my ex-wife. She doesn't even remember her, so don't mention her again when Piper is around."

"Oh, I'm sorry." Olivia blinked, her face indeed expressing just how sorry she was. "I didn't know."

"Exactly," he retorted, shoving his hands in his pockets. "There's quite a bit you don't know about what's happened here since you left, so don't come in all assuming."

Silence surrounded them and Jax wondered if she was going to apologize again. But, nope. There went that defiant chin he'd been introduced to earlier. Oh, and right on cue there went the squared, rigid shoulders. Olivia was now in fighting position . . . he'd do best to keep his armor in place.

"I came to drop this off." She dropped the sack between their feet and took a step back. "I was hoping we could talk, but maybe this isn't the best time. Does tomorrow work for you?"

"I have two flights tomorrow before Piper gets out of school and then another one around five. Tomorrow won't work."

Olivia crossed her arms over her chest, which only managed to press her breasts up even higher in that scoop of her tank.

Eyes up, Morgan. Don't show weakness in front of the enemy.

"Considering I'm pretty free while I'm in town, you tell me when you're available."

Jax thought to his schedule and really didn't want to find free time. If she wanted to chat about how she could assist or help fund the new-to-him Cessna he'd been saving for, then he'd be all too obliging. But, since she wanted to rip away his whole livelihood and pass over a check like she was buying a pair of shoes, he wasn't too quick to come up with a time.

"You're going to make this difficult, aren't you?" she asked on a sigh.

Jax shook his head. "I'm not the one being difficult. I'm doing my job, making sure my daughter has a happy, secure life. If you feel like this situation is difficult, maybe you should point the finger elsewhere."

Why the hell hadn't Paul put this place in Jax's name only? Paul was fully aware that Jax had nothing else immediate to fall back on, that this airport and flying were his life. Jax loved Paul like a father, and Paul had said more than once that Jax was the son he'd never had. They'd shared a bond, something so deep and meaningful. And it was out of respect for the man who'd helped Jax through the toughest times in life that he was being so cordial to Olivia. Well, as cordial as he was capable of, considering the circumstances. He was pretty damn proud of how nice he was.

"Listen." She dropped her arms and met his gaze with one of the sincerest look he'd yet seen from her. "I'm not trying to make your life harder. If you want to buy my half, fine. Otherwise, I'd really like to sell this place so I can be done in Haven and with memories once and for all."

Jax truly didn't get her disdain for what could've been her legacy. "Are you upset because I took over here? Were you wanting it?"

She jerked back, her nose wrinkling as if he'd just sprouted a third head. "Heavens, no. When I left, I never intended to come back. My mother made it clear that my dad chose this place over us. . . ."

She trailed off, her eyes darting over his shoulder to the plane. Blinking once again, she focused back on him. "My reasons don't matter. But no, I'm not upset he gave this place to you. I just want it out of my life."

There was no doubt she'd been misguided by her mother, because Paul had loved Olivia more than any airplane or this airstrip. When Olivia and her mother had left, Paul had been gutted and had thrown himself into his work even more. It was during that time that Jax really started hanging around more and taking on greater responsibility.

Paul had gotten so drunk one night and ended up spilling his emotions out in a tearful confession. How he'd e-mailed, but never knew what to say. How she did respond, but claimed she was happy in Atlanta. He'd worried he'd never see her again, that he'd driven her away for good. Paul had confided in Jax things that no one else knew, and Jax still held on to those secrets.

Olivia had a set opinion of her father and if she truly thought he hadn't cared about her, then she didn't deserve the truth.

"Daddy, this is the last juice box." Piper came running back into the hangar, breaking the moment. "Are we still going to the movies? Can I have pop?"

Jax shot his daughter a knowing look. "Have I ever given you pop?"

"If I keep asking you will."

Piper stopped in front of him and held out her juice for him to put the straw into it. Why these straws were made so flimsy and the holes so tiny was beyond his realm of comprehension. He was utterly convinced that people who made things targeted for kids had no kids of their own.

"When you're older," he stated, handing the pouch back to her.

"That's what you always say," she muttered. "I guess when I'm fifty I can have Pesi."

"Pepsi," he corrected with a grin. "And I was thinking more like sixty."

When Piper groaned, he smiled and turned his attention back to Olivia. She stood there just staring at Piper, and he had no idea what was going through her head. She looked almost . . . sad. Was she having regrets about coming here and all but demanding he sell? He sure as hell hoped so because she was going to be waiting awhile if she was holding out for a different answer from him.

"Livie?"

She jumped as if he'd broken her trance. "Olivia," she corrected.

Yeah, he remembered, but he liked to keep reminding her of her roots. Maybe he'd get through that thick head of hers just who she was and that running away didn't change the person.

He should know.

"I . . . um . . ." Olivia seemed to be at a loss for words. "I'll check back with you about our talk."

"You could go on a date."

Jax nearly choked on air at his daughter's declaration. And when he glanced to Olivia, her wide eyes suggested she was just as caught off guard.

"Honey, why would you suggest that?" Jax squatted down next to Piper. This was the first time she'd ever said anything like that before.

"Bella in my class said her mom was going on a date and that if they like each other she might get a new dad."

Jax's heart clenched. He had no idea she'd even had such thoughts as wanting two parents. For four years he'd been both mom and dad. He'd even watched YouTube videos to try to figure out how the hell to do her hair, but so far he'd only mastered the ponytails. He polished her nails and had let her polish his. Granted, she told him he couldn't take it off, so his toes were currently a vibrant shade of purple. Thankfully, he always wore boots or tennis shoes—he only prayed he wasn't in an accident.

"Honey, Olivia and I barely know each other. We aren't going on a date."

Piper's face fell. "But she's pretty, Dad."

That was definitely something he couldn't deny. Olivia was stunning, even when sneering at him.

"Piper." Olivia stepped forward and squatted down beside him. "Did you know my daddy used to own this airport? I used to run around here just like you. But, not every daddy has time for dating or relationships. And I bet your daddy is so busy flying clients and having fun with you, he wouldn't have time to take me anywhere."

Jax cringed. Not only did she just slam her father, she'd basically lumped Jax in with Paul . . . which was fine because Jax respected the hell out of the guy, but it was clear Olivia didn't.

Piper's eyes widened, as did her smile. "I'll just stay with Miss Mary. She always says she'll babysit anytime."

Jax rubbed his forehead. He truly didn't have the time, nor did he want to get into this conversation in front of Olivia, who clearly had a chip on her shoulder where men in general were concerned.

"Honey—"

"I'll go on a date with your dad if he wants."

Jax jumped to his feet. What the hell was she saying? He stared down at her and she merely glanced up to him and winked. Winked. What kind of game was she playing?

"But," she went on, focusing back to Piper, "we're just friends. I don't want you to get any other ideas."

Piper threw her arms around Olivia's neck. For a moment, Jax wondered if Olivia would return the innocent gesture, but she enveloped Piper and patted her back.

"I can't wait to tell Bella," Piper exclaimed as she pulled back and started sipping her juice.

Olivia stood and straightened her clothes. "Looks like we'll get to have that talk after all," she told him with a wide smile.

She'd cornered him and now he was looking at a date with the very last person he wanted to be alone with. Damn it.

"This shade makes me look like I have jaundice."

Olivia stared across the table at Melanie's nude polish. "No, it doesn't. You're just used to that pink you always wear. We were hoping you'd be a little more daring."

Melanie held her hands out, examining her glossy nails. "This is daring."

Jade rolled her eyes and stroked her mint green across her pinkie. "It's nude. You might as well wear nothing. It's a waste of product. Wear red or navy or even black. For pity's sake, mix it up."

Olivia still hadn't decided her shade. She stared at the variety from reds to pinks to bright summer colors. Nothing was hitting her; then again, perhaps she couldn't concentrate because she'd been set up on a date by a four-year-old. That little tot should grow up to be a politician or lawyer. She was a sneaky one and had them agreeing within seconds. Their piddly excuses to deny her had fallen on deaf ears.

"What's up with you?" Jade asked suddenly. "You've been frowning since you came back from the airport. Did he refuse to get your suit clean or did he feel you up again?"

Olivia reached for the bright red, deciding on something fierce. "He never felt me up to begin with, let alone again."

"That palm print on your ass says otherwise," Melanie murmured.

"Good one," Jade praised. "I'm so proud of the snark that's been coming out of you lately."

"I'm learning," Melanie beamed.

Melanie had been in a terribly abusive relationship. She was just coming out of the hellish marriage when she'd met Olivia and Jade. Melanie had been stifled for too long, beaten down—literally and figuratively—but she was starting to get her sense of freedom again. And Olivia was thrilled to see her friend grow and find herself.

Jade never had any issues with being sarcastic and speaking her mind. No, her issues stemmed from work, and so here they all were hiding from their problems back in Atlanta.

"So are you ready to spill about your second visit to see Jackson?" Jade asked as she resumed her polishing.

Olivia shook her bottle before uncapping it. "I met his daughter. She's so adorable and has lopsided blond pigtails."

"Oh, no. Do not let the cuteness deter you," Jade scolded. "You have a mission."

Olivia kept her gaze on her nails, not wanting to see either of her friends' reactions to her embarrassing turn of events. There was no way to hide the next bit of information, so she might as well just let them in on everything.

"I'm going on a date with Jackson."

She didn't have to look up to know both of her friends stilled. Silence settled so heavy between them, Olivia was almost afraid to say anything else for fear of her friends thinking she'd gotten sidetracked . . . even though that's exactly what had happened.

"If you think we don't want the backstory, you're

crazy," Melanie finally stated. "He asked you out and you agreed? Is this part of the plan to get him to sell?"

"Ooh, are you trying to seduce him to get what you want? Smart girl," Jade all but squealed. "But you can't actually sleep with him because that would be wrong. Maybe just flirting and some hot kisses."

An instant image popped into Olivia's mind. No, she was not going there. Jackson was hella sexy, but she wasn't about to stoop so low as to use her body to get what she wanted. She'd worked damn hard to get to the top of her company . . . well, almost the top, and she'd done so because she was damn good at her job and she worked harder than anyone in that company.

There was only one more rung on that proverbial ladder to climb and the promotion had come down to the final round. Olivia refused to lose this to some jerk who thought his balls were reason enough for him to have the position.

"Piper asked if her dad was going to take me on a date because she thinks I'm pretty," Olivia explained. "He keeps dodging me when I want to talk to him, so I pretty much agreed to a date. It's all still within my plan. I just took a different approach, that's all."

She glanced up from the first coat of bright red on her nails and met her friends' disbelieving gazes.

"What?" she asked, ready to defend herself. "That's all this is. I just want to discuss the property."

"And he agreed that easy?" Jade arched one perfectly shaped brow. "Maybe he's going to try to seduce *you* into getting what he wants."

Olivia laughed. "I doubt it. He's made it pretty clear he thinks I'm a spoiled brat."

"Then he doesn't know you," Melanie replied, all joking aside. "Maybe if you explain your reasons for wanting out of this—"

"He doesn't need my reasons," Olivia growled, but instantly regretted her sliver of anger. "Sorry, I'm not lashing out at you. I'm just frustrated, that's all."

"Maybe it's time for those cocktails," Jade suggested, then looked to Melanie. "Your nails are dry. Why don't you make the first round?"

"We're pretty limited." Melanie wrinkled her nose as she came to her feet. She crossed to the brown sacks on the counter and started pulling out bottles. "I found some wine of the twist cap variety, some questionable vodka, and the cashier winked at me and slid an extra bottle of flavored vodka into the bag."

Jade busted out laughing. "We're sending you every time, then. Free booze? That's perfect."

Melanie threw a glance over her shoulder. "The guy was at least seventy. Don't get too excited."

"If he thinks you're hot and wants to flirt, I don't see the problem." Jade blew on her nails, then stretched her arm out to admire them. "I think mint is definitely my color."

"Everything is your color," Olivia replied putting her last coat on. "You look stunning in everything. Your clothes, your polish, even when you crawl out of bed snarling before your coffee. It's not fair to be so perfect all the time."

"Remember my junior-year prom picture?" Jade leaned back in her seat and waved her hands back and forth to dry. "The hairstylist from hell and the dress that made me look twenty pounds heavier. Why didn't anyone tell me when I tried it on in the store?"

Melanie flicked on the blender, so Olivia yelled, "You didn't look heavier, it just wasn't the most flattering. So you had one bad moment? I cringe every time someone tags me on social media in a picture because I never know what I'm going to pull up. I either look great in a photo or I look like that hairy Oak Ridge Boy."

"Who?" Melanie asked as she shut off the mixer.

"My dad used to play their tapes in the hangar," Olivia explained. "It's an old country band."

"My parents listened to classical." She pulled out three glasses and filled each one. "I'm deprived."

"Trust me, the Oak Ridge Boys are not something you're missing out on. Except 'Elvira.' That's one catchy song."

Melanie sat the drinks on the table and took her seat. "So, when is your date and where are you going?"

Olivia reached for her glass and stared at the mixture. "What is in here?"

"Who cares," Jade replied. "Drink up."

Olivia took a sip, then a bigger drink when it didn't taste half bad. "Is that peach?"

Melanie nodded. "I put a little of that peach Bellini I mixed up earlier in it."

"This is pretty good, actually." Jade took another long drink, then swirled the remaining contents around in the glass. "Get back to the date. When and where? We need all the deets."

She should've kept her mouth shut. Olivia knew she'd never hear the end of this, but at the same time it's not like she could keep the date a total secret. At some point she'd have to leave the house and they'd know she was up to something.

Besides, in a town as small as Haven, someone would see them out and they'd instantly become the week's fodder for the gossip mill. That left her no choice but to suggest they go to a different town for their date. And by suggest, she meant demand.

Olivia sighed and eased back in her seat, clutching her drink to her chest. "I have no clue what's going on. He said he'd get with me when his schedule wasn't so busy. Piper made him pinkie swear that he'd call me within two days."

Jade laughed. "I love that little girl already. She's going to be a fun adult."

The spunky toddler would indeed, and an image of her in her teen years with Jackson trying to keep her under control was quite an amusing thought.

Piper was adorable, and it was clear she had her daddy wrapped around her finger. Olivia couldn't help but see the parallels once again with her own life when she'd been young. She'd thought her father walked on water, she was convinced he was the greatest person, and her very own superhero. He could fly, couldn't he? Definite superhero material.

But as she'd gotten older, her mother had told her things that made Olivia see her father in a different light. He hadn't always been there for his family. Her mother had often stated that clearly, they weren't enough for him, that the airport was all he needed. He'd chosen that dilapidated place over anything else . . . even his health, apparently.

Anger, resentment, even some guilt for not being enough coursed through her. Since her father passed, she'd run the full gamut of emotions. At the root of every single day, though, there was sorrow. No matter what happened in the past, he was still her father and she loved him. All those precious memories from her childhood kept replaying in her mind.

The burning in her throat, then her nose, followed by her eyes had her reaching for her drink again.

"We're going to need another for her," Melanie stated, nodding toward Olivia. "I know that look and she is about one second away from a meltdown. Quick, let's think of a movie we can watch. Something hilarious, nobody can die, and there has to be hot men."

Olivia shook her head and tipped back the last of her drink. "I'm okay. I just get nostalgic at times. Well, mostly since I came back."

She blinked away the moisture as it threatened to make an unwelcome appearance. "I'm still determined to sell this property. I have bigger things to worry about than this Podunk town."

So she kept telling herself, but every time she bashed the town out loud or even in her mind, that niggle of guilt rose once again. She seriously needed to get out of here and back to the life she'd created for herself. Returning to Haven might not have been the smartest move. She should've considered doing this business over the phone. Then again, what would she have done with all the stuff in her dad's house?

There was no good way to get closure. She'd simply have to endure it and hopefully she'd be somewhat unscathed on the other side.

"You're going to get that promotion," Jade assured her. She slid her barstool back and headed for the mixer. After surveying the bottles, she started making her own concoction. "That ass you work with isn't fit to be COO of Stennett Enterprises."

"The choice is obvious," Melanie agreed. "And I'm not just saying that because I'm your friend. I mean, I am, but I firmly believe you work harder and you are much more dedicated to your job."

Wasn't that the truth? She didn't recall the last real date she had been on and now she'd been set up by a toddler.

Olivia appreciated her own cheering section—she just wished she was as confident as they were. Examining her red nails, Olivia figured she might as well polish her toes the same shade.

She lifted her knee and propped her foot on the edge of her seat. "Well, they must see something in him or we wouldn't both be in the running."

"It's ridiculous and insulting that they even compare the two of you," Jade fumed. "He asked me out and when I turned him down, he attempted to tarnish my business. It didn't work, but he's such an arrogant jerk, he doesn't even deserve the position even if he was qualified."

Olivia had been with the company longer than Steve, but he'd brought in more business than she had. In her defense, he'd gotten sneaky when he'd pulled clients away from other agencies. Olivia didn't believe in being deceitful. She'd gotten this far in her career without being ruthless or flat-out lying. She worked her ass off, put in way more hours than Steve ever thought about, and had a legitimate love for the business and their clients. Steve basically loved himself and anything wearing a skirt.

"Are you still dodging the date question?" Melanie asked, raising her brows.

Olivia shrugged. "I don't know anything else. We didn't set a place, so for all I know we'll have takeout food in the hangar office."

"Or maybe he'll fly you somewhere fancy for a nice dinner," Melanie retorted with a wide grin.

"You're a hopeless romantic even after all you've been through," Jade stated as she added more ice to the mixer.

Melanie pulled her hair back and smoothed it all over one shoulder. "I have to be. I refuse to believe what I had was a typical marriage. I still feel that there's someone out there for me."

Jade threw Olivia a glance over Melanie's head. They both were too cynical and definitely not on the same page as Melanie when it came to men. Olivia and Jade were busy with their careers, proving they deserved their places and working toward higher goals. Even if they had time for men, they both had their reasons for not wanting to get into that.

Melanie, though, she was still on the lookout for Mr. Right. She wasn't one of those desperate women, though. She didn't hang on every word a man said just because he gave her attention, but she was hopeful. Maybe that's what made her so sweet, despite the fact her jerk of an ex continued to randomly rear his ugly head just to get under her skin.

"Well, I doubt there's someone for me," Olivia stated. "I'm not even looking anyway. My eyes are on this COO position and nothing else."

The knock on the front door had all three women jerking toward the front of the house.

"Expecting someone?" Jade asked, looking between her friends.

Olivia came to her feet and glanced down to her yoga pants and tank. Not what she'd normally greet guests wearing, because she prided herself on being classy and professional like her mother raised her, but her friends' outfits weren't faring much better.

"I'll get it," she stated as she swayed. "Wow. How much alcohol did we have?"

"Not enough if you're worried about it," Jade laughed.

Now the doorbell rang through the house and Olivia placed a hand on the narrow hall leading toward the entryway. With the porch lights illuminating the sidelights and etched glass door, she could make out the shape of a man. She had to assume it was a man from the broad shoulders.

As she got closer, she recognized those shoulders. She cringed when arousal curled low in her belly. She didn't want to be turned on . . . she couldn't afford to be.

What was he doing here? Did he think he could just drop by unannounced? Was this his game plan? To catch her off guard?

"Who is it?" Melanie asked from behind her.

Olivia glanced over her shoulder to see her two friends at the other end of the hallway, huddled together as if there were some serial killer who went around ringing doorbells before he chose his victims.

This was Haven. Their crime rate was pretty much nonexistent.

"It's Jackson," she whispered.

"I know you're in there."

Jackson's voice mocked her and she ignored Jade's laugh behind her. The spiteful side of her wanted to completely ignore him and go back into the kitchen with her friends. But the female in her wanted her to open that door and see the glorious man standing on the other side. Even if he was on the opposite side of what she wanted, she couldn't deny he was absolutely a joy to admire.

Olivia flicked the lock and jerked the door open. "Jackson. What are you doing here?"

"Jax," he corrected.

Those dark eyes raked over her and she trembled. Damn it. She didn't want to tremble from just one look. He hadn't even touched her and . . .

No. She refused to even entertain such thoughts. She'd been given a visual lick by sexy men before, no big deal.

But something about the way Jackson looked at her had her realizing nobody had actually *looked* at her who'd made her feel as if he was literally touching her. How the hell did he do that? If she could tingle from just one of his intense stares, what would happen if he ever actually touched her?

No. No touching allowed.

"What do you want?" she repeated.

He flashed that devilish grin and propped an arm on the screen door, which only drew her attention to his perfectly flexed bicep. "I'm picking you up for our date."

Chapter Four

There was something to be said for such a striking woman who demanded control—and then stealing said control from her.

Jax waited patiently while Olivia gathered her thoughts. She clearly hadn't been expecting him to show up at her door, which is precisely why he was here.

Jax hadn't wanted to set a specific time for their so-called date, a point he still needed to discuss with Piper. She was a sneaky one, and he was a bit proud of how quickly she'd manipulated Olivia. But still, he needed to talk with her about something deeper than her weaving this date.

Was his daughter already wanting a mommy? He had hoped they wouldn't have to have such a difficult conversation for a while. Now that she was in preschool she was seeing more kids with their moms and he should have realized sooner that this would be coming.

He'd delicately explained that her mommy had to go away and couldn't stay in Haven. He'd even lied and said she loved Piper very much, but sometimes people just had to go away. In truth, Jax had forced her to sign over her rights. If she didn't want to be here now, he didn't want to risk her coming back later and claiming Piper. The fact she signed over without too much of a fight proved exactly what type of woman she was.

Piper deserved better.

"I-I'm sorry," Olivia stuttered, blinking. "Date? It's late. Where's Piper?"

"She actually is staying all night with our neighbor. This is her second sleepover there."

"Who's your neighbor?" she asked, crossing her arms over a perfectly fitted tank. Damn it. Why did her curves have to look even sexier outside of those stuffy, rich-girl clothes?

With her hair down and loose curls lying over her shoulders, her leggings, and tank, she looked almost human . . . not at all like the business shark trying to steal his only source of income and future.

"An elderly lady who watches Piper for me sometimes. She has a granddaughter the same age and she was staying all night. They asked if Piper wanted to come over to make cookies and watch movies."

And that's all that needed to be mentioned for Piper to run and grab her favorite stuffed horse and pillow. She'd changed into her pajamas with unicorns, shoved her ladybug rain boots on, and promptly clomped out the back door with a wave of the hand. She was growing up on him, which he was proud of, but she could at least act like she'd miss him.

Jax dropped his arm from the door and shrugged. "I figured this was as good a time as any since I'm not busy."

Two women came down the hallway behind Olivia. Jax recognized Jade instantly. That woman was striking, she hadn't changed one bit, but she'd never done a thing for Jax. Even though she'd been older, too, when he was a preteen, nobody held a candle to Olivia Daniels.

Mercy, he was an idiot for allowing those juvenile thoughts to resurface.

"Jade, nice to see you. I'm not sure you remember me."

The redhead offered him a wide smile he was sure she'd used to trap many men into her web. "I do remember you. You've changed quite a bit since I saw you last."

That seemed to be the consensus of people who hadn't seen him since he was an awkward teen and hadn't weighed more than a buck fifty.

Turning his attention toward the blonde, he nodded. "I'm Jax."

"Melanie," she greeted with a shy smile.

This one seemed quite different from the outspoken Jade and the uppity Olivia. A beautiful trio, that much was for sure. If those three strutted down the streets of Haven, there would definitely be talk.

"Nice to meet you," he replied. "You ladies don't mind if I steal Livie, do you?"

Jade's smile turned into a smirk as she nudged her friend. "We don't mind at all. We weren't doing much of anything anyway."

Olivia's eyes widened as she stared back at him. "You can't possibly think I'm going on a date right now. I'm not dressed—"

"What you have on will be fine." More than fine because at least now he felt they were somewhat on the same level. He couldn't deal with her in those stuffy clothes, anyway. "We're not going far."

Olivia rubbed her forehead and closed her eyes. "Jackson—"

"Go," Melanie urged. "Jade and I are fine."

Jax waited for Livie to come up with another excuse, but she legitimately seemed at a loss for words. Maybe this wouldn't be as difficult as he first thought. Clearly, his plan of catching her off guard was brilliant. Now, if he could just keep this momentum going. He wasn't going to put much effort into this fight for the simple fact he didn't have to. He refused to sell, so there wasn't much she could do.

But he was going to hear her out because he was a gentleman and respected women. Livie was wasting her time, though.

"You may want to put shoes on," Jax stated, pointing down to her bare feet with the brightest shade of red on her toes. He would've pegged her for more of a French manicure type, something classy and simple. The red was a nice surprise and sexy as hell.

"I'll meet you wherever we're going," she replied, crossing her arms in defiance.

Adorable how she thought she could act like a child. He was quite used to that sort of behavior, so again, he had the edge here.

"That wouldn't be much of a date, would it?" he countered.

Livie turned back to her friends and Melanie held her hands out. "No argument from me. I'd love if a hot guy came and forced me on a date."

Oh, he liked this new friend already. She could be a useful ally. Jade remained silent, which pleased him. At least her friends weren't slamming the door in his face. They clearly wanted her to go, which spoke volumes about how lackluster her social life was. Apparently, they felt she needed to get out—or they thought she could persuade him into agreeing to a sale.

No doubt they'd all sat around and discussed this situation in depth and Olivia had been given advice and encouragement to go after what she wanted.

"Fine." Livie turned toward the left side of the door and slid on a pair of flip-flops before facing him once again. "Let's get this over with."

Jax held a hand over his heart. "I'm crushed you're in a hurry to get this over with."

Livie let out an unladylike growl as she marched past him. Jax flashed a grin at Jade and Melanie, who weren't even trying to hold back their laughter.

"Don't wait up," he told them.

Livie whirled around on the steps. "We won't be that long."

Ignoring her protest, he bound down the narrow concrete steps and headed toward his truck. He opened the passenger door and gestured for her to get in.

She plopped into the passenger seat and jerked her seat belt. "Don't take this date too seriously, Romeo."

"Oh, I'm just pushing your buttons because you're too easy to irritate."

Another growl escaped her as he closed the door. He gave her friends a mock salute as they stood on the porch and waved. Jax wasn't sure if this plan was brilliant or one of his more idiotic moves, but he was about to find out.

"What are we doing here?"

Olivia had no idea what to expect, but she didn't think they'd end up at the airport. Jackson's lights slashed across the darkness, landing on one of the old hangars.

"Our date. I figured this was the best place."

He was up to something, she just knew it. Whatever it was, she'd be ready. He'd caught her off guard once; she needed to be on her toes from here on out.

Once Jax killed the engine, Olivia opened her door. The creaky old truck needed some serious oil on those hinges, but that wasn't her problem. She slammed the door and set off toward the hangar.

Surprisingly, Jackson followed without one snarky comment. Once inside, she flicked the overhead lights, and once again that old Cessna sat proudly in front of her. Years of memories flooded her and Olivia already knew what angle Jackson was working.

She had to remain strong.

Jackson headed to the plane and started walking around doing an inspection . . . an inspection that one usually did preflight.

"No," she stated firmly. "Nice try."

Without missing a beat, he opened the tiny door and climbed in. With his booted foot dangling out, he grabbed the preflight checklist from the pocket of the door. He flicked controls on the panel, watched the wings tip, and moved on to the rest of the panel. Any seasoned pilot still always went through the routine of the preflight, but she wasn't having any part of this.

"Flying at night has always been my favorite," he stated, as if they were having a normal conversation. "Maybe it comes from my years in the Air Force, or maybe I just enjoy the peaceful time and the beauty of the lights below."

Olivia found herself crossing the space between them as he spoke. There was a different tone to his voice when he talked about flying. He came across almost nostalgic . . . laced with love. Definitely love. Still, she couldn't get in that plane and keep control over all the swirling emotions.

After a moment, Jackson hopped out of the plane and hit the switch for the bay door. The loud groaning of the track filled the space and the warm summer air swept in as the door lifted. He attached the tow and pulled the plane out and onto the pavement.

Damn it. Olivia knew if she wanted to talk to him, she'd have to get in that plane.

First, though, she had to take a deep, calming breath. The last time she'd been in that plane her father had insisted she fly and he ride as the passenger. They'd talked about nothing, really, and Olivia remembered being irritated because she'd wanted to go to a bonfire with friends, but she'd ended up letting guilt make her decision.

That was the last time she'd been in this Cessna, the last time she'd piloted. She hadn't given flying much thought since she'd left Haven; she'd tried to push that portion of her life behind her. But here she stood, literally face-to-face with her past when all she wanted to do was leave.

How had she gone so askew from her original plans?

"You want to fly?" Jackson asked, pulling her from her thoughts.

Olivia shook her head, holding her hands up. "Oh, no. I haven't flown since I was seventeen."

That devilish grin flashed her way once again. Why did he have to ooze charm and sex appeal? It wasn't fair that her adversary could make her tingle from across the room. Nor was it fair that someone who was so awkward years ago looked like he'd stepped out of a calendar photo shoot.

She had to work damn hard to attempt to stay on top of her weight, her wrinkles, her dark circles beneath her eyes. Jackson probably just slid out of bed and into his perfectly form-fitted jeans and tees and left the house. No regimen needed when you looked that good.

"I'd say you'd remember the second you got the controls in your hands." He closed the space between them and nodded toward the plane over his shoulder. "Come on. Aren't you just a bit curious to see how she still flies?"

A sliver of curiosity had crept up, but she had the willpower to ignore the unwanted emotion.

"I thought we were going to talk about this sale." There, she just needed to steer the topic back to the reason she was here. "We can do that just as easy in the office."

"Probably so, but I never get to just fly at night for my enjoyment." He leaned in closer, keeping that dark, mesmerizing gaze locked onto hers. "Fly with me, Livie. You won't regret it."

Oh, he could tempt the last piece of chocolate cake away from hungry women at a packed Weight Watchers meeting. He was too charming for his own good, and she truly needed to keep reminding herself she was here for one purpose . . . and it wasn't to get swept into his web.

"You can fly," she informed him. "I'll just enjoy the view."

He raked his eyes over her once more and Olivia braced herself for another of his comments. But after a moment, he nodded and headed back toward the plane. She pulled in a deep breath and marched ahead. She didn't want to think about the last time she sat in the tiny leather seat. She didn't want to flash back to the first time her father let her have the controls. And she certainly didn't want to spend more time in Jackson's company than she had to because . . . well, just because.

Olivia opened the passenger door, used the step on the wing, and climbed inside. That familiar scent surrounded her. The leather, the oil, the metal. There was no dodging the assault of memories. She gripped her hands in her lap as she waited for him to start the engine and do a final check.

Nerves swirled inside her. Not from flying, never from that. She'd actually loved the sport. So many people assumed the worst because the only press aviation received seemed to be when they crashed. But flying was safe, it was beautiful, peaceful. It calmed her in ways she couldn't explain.

But right now, being back in the plane she'd learned to fly in, the plane her father had babied for years, was a bit difficult. Not to mention being inches from her sexy rival worked over her nerves pretty well too.

"You've taken great care of her," Olivia stated, needing something to break the tension.

"She's paid my bills, so it's only fair I pamper her."

He maneuvered down the runway, radioed his takeoff information through the headset for any surrounding planes to hear, and got into position. The engines roared to life, and then they were jetting down the paved lane flanked by bright blue lights. Within seconds, they were airborne and Olivia looked out her side window. The tiny town of Haven was breathtaking, all glistening in various shades of light.

Jackson was right in saying the night was the most beautiful, the most peaceful. She'd taken this plane out a few times when she'd needed to think or when she just wanted to get away. Her time alone in the plane was limited considering she didn't get her pilot's license until she was sixteen, but she'd fallen in love even more once she got behind the controls.

"I wasn't aware you'd brought an entourage when you came to town."

Jackson's words sliced through her thoughts. "Jade and Melanie are hardly an entourage. They're my best friends."

"I remember you and Jade were always together. How did you meet Melanie?"

Olivia focused on the town below and not the way Jackson's aftershave or cologne seemed to mess with her senses. Couldn't he just smell like grease and sweat? That would make this so much easier. But no. She was enclosed in this tiny space with a man who smelled sexy and had charm dripping off nearly every word.

"We actually met at a marathon a couple years ago," she replied. Melanie's history was her story to tell, so Olivia wasn't getting into all of that. "She twisted her ankle right before the finish line and Jade and I ended up carrying her over it so she could finish. We've been friends since."

"Impressive," he muttered. He turned the plane toward Savannah. "So what is it you do in Atlanta?"

Olivia adjusted the mic on her headset. "I'm an accountant for a marketing firm, but I've been doing some work in PR as well."

"Sounds boring."

Olivia clasped her hands in her lap. "It's not boring. I stay busy and I have a very important position."

"Staying busy and being needed isn't the same thing as doing something you love," he retorted.

"I enjoy nice things, so I like my income." That may have been a vast understatement. "And I enjoy working somewhere that recognizes my talents."

"So you need material things and praise with your job?" he asked.

Olivia gritted her teeth. She wasn't shallow. She *wasn't*. Couldn't she be proud of the hard work she'd done? Why did he have to make her feel remorseful for having goals and reaching them?

"You won't make me feel guilty for my lifestyle."

When his whiskey-smooth tone didn't come back through the headset, Olivia glanced back out the window. She couldn't deny that she missed this. Flying was ingrained in her blood and no matter the person she was now, she was still the daughter of Paul Daniels.

"You remember Cash and Tanner?"

His abrupt question had her turning in her seat. "Of course. Tanner was in my grade, but Cash was a couple years younger. How are they doing?"

The lights from the panel illuminated Jackson's face. That hard-set jaw with just enough scruff to make her wonder what it would feel like beneath her palm . . . No.

She wasn't wondering. She didn't want to reach out and see how he reacted. What in the world was she thinking?

Maybe being confined in this small space was a bad idea. There was nowhere to go and she was literally at his mercy.

"Pretty good," he replied. "They have a plane in one of the other hangars. They went in on a Beechcraft Piston a few years ago. It's pretty nice."

She'd had no idea anyone else occupied the other hangars on the property. Her father had rented the space to recreational fliers, but Olivia never thought about Jackson doing the same.

"Do you have other renters?" she asked.

"A few. I have one guy who was going to leave town, but he ended up falling in love and is staying." Jax's laughter came through the headset. "I admit, I'm the one who set them up. But I've since learned they knew each other years ago. She was his late wife's nurse or something. It was an interesting story. Still, if I hadn't reconnected them—"

"You're a regular Cupid," she stated dryly. "What about other renters?"

"I still have space for two more, but aviation is a dying sport. I have a few teenagers who are interested in getting their license. They've talked to me about getting hours in and already started their online training. We'll see if they stick with it."

Olivia knew some people loved to fly, but once all that power was in their hands, they froze up. Some people scared themselves on landings or even takeoffs. She'd loved every minute of all the rush, the freedom. But the push-pull relationship with her father had tainted her love of the sport.

This entire airport had left a bad taste in her mouth when she'd left, and she hated to admit it, but the longer she was here, the more she was remembering the reasons why she loved it as a child.

She pushed aside the sentimental thoughts and returned her focus to the conversation. "Sounds like you're not doing too bad."

She hadn't meant to let that slip out. She didn't want to start getting invested emotionally into this situation. That wasn't smart business sense and she definitely knew better.

"I do all right." That low, rich voice filled her headset. "As long as I can provide for my daughter and do what I love, I don't care about extra."

Guilt slithered through her. Had he purposely thrown his daughter into the conversation to make her second-guess selling?

Olivia couldn't bear other people's crosses. She had her own issues and her own life to get on with, and she planned to get on with that life as soon as she put this portion of her past behind her once and for all.

"So you have your teaching license?" she asked.

"Yeah. I didn't necessarily have the urge to teach, but I'm always looking to learn more and better my skill. Things just fell into place, plus the extra money is nice. I have to watch the hours because of Piper and my regular flights."

A single father was not someone she had experience with. She wasn't sure what his life must be like. Olivia didn't have to worry about anyone else's schedule. When she wanted to do something, she checked her work calendar first and that was all.

Oh, no. She *was* shallow.

"Why haven't you flown since you left?" he asked.

Olivia stared at the controls in front of her. The urge to grab hold was strong, but she fisted her hands in her lap. Everything before her was the past, not her future.

"Probably for the same reasons you're not married."

Silence settled over the airways and she wondered if she'd stepped over the line. Obviously, she had, but she didn't want to delve into her issues any more than he did.

After a moment of tension-filled silence, Jackson's gruff chuckle came through. "You really don't want to talk about this, do you? Fine. I'm not married because when I was in the air force my wife gave birth while I was overseas. When she decided she didn't want to be a parent, I knew I had to give up my career and step up to the plate. She was a heartless mother and signed her rights over as she rushed to get out of town. So, I've been a little too busy to date, let alone remarry."

Olivia stared at the horizon where the darkness met the city lights. She wasn't sure what to say. She hadn't fully expected him to open up, so that was shocking in itself, but the picture he painted was heartbreaking.

His wife had left him and a newborn baby? She wanted to compare the parallel childhood she had to his instance, but she'd been eighteen when she'd walked away from her father.

"Nothing to say?" he asked. "You don't want to share with the class your little secrets?"

Olivia tucked her hands beneath her legs. Part of her wanted to feel those controls once again, part of her wanted him to land this thing because she couldn't handle being wrapped in all these memories.

"I don't know what to say," she murmured. "But no, I don't want to share anything. I just want to sell this airport. I can't have this in my life."

"Wanting to cut those final ties? I guess being a city girl now you're more concerned with promotions, getting to the top of that corporate ladder, and forgetting your roots."

Olivia knew anything she said would only make her sound like she hated this place, so she remained silent.

"I guess it's easier to move on than it is to water those roots, huh?"

Swallowing that lump of remorse, Olivia refused to answer. No, she didn't want to revisit the past. Obviously, that was the entire point of trying to get out from under this burden.

"You can buy my half," she suggested, as if that solution would wrap up this mess in a neat package.

"In a perfect world I would. But I have bills to pay and no extra cash."

"How about a loan?"

"My wife pretty much destroyed my credit while I was overseas. I'm still digging out of that mess."

Who was this woman he'd been married to? She left a newborn baby and had demolished Jackson's finances all while he was fighting for their country. What was wrong with people?

"I'm sure there's something we can work out," she murmured, more talking to herself than anything. She refused to believe there was no way around this.

"Why don't I get the property appraised and let's take it from there."

Jackson started their descent and part of Olivia was thankful their time was drawing to an end. The other part, the one she wished would shut up and get out of her head, wanted to learn more about the man who stood in her way. She wanted to know what happened after she left, how his relationship was with her father. Most likely Jackson was the exact child her father had wanted. With his love of aviation, Jackson made the perfect replacement once Olivia was gone. Hell, Jackson had been perfect while Olivia had still lived here. Maybe that was just another reason why her father stayed at the airport so often—he'd had someone to bond with.

Olivia couldn't deny the hurt. She couldn't deny that when she'd secretly wished her father would put her ahead of everything else, but instead he'd turned to the skies, to Jackson.

"You can do what you want, but you'd be wasting your time." His voice came through seconds before he tapped the control and announced his landing. "This is my life, Livie. You wouldn't like it too much if someone showed up at your place of employment one day and told you to give everything up."

"This isn't the same thing," she argued.

"It's exactly the same thing, I just reversed the scenario."

He wasn't going to make her feel guilty. Hadn't she already had that pep talk with herself? The whole single father, ex-soldier, small-town hunk was too damn appealing on levels she couldn't even address in her own mind. She refused to let him get to her, but that grip she had on the control was starting to slip. If she didn't watch herself, she'd lose more than just this sale.

As he lined up with the airstrip, Olivia's trained eye instantly went to the lights to the left of the runway to make sure all three were green for a safe landing.

"You're a great pilot," she found herself saying. "You can tell you have a passion."

"I would've still been in the air force had my life not taken a different turn," he explained. The plane made a gentle bump as the wheels hit the pavement. "But Piper is the best thing that's ever happened to me and I wouldn't change a thing."

"Not every parent would have given everything up like that."

"I never walk away from what's mine. Not even when

my marriage was falling apart. I would've stuck it out to make things work."

Olivia didn't understand that type of dedication. She'd never been shown such devotion or love. She couldn't help but wonder if he loved his wife that much or if he was just determined to give his daughter the best life he knew how. No matter, she didn't need his whole backstory. She didn't need to know what made him tick to move forward with her plans. Selling this airport was nonnegotiable.

"Let me buy your half, Jackson. I would make it worth your while and give you enough until you found something else."

He taxied around the runway, slowing the plane down and letting the engines cool. Olivia waited on him to flat-out refuse once again. It seemed to be their song and dance. But she wasn't giving up . . . then again, neither was he.

"Not everything is a business decision," he finally stated. "You don't even bother getting to know someone before you try to turn their life inside out. You know the young boy I used to be. You see me as some sort of replacement for you in regard to your father. If you only knew how he was after you left, you might not be in such a hurry to sell his legacy."

The unwelcome burning in her throat had Olivia swallowing hard. Those emotions she'd once thought buried kept creeping up at the most inopportune times . . . and even more so since she'd been back. Living in her childhood home, sleeping in her old bedroom, and dealing with Jackson really thrust her into dealing with things she'd rather run from. But she'd been running long enough. She was a big girl now—time to act like one.

"You only saw my father's side of things," she explained. "I'm sure you think you know the situation, but I promise you don't."

As they neared the hangar, he slid off his headset and placed it between them. Bringing the plane to a complete stop, he turned to face her.

"Then tell me," he stated, as if things were that simple, and that open, between them. "Tell me what it was like. Because I assure you that you also don't know all the sides of the story. You have no clue that your father kept those little overalls you used to wear as a toddler hanging in his office behind the door until he died. You have no clue that he was sick when you left, and you can't possibly know that he busted his ass to hold on to this when his medical bills had become so much that he almost had to sell. He stayed at the airport more than usual because he didn't want you and your mother to see how run-down he was from the illness."

Shock flooded her as Jackson eased the plane back to the front of the hangar. She sat in utter silence, letting his words penetrate her mind. Once they were parked, he shut the plane down and abruptly exited as if he had nothing else to say to her. Olivia let him go, because she truly had no clue how to respond.

Tears pricked her eyes and she knew she was at a point where she was going to have to get some answers before she could fully move on. She was going to have to revisit that time when she'd left, and Jackson was going to have to fill her in because, no, she'd had no clue her father had been sick.

And that bit of information just changed the dynamics of this entire situation.

Chapter Five

Jax didn't give a shit what Olivia did. He'd put the plane up later. She could call a friend to come get her or she could come in and ask him. But right now, he just needed space.

It wasn't a stretch to say that Paul Daniels was like a father to Jax. With both of Jax's parents deceased, he'd grown up with his grandfather, who was wonderful, but he was older and tired. Paul had been amazing, teaching an eager Jax everything he'd known about planes and flying.

Jax had started tinkering after school, and then that turned into the weekends and summer breaks. He'd learned to fly a plane before he knew how to drive a car and he knew much more about the engine in a Skyhawk than he had about the one in his old Mustang.

But when Paul had gotten sick, Jax wondered why he hadn't told his wife and daughter. At the time Jax had only been thirteen, so he didn't feel it was his place to step in and say anything. Paul had his reasons, stating he didn't want them to stay out of pity. He'd been a proud man, a man of integrity and compassion. Jax absolutely hated that Livie thought the worst of her father. The man would've done anything for her, but in the end, time had run out.

Jax paced the empty hangar, raking a hand over his hair, then rubbing his jaw. The bristles scraping against his palm reminded him he hadn't shaved in a couple days. Having Olivia show up had thrown him off, and he was never thrown off his game.

Something about the hoity-toity city woman he'd once had a school-age crush on had set him into overdrive. Part of him wanted her to get the hell out and never return, just leave him alone with his business. But the other part, the strictly male part, wanted to kiss the hell out of her and mess up that perfect persona she portrayed.

Jax knew that same girl who used to have grease beneath her nails as she helped her father with his planes still lived in that big-city-girl body. She'd loved flying when they'd been up. He'd seen her gripping her hands and he knew she wanted to take the controls. Something that deeply rooted didn't just disappear simply because you wanted it to.

"You can't just drop news like that and walk away."

Jax kept his back to Livie. Her footsteps echoed in the open hangar. "I shouldn't have told you anything," he stated. "Your father didn't want you to know."

"Why the hell not?" she demanded.

Jax spun around and for the first time since she'd come back, he saw something he didn't think existed in Livie . . . guilt. That's exactly what Paul didn't want.

"He didn't want you or your mother to stay out of pity." Jax figured now that Paul was gone, revealing the truth wouldn't much matter. Maybe if Livie saw exactly how things went, she wouldn't be so bitter. "He loved you both. Yes, he had an odd way of showing it, but you have to know that everything he did was for you."

Livie crossed her arms, pushing her breasts up in that scooped tank. Damn if she wasn't one of the sexiest women he'd ever seen. That crush as a preteen and teenager had been mild compared to the ache and need he had flooding him now.

But he'd gotten tangled with a beautiful woman once before and Livie wasn't sticking around. She wanted the hell out of Haven once and for all.

"Since you know so much about my father, please, enlighten me."

Propping his hands on his hips, Jax pulled in a deep breath and willed himself to remain calm. "It's a moot point now, Livie. He's gone. We're at a standstill until you can come to grips with the fact that I will never sell. Ever. There's no money you can wave in my face, there's no way you can mastermind your way into this sale. The airport, flying, and the people that need these services are the second most important things in my life."

Her eyes never wavered from his and he wondered if he was actually making headway with her. Was she grasping exactly what he was saying? He was done playing games, he was done trying to be nice about the situation. She was wasting her time and she was wearing him out.

"What happens if I go back to Atlanta?" she asked. "We're still legally partners in this business. I should have equal say."

Jax laughed. He couldn't help himself. "So now you want to be partners? As in, you want to decide what's best for the airport so you can rake in half the money? I assure you, it's not much."

He'd been scraping every extra penny and dime for years to get a new Skyhawk. He'd managed to squander away a good amount so far, but planes were damn expensive, even used ones. But he knew this Cessna wouldn't last forever. No matter how much he babied the beautiful piece, it was nearing time to retire. He wanted to invest in the future, in a plane that would hopefully be something he passed to Piper as she grew older. If she loved the sport as much as he did and opted to turn it into a career, he wanted to be able to give her something nice.

"You can keep the money, but this place needs some sprucing up in a major way."

"There you go with the material things again," he told her as he took a step toward her. "As long as my plane flies and my clients get to where they need to be, they don't care if the building needs paint or if the weeds are out of control. It's a small town, Livie. I work by reputation alone, not the beauty of my building."

"Our building," she corrected.

Jax stepped forward once again, towering over her. Her eyes flared as she stared up at him.

"Is that how you're going to play this game?" he murmured, raking his eyes over each one of her striking features. "You think you're going to keep up your half of this legal binding?"

Livie's tongue darted out to lick her bottom lip and he couldn't help but track the seductive movement.

"I don't know how to play this game," she admitted. "We both want different things and I'm used to getting what I want."

Her floral scent hit him in just the right, or wrong, way. Arousal churned deep in his gut and he hated that he had this strong of a pull toward someone so hell-bent on stealing his life.

"Ironically, I'm used to getting what I want, too."

That was all the warning he gave her before he crushed his lips to hers. He was done listening to her talk, he was finished with this conversation that was obviously going nowhere. He'd wanted to kiss her for years and now that she was right in his face, why the hell not?

When she opened to him and leaned into his body, that was all the green light he needed to wrap his arms around her and thrust his hands into all that silky hair. She clutched his shoulders, her fingers bruising him, but he didn't care. There was a fine line between hate and desire. He'd obliterated that invisible barrier the second he touched her . . . maybe before. Maybe when he'd shown up at her house with this insane plan to take her up in the plane.

But he'd wanted her to get that smack in the face from her past and see exactly what she was doing.

Instead, his control had snapped and now he had his arms full of Livie. Jax slid one hand down to the small of her back and leaned over her. That grip she had on him tightened even more as she was only being held upright by him. Again, he wanted her to know exactly who was in control here.

When she moaned and arched against him, Jax wondered exactly who held the reins because he was drowning in this woman and that was a damn problem. This was the first kiss they'd shared . . . but he knew it wouldn't be the last.

Livie tore away from the kiss and stumbled back, leaving him cold and aching for more. One shaky hand went to her lips—his ego liked to believe he'd made her shaky and just as needy.

"Why did you do that?" she whispered.

"I wanted to."

Her eyes were a darker shade now—from arousal?

No matter, he'd never seen a sexier sight than Livie with her hair in disarray from his hands, her lips swollen from his touch, and her body trembling. Yeah, there would definitely be a next time.

"You can't—we . . ."

She shook her head and spun around. Jax waited while she gathered herself. Another boost to his ego. She smoothed her hair with her fingers, straightened her tank, and squared her shoulders before turning around. Sure, she could try to get back to that stuffy Livie, but her moist lips puffy from his assault couldn't be so easily tamed.

"We just did," he countered with a grin he couldn't suppress. "And I plan on doing it again."

One perfectly arched brow lifted. "Is that a threat?"

"More like a promise."

Livie marched past him. "Take me home."

Jax turned, reached out, and snaked an arm around her waist, hauling her back against his chest. He must have been a masochist because he should have just let her walk away—but he could still feel her lips, her body, against his.

"Are you offended because I kissed you or because you liked it?" he whispered in her ear.

Her body stiffened against his, but he didn't turn her loose. "I didn't like it."

Jax laughed, brushed her hair off her neck, and replied, "I bet I'll have bruises on my shoulders that say otherwise."

"Don't flatter yourself."

He released her long enough to spin her around. "I don't need to flatter myself. Not when you were arching that sweet body against mine and moaning. I bet those uptight city boys don't even know how to treat someone like you. I bet they take you to a fancy restaurant, bring you flowers when they pick you up, and give you a polite kiss good night."

She blinked and tilted her chin in defiance and he knew he'd hit the proverbial nail on the head.

"No wonder you responded so passionately."

Livie narrowed her gaze. "You're not my type."

"I'm not asking for you to walk down the aisle with me. I already did that and it was a disaster." He leaned in just enough to torment himself with that floral aroma once again. "Although I'm positive you don't even know your type."

"It's not someone too young for me."

Her weak defense was muttered, which only proved she was losing her grasp on her self-control.

"Baby, I'm not young," he corrected. "I've seen and done things you could never imagine and I assure you, you weren't thinking of my age when you had your hands all over me."

He leaned in just a bit closer, pleased when her eyes dropped to his mouth. Jax came within a breath of her lips, she parted . . .

"I better get you back home." He skirted around her and headed toward the door. "Your roommates will be worried."

As he stepped out into the night and headed toward his truck, Livie followed behind him, muttering under her breath some extremely unladylike expressions. Jax had a difficult time keeping his laughter under control.

He wanted her to be achy because he was damn uncomfortable. She couldn't throw their ages in his face and she couldn't lie, either. She'd been just as invested in that kiss as he had.

Jax would drive her home and he'd lay money on the fact she wouldn't get any sleep tonight. She'd try to rationalize that kiss, question why she liked it so much, and start formulating some other plan to get what she wanted. She could try, but he planned on kissing her again, he planned on keeping her thrown so far off her game she forgot why she came, and he sure as hell planned on keeping this airport.

* * *

Olivia practically crawled down the stairs the next morning to the blissful aroma of coffee. After being awake nearly all night, she was going to need copious amounts of caffeine today.

She jerked her hair up into a loose knot and wrapped a thick band around her mop to hold it out of her face. She was not in the mood today for hair, for real clothes, for . . . well, anything. Except caffeine, in which case she could use an abundance.

With a yawn, Olivia padded into the kitchen. Her friends' chatter didn't even lift her mood. Nothing was helping because for once in her life she was at a complete loss. The kiss was one thing, but it was all those damn emotions that assaulted her after that had her so disoriented.

How could she have enjoyed his touch? Why had her body betrayed her, because she knew full well she'd arched into him and groaned?

Ugh. The groan. That should've never slipped out. Now she was working backward because how could he take her seriously when her actions indicated she was easy to manipulate.

"Well, look who's up," Jade said around her mug that said THROTTLE IT UP, BABY. Her father always had silly mugs and tees with random sayings. She used to find all of that embarrassing, but now . . . well, she kind of found it humorous.

"No walk of shame this morning?" Jade asked. "I was so hoping you'd take advantage of Jax now that he's all grown up and looking damn fine. Why didn't you tell us exactly what you were up against? Did you see that set of shoulders?"

Had she seen them? She'd clung to them while he'd practically made love to her mouth and had her forgetting everything, including her own name for a minute.

"No walk of shame," she grumbled, sliding onto one of the empty barstools. "I'm not here for booty calls, Jade. I need to wrap this mess up and get back to my life."

Melanie sat a steaming mug of coffee in front of Olivia. "You look like you need something stronger than this."

"I need to get my head examined," she muttered as she took that first sip, which touched her soul. "I mean, he can't just kiss me and think that I'll—"

"Whoa." Jade sat her mug down and slid in beside Olivia. Mel instantly flanked her other side. "Start from when you drove away from the curb and leave nothing out. Extra details about his lips, too, for those of us who aren't kissing anyone lately."

Olivia gripped her mug and shook her head. "We argued, we took a flight, he told me my father had been sick when my mother and I left years ago, and then the jerk kissed me."

"Was it a bad kiss?" Jade asked, her nose slightly wrinkled.

"What did he say about your dad?" Mel chimed in.

Olivia truly didn't have the emotional stamina to keep up. "I don't know what was wrong with my father. Mom and I had no clue anything was wrong when we moved. And the kiss . . . well . . ."

"I knew it." Jade pumped a fist in the air. "So awesome it left you speechless. I'm guessing that's why you're so grouchy today, because he left you frustrated. I've been there."

"Shut up." Olivia took another sip of her coffee and refused to look at her friend, whom she knew would be smirking. "I need to figure out how to get him to sell. If half is mine, I want my money and I want to sign it over to someone else."

"This isn't about money," Melanie stated softly. "Don't kid yourself."

Olivia shook her head. "Not completely, but I feel that it's owed to me."

"No, you don't," Jade interjected. "That's the hurt talking. We know you're a shark when it comes to your career, but this is personal and you're still facing these feelings from the past."

Yeah, she was. There was no way to dodge them . . . she'd tried.

"What am I going to do?" she asked, setting her mug back on the counter. She ran her fingertip over the crack in the handle. "I have half an airport that I don't want and Jackson clearly isn't budging either. It's impossible for both of us to get our way."

Well, except for when his lips were on hers, but that was another matter entirely. There was no denying they'd both wanted that. Unfortunately, the sampling of Jackson Morgan only left her wanting more, and acting on her wants and needs and this damn achiness was only a recipe for disaster.

"Why don't you join as partners?" Melanie stated simply, as if that were the answer for them all.

Olivia came to her feet and circled the old island. She grabbed a granola bar from the counter and ripped the wrapping off before taking a bite.

"This tastes like sawdust," she muttered around the dry bite.

"That's mine," Jade growled.

"Well, it tastes like I'd rather be fat." The second the words were out of her mouth, Olivia turned to Melanie. "I'm so sorry. That was uncalled for and insensitive."

Mel waved a hand and smiled. "You're having a rough morning and I love you. You get a free pass at any fat jokes."

If there were ever a real-life saint, Melanie Ramsey was it. She forgave easily, loved freely, and was always the peacemaker. Which is most likely how she remained in an abusive marriage and overweight for too many years. She'd taken the attention offered by a ruthless man and mistaken it for love. It was only after they married that the verbal and physical abuse started. Melanie was stronger than she thought because she'd not only escaped that nightmare, she was thriving.

Olivia tossed the bar onto the island in front of Jade. "You can have the rest."

With a shrug, her perfectly fit friend finished the bar claiming to be akin to s'mores. The next time Olivia had a s'more, it better be with a campfire and a stick with a gooey marshmallow on the end.

Olivia leaned back against the counter and sighed. "I guess while I'm formulating a game plan, I'll start cleaning out these closets."

"We're here to help," Jade stated. "My morning run is done. It was actually nice with the warmer temps; I didn't need to pack my inhaler. So, use me where you want. I'm yours the rest of the day. Unless some hunk knocks on the door and offers to take me out."

Rolling her eyes, Olivia glanced to Melanie. "What about you? You ready to tackle my demons with me?"

"Do we need to go ahead and open the wine and get tissues?"

Olivia pushed off the counter with a laugh. "It might not be a bad idea, but let's do champagne and at least call them mimosas. Hold off on the tissues. I'm going to try to keep it together and get this done."

Jade turned her attention to her phone as Melanie started working on their cocktails. Olivia hadn't bothered to bring her phone down. She didn't want to look at e-mails or texts from work. She had to finish putting together an ad for one of her top clients, but she was nearly done and she planned on doing that after she tackled the past.

Leave it to her to use work to unwind and relax. She truly needed to get a life, but she was happy with the one she had . . . wasn't she?

Damn it. She never questioned her happiness in Atlanta before coming back . . . and she'd only been back a few short days.

"Maybe we should book a few days at Bella Vous before we leave," Jade suggested as she kept scrolling through her social media. "Or at the very least get some massages."

Bella Vous had the most remarkable masseuse and despite the fact the resort was booked for months in advance, they knew Cora and she would squeeze them in.

Going to the old antebellum estate was relaxing enough even without the massage. The grand home had been transformed into something from a magazine.

Olivia and Jade had gone to school with the Monroe boys and nothing shocked Olivia more than knowing those guys had managed to pull off such a remarkable business. Of course, maybe that had something to do with the women in their lives, but who knows.

"I could definitely use a hot stone massage," Olivia stated. "But the resort is getting so popular with the tourists coming in from Savannah, I'm not sure we could get in."

With a shrug, Jade replied, "I'll at least try."

Melanie sat three glasses on the bar and poured their drinks. "Did you guys hear the rumor about the movie crew coming to Haven?"

Georgia was well-liked by the film industry because it was less expensive to shoot in and the scenery was simply gorgeous. Olivia wouldn't want to live anywhere else; she just preferred the city over the small town.

"I didn't know one was coming to Haven," Olivia replied. "Where did you hear that?"

"When I grabbed the paper off the sidewalk this morning, I overheard your two neighbors talking."

"Gray-haired neighbors?" Jade asked.

"Yeah."

Olivia shot Jade a smile. "Those two are always gossiping about something. I swear, they were old and gossipy sixteen years ago when we lived here."

"They didn't see me, but I just heard one of them say the film crew would be here in two weeks to start scouting locations in town."

Haven had some beautiful areas. The park, the round-about in town with a massive clock in the center; the courthouse was also a stunning structure. Definitely the new resort and spa. Those grounds were remarkable and the home itself just screamed Southern plantation. She wasn't sure what type of film was being shot here, but if it was an historical or a small-town love story, Haven certainly fit the bill.

"I need to get to work or I'll never get it done." Olivia took her glass and headed toward the back set of steps that led to the bedrooms. "Save yourselves, run now. I can't promise there won't be tears and throwing things."

Jade and Melanie grabbed their drinks and followed. Apparently, her warning wasn't necessary. She'd informed them before they came to Haven and they'd assured her they were here for her, but Olivia knew they were here for one another. It was almost as if they took turns leaning on one another. Melanie definitely had used their shoulders to cry on. And Jade, well, Jade was proud, but she'd break soon. She was dealing with some ugly things and it wouldn't be long before she'd need them. When that time came, Olivia knew there was nowhere else she'd be but by her friend's side.

Chapter Six

"Damn it."

Jax wiped the grease on his already-stained jeans and stepped back from the leaking fuel drain. The rubber plug had been a bit difficult to get in, something he didn't typically have an issue with.

"Another exhilarating day on the job?"

Jax spun around to his older cousin's snarky comment. "Don't you have parking tickets to write?"

Tanner Roark crossed the hangar and shrugged. "I did that yesterday. Today I'm taking a breather and letting my writing hand rest."

Jax turned back around to the pan of fuel he'd drained. "Did you come to help with this leak or to just be a pain in my ass?"

"I can do both," Tanner replied. "I'm excellent at multi-tasking. Comes with the badge."

Tanner was an officer for Haven and was rarely seen out of uniform. Jax believed his cousin most likely wore it to keep the attention of the ladies. Tanner had always been quite the ladies' man and didn't make any apologies about the fact.

Quite the opposite of Jax and their other cousin, Cash.

The three were not only cousins, but also best friends. Jax and Cash had gone through ugly divorces. Tanner had sworn never to get himself into such a predicament as marriage. Jax figured he was the only smart one out of the bunch.

"You want a pair of coveralls?" Jax asked.

Tanner stepped up beside him and propped his hands on his hips. "Nah. Is this Bill's plane?"

"Yeah."

Bill was just one of the renters who occupied a portion of one of the hangars. Oftentimes Jax would do maintenance on others' planes to help out when he could. Now he was wishing he'd not taken this on because he was a greasy mess and he had to go to Piper's school this afternoon for some ceremony because Piper had entered a poster contest and was about to find out she'd gotten first place.

He hoped he had time to shower and not look like a complete slob, but at the same time he needed to get this job done because Bill was planning a flight for five this evening.

Jax would find a way to make it work. He always did. His new life motto was "it will all work out" and so far everything had. Maybe not in the way he'd planned, but there was only so much he could control.

"What do you need?" Tanner asked.

"This pan needs emptying."

"Do you want me to do that first or do you want to discuss the fact that Olivia Daniels is back in town?"

Jax swore beneath his breath and shook his head. "I'd prefer to just get this job done and ignore the locker-room gossip."

"Too bad. Start talking."

Since Tanner made no move to get that pan out of the way, Jax slid the cardboard beneath the mess to the side. "Livie is back. She wants to sell the airport and pretend this never existed in her life and be done with the last memory of Paul."

Tanner let out a low whistle. "Sounds like a bind. Did you tell her about Paul or did you opt to close up and just be stubborn?"

Being stubborn might've been a smarter option considering when he'd opened just enough to give her a glimpse, they'd ended up kissing and he could still taste her on his lips.

Damn it. He'd tried to get that moment out of his head, but there it was again. Jax didn't even have to concentrate and he could feel her sweet curves as she arched against him and returned his kiss. As a teen he'd dreamed of what that moment would be like, but now that he was older, more experienced, finally getting a taste of Livie Daniels only left him aching for more.

"She knows all she needs," Jax explained going back to examine the plug. It was holding; now he just needed to repair the line. "Nothing is changing her mind."

"She still hot?"

Jax snorted and shot his cousin a glare. "Are you kidding?"

Tanner shrugged. "That question is from Cash. He's busy at the gym until this evening."

Picking the new line from the floor, Jax leaned into the Cessna. "You two are worse than a bunch of old ladies. I'm not thirteen with a crush and a hard-on anymore."

Well, he had gone home rather uncomfortable after that kiss, but he wasn't an adolescent. He was a man and he needed to act like one. He could start by figuring out a way to get Livie to back off, which was damn hard when he was busy sampling her mouth and feeling her up.

Tanner grabbed the pan with fuel and headed out the open bay door. "Cash said he heard Livie has friends with her. You see them?"

"Jade is with her and another woman I met the other night. I think her name was Melanie."

"Jade was a year younger than me in school, but I took her out a couple times."

Jax slid the new line into place, thankful this was going smoother than the first part. "Is there anyone who's crossed through this town that you haven't taken out?"

"That other lady you mentioned," Tanner stated as he walked out to dump the fuel.

Jax got busy on the line and had it changed out and ready to refuel. Tanner came back in and was silent for a while, doing something on his phone, most likely making a date.

"You free this evening?" Tanner asked.

Swiping his hands on his pants once again, Jax climbed down and nodded. "Should be. What's up?"

"Cash texted and said he had a client give him a bunch of steaks from their farm."

"I could use a steak, but if he thinks this is going to turn into me spilling my guts, he's wrong."

Tanner shoved his phone back in his pocket. "I don't care what he thinks so long as he brings meat."

"Tell him to be at my place around five. Piper and I will make something to go with it."

Jax headed out of the hangar, making his way toward the office where he could wash off the mess somewhat before heading home to shower and change. Tanner followed at his side.

"How's she liking preschool?"

Jax opened the office door and gestured his cousin inside before he stepped into the refreshing air-conditioning. "She loves it. I'm going to head to the school in about an hour to some awards thing. I guess she won a poster contest, but she doesn't know about it yet."

"That's awesome," Tanner stated, crossing his arms. "I bet she's making all kinds of friends. You'll be having little slumber parties before you know it."

Jax cringed at the thought of squealing little girls overtaking his home. Soon enough that would happen. He had a feeling he'd have makeup on his face and polish on his hands. But being the dad of a spunky little girl was the greatest job he could've ever asked for. He wouldn't trade it for anything.

"Let's focus on tonight," Jax stated, stepping into the bathroom to wash off his hands and arms. "Warn Cash not to start talking too much about Livie. Piper already thinks she's gorgeous. Somehow she manipulated us into a date."

"The hell?"

Damn it. Jax hadn't meant to let that part slip out. That was just another reason he'd taken Livie out in the plane last night, because it was private where nobody would see them and there would be no gossip. Of course, now that Tanner knew, there was no way in hell he wouldn't tell Cash.

"Forget you heard that," Jax muttered, lathering up his hands and scrubbing like hell to get that grease off so he didn't go to school looking like he'd never bathed. "There was no date."

"Spill it, Jax. You know I'm not going anywhere until I hear what happened."

He refused to glance up and meet his cousin's reflection in the mirror over the sink. The bathroom was so tiny, he knew Tanner stood directly behind him. Jax was essentially trapped and there was no need to deny or even lie. Tanner would draw his own conclusions and share them with Cash like some damn old gossipy lady. Jax had to give him something though.

"It was nothing really."

Except the kiss, but there was no way Jax was going to get into that portion of the evening.

"Piper said something about her friends having mommies, then she asked if Livie was here to go out with me, and that all snowballed. Basically, we agreed to appease Piper and we used the opportunity to talk."

"You said that twice, so what else happened?"

Why did he have to be so damn intuitive? Talk didn't always mean something else.

"Are you always in cop mode?" Jax growled as he shut off the squeaky faucet. "Because we talked, we argued, I drove her home."

Tanner stepped back and let Jax pass through, but the mocking laughter followed. He didn't care how much his nosy cousins prodded, because there was no doubt that Cash would jump on this bandwagon. Jax was not spilling any details because talking about the kiss would make it out in the open and no longer a secret. Jax was positive Livie didn't want anyone to know what happened between them and he sure as hell wasn't about to give Cash and Tanner fodder for endless jabs.

"Maybe you just need a few beers to lighten up," Tanner replied as if he had the answer to the mystery.

"You know better than that. It takes more than a few beers to get me talking and I don't drink that much with Piper home."

Priorities had changed since he'd come home and started parenting. By far a totally different lifestyle from what he was used to and there had been a major adjustment, but Jax loved every minute. Being a single parent was by far more difficult than anything he'd ever done, but Piper was worth it. She was his entire life. This airport was how he paid for everything to secure her life, and that was just the monetary aspect. He and Piper shared a bond here, they would chat about planes, about flying, and the future here. She was only four years old, but she had a vision for a future and that future was right here.

"You know we're going to get this out of you." Tanner

pulled his cell from his pocket. "Cash and I will be over this evening. Don't think we won't revisit this topic."

"You'll be wasting your time."

With a shrug, Tanner focused on his phone as he sent a text. "I have no other plans tonight. Piper has to go to bed at some time. We'll get you then."

Jax laughed and grabbed his keys off the old scarred desk. The same desk Paul used when he took over here years ago. "When Piper goes to bed, that's when you two losers are leaving."

Tanner headed out with Jax and stopped beside the old beat-up truck Jax so loved. "Was there something you wanted when you stopped by?"

Shoving his hands in his pockets, Tanner rocked back on his heels and nodded. "I wanted to talk to you about a job prospect."

Intrigued, Jax crossed his arms and leaned against his bumper. "For you?"

"I was given an option of transferring units."

"Where's the other unit?"

Tanner pulled in a deep breath, his broad chest expanding beneath the gray T-shirt. "In St. Perry."

Stunned, Jax absorbed the information. "Two hours away. What made them offer that to you?"

"You know I passed my exam to be promoted to sergeant?"

Jax nodded.

"Well, there's an opening coming up there and I was offered first. I'm supposed to tell them within the next couple months. It's a long gap, but they want time to look for others if I'm not interested."

Raking a hand over the back of his head, Jax truly had no clue what to say. "Do you want the job?"

"I want the pay and the position, but I don't want to be in St. Perry."

"You talked to Cash?"

Tanner shook his head. "Not yet."

"Well, whatever you decide, we'll support you. I know we were both proud of you for passing. You'd make an excellent sergeant."

Tanner kicked at a pebble with his work boot. "I'd prefer to be excellent a little closer to home."

"Well, you can always take the position and wait for something to open up here."

Tanner simply nodded and Jax knew he was torn up over the life-changing decision looming over him. But Jax would have his back no matter what. It would suck to have his best friend move, but two hours wasn't terrible. It wasn't down the street like they were used to, but it could be worse.

"I need to get to the school," Jax stated. "I'll see you this evening and keep your mouth shut about Livie around Piper."

Tanner tossed a dimpled grin. "I know how to handle a toddler. It's Cash you need to worry about."

Jax ignored the warning and climbed into his truck. Cash and Tanner had been there for Jax from the beginning of this whole parenting thing. The three of them often took Piper out fishing or to the park and on occasion they'd all pile into the movie theater. Nothing like three guys and a little tomboy heading in to see the latest kiddie flick.

Jax was convinced Tanner liked to use Piper to pick up ladies, but Piper was so damn adorable, it was impossible to ignore so much cute.

As he drove away, his mind circled back to Livie. She'd melted when she'd spoken to Piper and Jax couldn't deny a piece of him had softened. The way she'd squatted down to speak to Piper on her level stirred something deeply within him. He didn't want anything to stir, he didn't want to find Livie even more attractive. Between the kiss and the way she seemed to adore Piper, Jax was having a difficult time remembering they were on opposite sides of the spectrum.

Tonight he was going to have to answer to his cousins. There was no way in hell Tanner wasn't spilling everything to Cash. Most likely they were on the phone now chatting.

Regardless, he had more important things to address than what they thought. Livie wasn't going anywhere and it was only a matter of time before he was face-to-face with her again. Jax doubted anything would prepare him, because as much as he wanted to end this property dispute, he wanted to touch her, kiss her, and forget they were technically enemies.

Chapter Seven

"Sweet tea?"

Olivia glanced up from her laptop and smiled at Jade. "Perfect timing. I just submitted the quote."

Jade sat two glasses of sweet tea on the small table by Olivia. Jade folded her lean frame on the chaise and let out a sigh.

"Where's Melanie?"

"She said she was going into town."

Into town was code for Haven. There were many cute specialty shops that had popped up since Olivia had left years ago. The once run-down, sad area was now thriving with day-trippers from Savannah and the locals who appreciated their beautiful, quaint area.

Olivia took a sip of her tea and welcomed that extra kick of sugar and caffeine. After working all day in the bedroom closets, she was more than ready to relax.

"I've been thinking," Jade stated in a slow, careful tone. "Just hear me out before you shoot down my idea."

Olivia sat her laptop beside her on the cushion and gripped her cool glass. "When you lead in like that, you're already making me nervous."

Stretching her long legs in front of her, Jade crossed

her ankles and stared out into the spacious backyard. "I had an epiphany while going through your guest-room closet. Maybe I was trying to figure out a way to find a happy medium with the airport or maybe I was trying to distract myself from pictures of you with a bad perm, I don't know. Regardless, something kept sticking out in my mind and I think it's worth surveying."

Olivia sipped her drink and was almost afraid to hear the rest of Jade's line of thinking. Her friend was a brilliant businesswoman and she was always working her mind in overtime. She was successful, but lately had been second-guessed and really put through hell at work. Some may say she was running from her problems, and she may have been, but getting Jade out of Atlanta so things could die down was the smartest move right now.

"Let's have it," Olivia sighed.

"Don't sell the airport." As soon as Olivia opened her mouth, Jade closed her eyes and held up a hand. "You said you'd hear me out."

"I said no such thing," she argued.

"It was implied." Jade waved her hand and crossed her ankles. "As I was saying, don't sell the airport. You're half owner, so anything you do would benefit you as well."

Olivia laughed. "Have you seen the place? I'm sure Jax barely pulls in enough to keep himself afloat, let alone give me half."

"You haven't heard my idea," she stated, her voice suddenly taking on almost a sinister tone. "You're going to turn that airport into something like this town has never seen."

Olivia nearly choked on her tea. "Excuse me? You not only want me to keep this part of my past that I want out of my life, but you also want me to get fully involved in it and . . . what? What exactly is in that marketing brain of yours?"

Jade was a mastermind when it came to business. She

had taken more than one dying company and breathed it back to life, but Olivia didn't want Jade breathing in the direction of the airport.

"Haven has seriously grown since we lived here. The tourists are flocking in from Savannah, the resort is really pulling people in, and with the film industry flocking to this state, Haven is the perfect town for even more."

Olivia registered every word, but she didn't even want to entertain the idea of renovating the airport or making it into something spectacular. None of that ever even entered her mind, because she wanted out. How many times did she have to keep telling herself and her friends that? Maybe if she kept replaying the main goal in her head, she could make it a reality.

"They'll have to fly into Savannah or another city and drive in," Jade went on. "Why not make it where people want to come to Haven instead of into other places? I don't know the full dynamics yet, but Haven is growing. Why shouldn't the airport? We can make it something that will not only keep Jax more than in business, but will create revenue for you as well. You don't necessarily have to be here. There's no reason you can't oversee from Atlanta."

Olivia's head started spinning. "What did you put in this tea?"

"Sugar and more sugar. Oh, and ice."

"No alcohol? Because that idea of yours doesn't sound terrible . . . except the part where I have to be involved at all. I'd rather just be done here."

Jade swung her legs over the side of the chair and sat her glass on the table. "Maybe you should discuss this with Jax. What if you two can collaborate . . . or at least share another kiss?"

Olivia groaned and took another drink. There was no way she could work with Jax on anything. Just being near that man made her . . . well, she couldn't figure out the exact term for all her feelings. Maybe one didn't even exist.

And why did she instantly think of him and have tingling lips? Damn that man for making her get sidetracked.

Olivia cursed Jade, too, for planting these thoughts of a renovated airport. She didn't have time to babysit contractors, come up with plans, or work with Jax in an intimate manner . . . because any job of that caliber would consume much of her life and require one-on-one time that she simply didn't have the emotional stamina for.

"We're not sharing anything," Olivia demanded. "I have a promotion to get back to. I have a corner office that's just waiting for me and my new nameplate."

"You're not a shallow person, don't start now."

Her childhood friend knew her so well. Still, there were times she did look forward to the material things and accomplishments of life. She'd worked hard to get where she was and if she wanted to be shallow for a bit, then she would.

"You said you put that quote in," Olivia claimed. "Did you overcompensate for all of this grand designing you're talking about?"

"It's all taken care of and on paper," Jade stated confidently with a wide grin.

Olivia smoothed her hair back over her shoulders and wished she had some magical crystal ball to see all the answers. She was at a complete loss as to how to move forward. There was her path and then there was Jackson's path and the two went in opposite directions.

"Your idea sounds great, honestly." Olivia sighed and chose her words carefully. "If I were a different person, if I didn't already have ties to that place, and if I weren't so busy at work, then maybe I would find a way. But there are just too many factors."

Jade came to her feet and picked up her glass. "Don't shut it down completely. You really should think about this option. Melanie and I would both help and I'm sure Jax would rather that than to get rid of it altogether."

Most likely he would, but he wouldn't have any money to invest in the initial renovating process. She had a good chunk saved, but even that would only go so far. They'd have to get grants and loans if they wanted to do everything up right.

"I see the thoughts going through your head."

Olivia glared up at her friend. "I hate you right now."

With a laugh, Jade shrugged. "I know that's best friend code for how awesome I am. Seriously, Liv, I'm here for you. No matter what you decide, no matter if you want to run away from everything or stay and make it work, I'm here."

Olivia swallowed the lump in her throat and nodded. "I know you are. There's just so much to figure out and I'm not in familiar territory."

"Meaning you always do business without getting your heart involved. It's time to use that organ, you know."

She grabbed her tea and came to her feet. "I'm not sure it works," she muttered. "I've purposely kept feelings out of my career."

"Well, the airport isn't your career. It's part of who you are whether you want to admit it or not."

Olivia didn't want to admit it, not even to herself. She wanted her father to still be alive, to still have the reins on the property. She hadn't seen him in . . .

Tears pricked her eyes and try as she might to blink them away, they slipped down her cheeks in a steady stream.

"Oh, no." Jade slipped the glass from Olivia's hand, sat it on the table, and wrapped her arms around her.

"Where's Mel when we need her? She's better with tears than I am."

Olivia attempted to laugh at her friend's accurate statement, but it came out watery. "I'm sorry," she cried. "I hate this."

Jade patted her back. "Yeah, well, we need to deal with everything no matter how uncomfortable you are and that's why we're here. Talk to Jax tomorrow."

She didn't want to talk to him. The childish side of her wanted to avoid him at all costs. But the feminine side of her wanted to see him, wanted to know if that spark would still be sizzling when she looked into those bright blue eyes. Would he touch her? Would he try to kiss her again? Part of her wished like hell he would, but that would only complicate matters further.

Olivia eased back from her friend and swiped at her damp cheeks. "I'll think about your plan. I can't talk to him until I have a firm idea of what to say."

"Actually, I already drew up a spreadsheet." Jade flashed that megawatt smile that always indicated she was up to something. "I mean, it's obviously rough because I literally just had the idea a few hours ago, but it's on my laptop."

Olivia narrowed her gaze. "I thought you were cleaning out the closet."

"Well, I was, but then I got a text from one of my coworkers and slid back into work mode. One thing snowballed into another and I got to thinking about the film crew coming in. It was pretty easy for my mind to wander into your problems and mesh them with something fantastic."

As Olivia listened, she couldn't help but laugh at the way Jade's mind worked. Of course she'd want to focus on someone else's problem. Her own were a nightmare and there was no end in sight. Jade was one strong woman, but being the victim of harassment at work from the CEO was something she couldn't hide from forever.

Right now, though, Olivia had to deal with her own pressing mess. Thoughts swirled around in her mind, bouncing off one another—or more like fighting one another. Part of her wanted to forget Jade ever mentioned such a plan, but the other part of her knew that Jade was brilliant and the idea definitely had merit. Jade also never would've brought it up if she didn't think it would work.

"I think I'd rather tackle boxes in the attic than deal with making such a decision," Olivia muttered.

"Then let's go." Jade headed toward the back porch, her long red hair swinging halfway down her back. "We'll run the idea by Melanie once she returns and get her vote."

Melanie was always their voice of reason, but Olivia already knew what she'd say. There was no way she was going to avoid talking to Jackson, but she knew she'd better have a rock-solid plan before going in. She couldn't afford to get sidetracked again by his charm . . . or his lips.

Piles of pictures, papers, childhood school papers . . . there was so much stuff. Clearly, her father hadn't tossed anything out. Had he held on to all of this because he just didn't want to go through it or because everything held some sentimental meaning?

The front door slammed and Olivia jerked to glance at Jade.

"If that's Mel, she's pissed," Jade stated, setting her stack of papers aside and coming to her feet. "She doesn't slam doors."

Against the protest of her sore backside, Olivia stood and stretched as she headed toward the bedroom door. They'd been working in the room where Jade was sleeping, but so far everything was pretty much garbage. Well, she'd keep the photos in a box, but she didn't need the papers she'd scribbled on in kindergarten.

"We're in Jade's room," Olivia called.

Melanie stomped up the steps and the second she came into view, Olivia was shocked to see her friend's hair all in disarray.

"Something wrong?"

Mel rolled her eyes at the obvious question. "I just met this jerk who pulled me over for speeding. How was I supposed to know the limit in this town was twenty-five? That shouldn't even be a thing."

Olivia bit the inside of her cheek to keep from laughing. "Well, we do have a lot of people who walk and there's more tourists now than ever before. How fast were you going?"

"Forty."

Cringing, Olivia said, "That's going to be a hefty fine."

"I also got charged with reckless op."

"Do you have to go to court?" Jade asked, stepping out into the hall.

"No." Olivia sighed and raked her hands through her hair, which would explain how it got in its current state. "I'll just pay the stupid fine."

"Sorry," Olivia murmured.

Melanie glanced into the bedroom, her eyes widened. "You guys have been busy."

"I'm channeling my emotions in here for now." Olivia turned toward the room, realizing it looked much worse from this angle than when she'd been sitting in the midst of her piles. "Jade's mind has been working in overdrive and now I'm even more torn than before."

"My idea is brilliant, if you ask me."

"I didn't," Olivia told Jade.

"Well, tell me," Melanie demanded.

Olivia went back into the room and sank down in the

circle where she'd been surrounded by photos and papers. "I'll let Jade tell you. I'm still trying to wrap my mind around it all."

As her friends settled into the room, Jade started all over again explaining about the newly revamped airport catering to a higher class of clientele. Even the second time hearing this didn't make it any clearer in Olivia's mind.

She shuffled through the pictures, realizing she couldn't bring herself to get rid of any. They each captured a moment that she'd never get back, and with each one she was instantly thrust into an exact time and place. The clothes were familiar, the smiles were so real she could hear the laughter. There were definitely good times in her life, or maybe she'd been so young her mother had shielded her from the sadness.

What the hell was Olivia supposed to do with all this stuff? Her condo in Atlanta wasn't exactly the place she wanted to bring all these boxes. When she went back—and she seriously prayed that was soon—she wanted to be free of all these things, all this stuff she'd lived without since she left the last time.

"That does sound rather impressive," Melanie finally stated when Jade was done with her marketing plan. "Time-consuming, costly, but definitely a risk that could pay off in a big way."

Olivia dropped the stack of old pictures into her lap and glanced to her friend, who sat on the edge of the four-poster bed. "I'm aware of the pros and cons. Believe me, I've made a spreadsheet in my head. I just . . . damn it, I wish my dad wouldn't have left me his portion of the airport. Or, I don't know, at least know what he expected me to do with it."

Melanie wrapped her fingers around the dark wood post and shrugged. "Maybe if you listen, he's trying to tell you."

Confused, Olivia asked, "What do you mean?"

"I believe in signs," she explained. "Pay attention to what's going on around you. Don't make this about you trying to get in and get out. Think about what's going on, how it will affect you and everyone involved. Maybe there is an answer that will work for everyone and maybe your dad had something in mind and that's why he left it to both you and Jackson."

Olivia didn't want to wait for some sign. Time wasn't on her side at the moment. There was only so long she could work away from her office in Atlanta. Even though she was doing her job just the same, it was different to be face-to-face with her boss. Olivia wanted that promotion and needed to get back in order to make sure the right person was appointed.

"I'll talk to Jackson," she finally conceded. "But don't get your hopes up. I can't see him letting go of his small-town-feeling airport. Plus, he rents the other hangars to local pilots so I'm not sure how all of that would play out or if more hangars would need to be added. There's quite a bit to take into consideration."

"Just make sure you know what you want and what will work for you before you go to him," Jade added. "You don't have to go along with this plan at all. You can forget I said anything."

Olivia rolled her eyes and tipped her head toward her friend. "I can't forget now. It's a smart plan; I just don't know if it's something I can be part of. Talking to Jackson is the next step."

"I'd rather discuss your date the other night." Melanie produced a wide smile and raised her brows. "He is rather sexy. Not that I'm looking for anyone at this point in my life, but I can live through you."

Waving a hand, Olivia muttered, "No reason to live through me."

"Considering that's the closest any of us have had to a date in quite some time, we are going to have to use this as a real date."

Olivia sat the stack of pictures aside and sighed. "You know everything. We flew, we argued, he kissed me."

"Skip the first two and tell us about the third point."

Jade laughed and patted Melanie on the back. "I feel we're raising you right."

"I legitimately want to know," Melanie laughed. "Because it sounds like he's interested in you."

Olivia shook her head, refusing to even contemplate that notion. "He's not interested. He's trying to distract me and throw me off my business game, that's all."

And it had worked . . . temporarily. "It was nothing. I mean, it was a kiss, but it meant nothing and it won't happen again."

"Then why are your cheeks pink?" Jade asked. "And the way you keep denying it makes me wonder just how much you even believe it yourself."

Olivia came to her feet and brushed off her capris. "Shut up. I'm done here. If you two want to stay and get things into piles, great. I'm going for a walk."

"She's daydreaming about the kiss," Melanie whispered.

"Oh, I think at this point Jax is the star of her fantasies. Just let her go."

Olivia growled and left the room, her friends' laughter following her down the steps. She slid into her flip-flops and headed out the front door. It was a beautiful, breezy spring evening and Olivia seriously just needed some air. She needed to get away from the house, away from the mocking of her friends—no matter how true their assumptions may have been—and she needed to think about her next move with Jackson.

He'd be waiting for her, no doubt. He'd have some new, charming move to catch her off guard. But she'd be ready.

Olivia had handled multimillion-dollar business deals and dealt with charming men on a daily basis. Jackson wasn't going to throw her off or get her to back down.

Maybe this new plan of Jade's would spark some interest with him and they could both get what they wanted. Then again, this may also keep them on opposing sides.

She glanced to the time on her cell. *Might as well get this over with.*

Chapter Eight

The rain falling on the metal roof was enough to have Jax wishing he'd just headed home. Instead, he sat in his office, looking over finances while Piper slept on the old, worn brown sofa. He kept a sleeping bag here for her because the couch wasn't the softest fabric and he wasn't investing money to upgrade it.

His sweet girl lay curled up, her blond hair sliding out of her pigtails. The bibs she wore were too large for her tiny frame, but she always insisted on wearing them.

Those bibs were a constant reminder of who truly had the power here. They'd hung on the back of this office door for years and Piper always loved playing dress-up with them, because dress-up to her wasn't becoming a princess.

She wanted to be a plane mechanic and pilot like her daddy, and he couldn't fault her one bit. He loved his job, loved when he'd been in the air force, but enjoyed the place he was at now in his life.

This airport was so much more than a means to pay bills. This place had been here when he'd needed somewhere to go. When he'd had few options and no time to go on the hunt, Paul had taken him back in an instant.

The click of the hangar door caught his attention. It was after eight, closing in on nine, so who would be here? Glancing at Piper, he saw she was still fast asleep. Jax slipped out of his office and gently pulled the door behind him before turning to see who had popped in. Shouldn't have been another pilot, not with the weather taking on a nasty turn this evening.

Pilots were constantly watching the weather whether they were taking off or not. It was just something ingrained in them and Jax didn't even think anything of it anymore. Georgia was especially tricky in the spring. The pop-up storms were too common to be careless.

Jax rounded the corner from his office to the main area, which might be considered a lobby, and came to stop when he saw Livie squeezing the water from her hair. Part of him wanted to laugh at her water-logged appearance, but the other part of him, the completely male part, was too busy taking in the way her clothing had molded to her body.

The black legging capris and plain red tank showed off the fact that she didn't just sit behind a desk and push papers all day. This woman was in shape and had curves in all the right places . . . places his hands itched to touch.

Damn it. He'd wanted that kiss to be some one-time event when it came to his hormones. Unfortunately, one look at her, frazzled as she may have been, and he was confident there were going to be more kisses, more touching. He couldn't wait.

Livie looked up and jerked back. "Oh, I didn't see you standing there."

She flung her damp hair back over her shoulder and attempted to swipe the moisture from her clothes. Jax crossed the space between them, never taking his eyes off her. Somewhere between her demanding he sell and their plane ride, he'd gone from loathing to wanting. It had been a damn long time since he'd felt an attraction this strong, but how could he ever trust that gut instinct again? He'd thought Carly was the one for him and she left him with a two-week-old baby. Clearly, where women were concerned, he wasn't the best judge of character.

"What are you doing here?" he asked.

She glanced around the open hangar, then back to him. "I was just out for a walk and ended up here."

Stunned, he took a step closer until there was little space between them. "You walked five miles?"

"I guess so." She shrugged. "I was cleaning out my house and needed air. I didn't have intentions when I left."

"Yet here you are."

Her eyes held his as she nodded. There was no way she could've known he'd be here. He never knew when he'd be late either. He'd actually had a flight for this evening, but had to reschedule it due to the unsteady weather system.

"Did you need to see me or just come here to think things through?" he asked.

A droplet of water slid down her neck, disappearing into that scoop of her tank. His body tightened, stirred, as he brought his gaze back up to hers. The woman was torturing him on every possible level and he was human . . . at some point he was going to crack.

"Both," she murmured.

"Piper is asleep in the office. We can talk out here or go out to the bench under the awning."

"Let's go outside," she told him. "I've always loved a good storm."

He remembered Paul saying that about her. She'd sit on their back porch and watch a storm for hours until they made her come inside.

Jax wasn't too concerned about Piper waking. She was such a sound sleeper, but he propped the door open to the outside, so he'd be able to hear her if she called for him.

The rain came down steadily, bringing with it a scent

he only associated with storms. There was something so relaxing and calming about a good hard rain, the rumble of thunder, and the flash of lightning.

But Jax wasn't too relaxed or calm right now. He was too keyed up with Livie showing up unexpectedly. Something was on her mind, but he had no clue as to what. Something had brought her here and he only hoped she'd had some grand epiphany and decided against selling his life out from under him.

Jax took a seat next to her on the bench and leaned forward with his elbows on his knees. He stared down to his hands dangling between his legs and figured she'd start talking soon. He was content to wait her out.

He was rather intrigued she'd opted to come to him, especially considering how they'd left things.

"Why did you kiss me the other night?"

Okay, definitely not what he thought she'd lead with, but a topic he didn't mind answering honestly.

"Because I wanted to."

Hadn't he warned her he got what he wanted? Livie was no exception. He'd wanted her since he was thirteen years old . . . granted those wants turned from a crush to a full-blown aching need only a man can fully appreciate.

"You don't like me," she argued.

"I never said I didn't like you. I don't like the reason you're here."

Olivia folded her arms over her chest and leaned back against the bench. Jax threw a look over his shoulder, but Livie was lost in thought as she stared at the rain dripping from the overhead gutter.

"Are you happy here?" she asked, finally searching his face. "I mean, if Piper wasn't in your life, if you were just a bachelor—"

"She is part of my life," he stated. "I never think about her not being here. She's the best thing that's ever happened."

"I didn't mean it like that," she corrected. "I just want to know are you doing what you love? I know you want to fly, but here? Why not for some major airline where you can travel the globe?"

Jax laughed and leaned back beside her, his shoulder brushing hers. "You still don't get it. This place is my life. It's everything to me. Going somewhere else doesn't even cross my mind, so yes, I'm happy."

Livie nodded as she chewed on her bottom lip. Something was racing through that mind of hers. She clearly had an issue she was sorting out and he figured it was more than just how to sell this piece of her past. It was clear she was battling herself and he didn't want to intrude. Besides, sitting here listening to the rain with a beautiful woman wasn't a bad way to spend the evening.

"Jade came up with an idea and part of me wants to run fast and far, but the other part makes me wonder if this is the answer we'd been looking for."

Actually, he hadn't been looking for an answer considering he had no intention of selling, but her words intrigued him.

"What did she say?"

"For us to renovate the airport and cater to a higher class of clientele." Just as he opened his mouth to argue his clientele was just fine, she held up a hand. "Wait. Nobody would take away what you've already got here. But, with the film industry in this state, why not tap into that?"

Why not? He could think of several reasons.

"Money, time," he murmured. "The legal side of upgrading the airport would be costly on top of the actual renovations. We'd need more hangars, employees who would want to be paid. There are so many cons, I can't even get to the pro side of the list."

"That's why we need to talk," she retorted. "I'm not

saying I'm one hundred percent on board with this plan, either, but it's worth discussing."

Scenarios ran through his head. What did he know about high-profile clients? No doubt they'd have their own private planes and this airport was only set up for a certain size to land. There were just so many negatives and the idea had only been in his mind for all of two minutes.

"We'd have to work together to see this through," she began.

Jax flashed a smile. "I wouldn't mind some one-on-one time."

"You've got to be kidding." Livie's brows rose. "You think we're just going to pick back up from that kiss? I'm trying to have a serious conversation here."

With a shrug, Jax turned back to watch the rain puddle in on the uneven sidewalk. "One has nothing to do with the other. I'm attracted to you, you're attracted to me. The airport doesn't affect my emotions."

Livie came to her feet, hands on her hips as she stared down at him. "Are you always this direct?"

"I'm not going to dance around the topic, Livie. Whether you want to admit it or not, there's an attraction. Whatever business you want to conduct is a whole other issue."

She continued to stare at him, her eyes wide, her hair hanging in damp ringlets. Livie Daniels had a feisty side, but she was also easy to read. She was afraid of this tension between them. She wanted to focus on why she came to Haven to begin with, but here she was thrust into an unwanted attraction just the same as he was.

"Listen, I'm not thrilled about this either," he went on. "I was getting along just fine before you came into town. I have a daughter who is my number-one priority. I haven't dated since her mother left because I've been too busy.

But here you are making me want and damn it, I'm not ready for that."

"You think I like this?" she demanded, throwing her arms wide. "I have more important things to do than argue with you about this place or that kiss."

Jax came to his feet, standing directly in front of her. He leaned over until she stepped back. He snaked an arm around her waist and hauled her flush against his body. Mists of rain hit them, droplets landing on her smooth skin.

"You think my life isn't important? That I'm not filled with things I'd rather be doing than constantly replaying how your lips felt against mine?"

Her hands went to his chest, but instead of pushing him away, she curled her fingers and gripped his shirt. "You haven't—"

He tightened his hold. "I have. I've thought of you, of us. You think all those years ago I wasn't infatuated with you? I'd see you strut in, totally ignore me, and waltz out like the princess of the palace."

Damn it. He didn't want to just expose every single thought he'd had about her. She made him forget every pep talk he'd given himself and she totally tore through the red flags waving around in his mind.

"If you want to work together, then by all means, let's work." He nipped at her jawline, pleased when her head tipped back. "But I'll give you this one and only warning— I want you and I intend to have you."

When her eyes widened, then darted to his lips, it took every single ounce of willpower for him to pull back and release her. His body protested at the loss of her touch. But he wanted her to be just as aching, just as frustrated as he was. Only then would he get to see the real side of Livie, the side he'd wanted to expose since she stepped foot into that hangar wearing her proper suit.

"If we're going to really dig into this idea, we can't be . . ."

She waved her hand between them. Amused, Jax reached out and wiped a damp tendril from her forehead.

"Can't be what?"

Her eyes narrowed. "You know," she said, swatting at him. "Stop touching me."

"You just arched your body against mine and moaned. Now you're choosing to say no?"

"I didn't arch or moan," she argued. "Maybe we should have chaperones when we discuss renovating."

Jax couldn't stop the laugh from slipping out. "You think someone in the room will stop me from doing what I want? You don't know me very well."

"I don't know you at all," she all but shouted over the pounding rain. "I know you worked for my father, now you're a single dad, and you make me—"

"What?" he asked, more intrigued than ever.

She let out the most unladylike growl. "Forget it."

Jax wasn't sure if she was talking to him or herself, so he merely shrugged. "I'll drive you home. Let me pull my truck into the hangar and put Piper in."

Livie opened her mouth, then closed it.

"What?" he asked. "You want to argue about that, too? You don't honestly think I'd let you walk home in this rain, do you? Besides, it's pitch-black out. I'm a Southern gentleman, Livie. I'll make sure you're properly taken care of."

Her swift intake of breath was all he needed to know he'd hit his mark with that last line. He wasn't messing around. She may have thought this talk of attraction was done, but he'd barely gotten started.

Suddenly, Livie's eyes widened as she peered over his shoulder. Jax turned, catching sight of Piper standing in the doorway with her lopsided ponytails. She rubbed her eyes and yawned.

"Hey, sweetheart." Jax crossed the cracked concrete and lifted his sleepy girl into his arms. "You ready to head home and get tucked into bed?"

"You promised to read the Amelia Earhart book tonight," she whined as she lay her head on his shoulder.

"I did, but I didn't know we'd be here so late."

The kid couldn't remember the daily ritual of brushing her teeth, but she sure as hell wasn't about to forget a promise he made last minute as she hopped out of his truck for school this morning.

"Daddy." She wrapped her little arms around his neck. "You can't break your promise. That's what you always tell me."

Sometimes he really felt he was nailing this parenting thing, and other times he realized his guidance came back to bite him in the butt.

Jax glanced to Livie, who still hadn't moved, hadn't taken her eyes off Piper. And then it hit him. The bibs.

"They've been on the back of the office door since you left," he reminded her. "She's just started wearing them recently. They're a little big, but . . ."

He truly had no idea how to approach this, and from the look on Livie's face, she didn't either.

"If you'd rather she not—"

"No, it's fine." Livie blinked, as if she were pulling herself from some trance. "I forgot about them until you mentioned them the other day, but I hadn't seen them yet. I'm just surprised, that's all."

"Are you having another date?" Piper mumbled.

Jax shot Livie a wink. "Not tonight," he said, patting Piper's back. "Livie needs a ride home, though. Can you stand here with her and I'll go get my truck so you two don't get so wet?"

She nodded against the side of his neck, her wild hair tickling his jaw. He sat her down, but Piper immediately went over to Livie and extended her arms. Livie froze, not enough for Piper to notice, but Jax was pretty in tune with Livie. She didn't want to get too wrapped up in this place, with him or his daughter.

"Be right back."

Jax didn't offer any reason to Piper why Livie wasn't picking her up, and as he walked back in to get his keys and shut off lights, he threw a glance over his shoulder. Piper was firmly resting in Livie's arms. In that second, something tripped inside his chest and he had no way to even describe the emotion.

Turning from the scene behind him, Jax couldn't let any of this get too personal. No matter how strong the pull of attraction was toward Livie, he had to keep reminding himself of how Carly had also tugged him into her life only to stomp on his heart and walk out without a regret.

Jax turned off the lights, set the alarm, and headed to get his truck. He wasn't looking for a relationship. A little flirting, kissing . . . whatever else may arise was fine, so long as commitment stayed out of the equation. If they had a business deal, fine, so long as they both agreed to it. But anything deeper, forging a stronger bond, was out of the question. After all, he not only had his own heart to protect, he also had to look out for his daughter.

Seeing those bibs had been like a slap to the face from reality. She'd worn those every day when she'd go to the airport to work with her dad during summer breaks and after school. They'd been big and baggy at first, then she'd grown into them. By the time they were getting too small, Olivia didn't want to wear them anymore.

But they held a special place in her memory bank, she

couldn't deny that fact. Seeing Piper in her messy ponytails and the baggy bibs with cuffed hems churned something in Olivia. Those nostalgic memories were starting to consume her. With each passing day, she questioned whether she was making the right decisions. There simply was no good answer and no one to tell her how the future would play out.

"Olivia, did you hear me?"

She gripped the phone and stared down at her blank paper. The pen lay to the side untouched.

"I'm sorry, what?" she asked.

Since Jax had brought her home last night she'd had a difficult time concentrating. Thankfully, Melanie and Jade had been out on the back porch and didn't know Jax had driven her home—she'd never hear the end of it if they knew.

Now she was trying to concentrate on work, but she just didn't have the heart. What was happening to her?

"I said, rumor has it the decision for COO will be made as soon as next week," her assistant whispered.

Olivia could always count on her assistant to keep her updated on the current rumor mill. Nerves and anticipation spiraled through her. She could practically taste the victory.

"I should be getting an acceptance from the VanKirk Agency today," Olivia said. "I e-mailed the plans to them, great job working on that, by the way."

"You did most of the work, I just drew up the actual proposal."

Olivia picked up the pen and started to draw. "We make a great team. I'm sure they'll love what we came up with and once I land that account, there's no way I'll be denied the promotion. We've been trying to get the attention of Patrick VanKirk for years."

Yes, the victory was going to be so sweet. Considering

her opponent thought she was incompetent because she was a woman, that was all the fuel she needed to work her ass off toward this promotion. What did boobs and lack of a penis have to do with her job anyway?

"I'll be sure to let you know as soon as I hear from them," Olivia said as she slid her pen over the paper. "They wanted things wrapped up by the weekend, so I should be getting word anytime."

"When are you coming back?"

Olivia sighed and continued doodling. That was the proverbial million-dollar question, wasn't it? She truly had no clue. Especially now with this brainstorm of Jade's, Olivia had no idea what the future held. All she knew was she needed to be in the office for the announcement of her promotion.

"Soon." There, that sounded like she knew what was going on, right? "Text, e-mail, or call anytime. I still have a few things to get done here and I'll be back as soon as I can. Believe me, I miss you all."

Although, over the last couple days she hadn't thought so much about work. Her mind had been preoccupied with one very sexy, very charming pilot who constantly caught her off guard with his touch. And he did have that whole gentlemanly thing going. Why couldn't he be rude or ugly? Yeah, ugly would really help.

No, he had those broad shoulders, dark hair, tanned skin, striking eyes. He was the perfect poster boy for small-town hunk. The fact he was a caring single father was so charming and sweet, she wanted to find something that turned her off . . . but she kept drawing a blank.

"Have I lost you again?" her assistant asked.

Olivia closed her eyes and sighed. "Sorry. I'm just overwhelmed at the moment."

More like daydreaming about a man who was driving

her out of her mind and keeping her awake at night. Not to mention the adorable toddler who had pretty much stolen her heart.

"It's okay," she replied. "Just don't get too wrapped up in that town and forget to come back to us."

Olivia laughed. "That would never happen."

But as she glanced down to the paper, she stilled. She'd drawn her Cessna. No, not *her* Cessna. Jax's Cessna. That was his plane now; she had no ties to it. Well, legally she did, but it wasn't the plane she wanted.

What did she want, though? Because she thought she knew, but now she wasn't so sure. She still wanted the coveted promotion; she'd worked too hard to just walk away. But part of her wanted that airport to be everything Jade suggested. Was it even possible to have both?

Olivia disconnected the call and sat her cell on the desk in the formal living room. Jade and Melanie had gone out for a run. They'd begged Olivia to join them, but she knew she had too much work to catch up on this morning. She needed to run, though. It was the only thing that kept her sane and cleared her thoughts. Nothing was as therapeutic as getting fresh air, working up a sweat, and pounding the pavement.

Getting in a good workout with her friends sounded ideal, but she wasn't so sure she'd be good company.

Olivia leaned back in the creaky old leather chair and stared at the plane. Melanie had said to look for signs, something Olivia didn't necessarily believe in, but if she did, was this a sign? Was Piper wearing Olivia's old bibs a sign?

What exactly constituted a sign? Because Olivia would seriously love some help right about now.

Olivia couldn't help but think about how sweet little sleepy Piper felt in her arms. The way she just relaxed and gave in to the state of exhaustion. Olivia couldn't recall the last time she was ever relaxed or even leaned on someone with such trust and abandon.

Maybe as a child. Perhaps when her mind was still filled with puppy dogs and rainbows. Before her parents split she was definitely a different person. Once she graduated and she and her mother moved to Atlanta, Olivia started to gain some of her happiness back. College was a great escape and fresh start, especially with her best friend at her side.

She and Jade had been through it all together. Then they'd met Melanie a few years ago and carried her into their happy circle. Olivia guessed she had them to lean on. She knew she could always count on them for anything she'd ever need. They depended on one another, though, and that's what made them so perfect for one another. They were like their own little army.

Olivia glanced back down to the image she'd drawn. Not that she was some grand artist, but she'd always loved doodling. Most often it was nothing of any importance, just a way to pass the time or relieve stress. Her planner had random ink sketches all around the borders.

Pushing her chair out, Olivia came to her feet. She couldn't sit here all day and evaluate life or try to dissect all the chaos inside her mind. There wasn't enough time for the mess that was her emotional state.

There were boxes to pack and memories to face. She'd finally made a dent in the spare room early this morning before her phone calls and e-mails. So far she had several bags of old school papers she was going to trash, but the pictures were sitting in a box until she could figure out the best approach for those.

Her mother had moved on, remarrying and settling down in Charlotte. Olivia rarely saw her, but they'd text and chat on the phone. They were close, not like they were when they'd first left Haven. Part of Olivia wondered what had happened, but deep down she knew. Her mother had literally moved on. When she'd wanted to leave Olivia's dad, she had. Then when she wanted to leave Olivia, she had.

Weighing her mother's actions wouldn't change anything and Olivia was an adult. She didn't need anyone, but she sure would like to know how to move forward. Was it even possible to get the promotion, increase her workload, and simultaneously work on revamping a dilapidated airport?

She must have been out of her mind for even considering it. But the possibilities were mounting so fast in her head, and she was the budgeting manager over marketing, so she saw this type of work all day, every day.

Before she could talk herself out of all the reasons not to, she jotted down a list. What started out as pros and cons quickly turned into pros and quickly escalated to grand ideas.

Seeing things on paper always made them seem more real. After glancing over all her notes, Olivia knew in her heart she wanted to pursue this plan. Jackson may not be too keen on it, but moving ahead to something bigger and better was at least going to keep him in the business he wanted. This was obviously the happy middle ground Jade had suggested.

Now Olivia just had to figure out a way to make sure Jackson knew this plan was brilliant and would benefit them both. That wasn't even the most challenging part. She had to face him and hope he kept his roaming hands and talented lips to himself, because she was fighting a losing battle and each time he touched her, she craved even more.

Chapter Nine

"You win, again," Jax declared.

Piper squealed and pulled the cards across the table. "You guys are terrible at Go Fish."

"Why do I feel like I'm raising a card shark?" he muttered as he came to his feet.

"Because you are," Cash replied.

Cash and Tanner had come over about an hour ago. They'd eaten and settled into Piper's favorite game, but it was getting later and he needed to get Piper into bed.

When they were home at a decent hour, he made sure she didn't stay up late. There were circumstances where flights held him up, but even then his faithful babysitter and neighbor was always good to get Piper home and in bed.

"One more game." She stared up at him with those big brown eyes and shoved that bottom lip out. "Please, Daddy?"

He laughed. "Nice try, darlin'. Go in and get your pajamas on and I'll come tuck you in."

"And read my story," she stated climbing down from the kitchen table.

Cash stood and scooped Piper up. "How about I read your story? I haven't tucked you in for a while."

"Yay, but when you read, you're not allowed to do funny voices," she told him, patting his stubbled jawline. "This is a serious book."

He gave her a mock salute. "Yes, ma'am. Let's go."

Tanner remained at the table and started straightening the cards. "You talked anymore to Livie?"

Jax opened the fridge and pulled out a beer. "You've been dying to ask that, haven't you?"

Tanner shrugged. "You going to get me a beer?"

"No." Jax popped the cap off and took a long, refreshing pull. "Piper barely got out of the room before you already started in on me like some gossipy old lady."

"Call me what you want, but I'm still waiting to hear. You must've seen her again or you would've already told me no."

Jax had seen her in person, as well as in every single dream since she'd stepped back into town. And she'd texted him earlier to inform him she wanted to sit down and discuss the airport. Heaven help him, she was going to test every bit of patience he had.

"No, wait. Don't say anything." Tanner stood and circled the table. "Cash will want to hear this too."

He nudged Jax out of the way and took his own beer out of the fridge. Jax hadn't told his cousins about the idea Livie had run by him. He was still trying to process it all himself. There wasn't a doubt in his mind that she was full-blown into this concept and was probably home making spreadsheets or a PowerPoint presentation to go over with him tomorrow.

Well, he knew of one way to distract her if he didn't like how their little meeting was going.

"Anything exciting happening in Haven I don't know about?" Jax asked, hoping to deflect the conversation away from him.

Tanner pulled out one of the kitchen chairs and sank

into it. Resting his elbow on the edge of the table, he took a drink before setting his bottle down. "Not much. I get nervous when it's this quiet, though. It's like the calm before the storm."

"It's Haven," Jax stated. "Nothing too wild goes on here."

Tanner winced. "Don't say that. When I start getting too comfortable, that's when something strange happens. Last month I had a call that there was a guy in a pool trying to have sex with a blow-up floatie."

Jax was so glad he wasn't taking a drink right at that moment. "How the hell is that even possible? I guess whatever people want to do in their pools is their business, but that's gross."

"It wasn't his pool," Tanner corrected. "The lady came home and found a guy in her backyard with one of her floats."

"Brings a whole new light to breaking and entering."

Tanner shot him a narrowed glance. "You're hilarious."

"I think so."

"I did pull over a woman the other day who was pretty hot and I hadn't seen her in town before. That rarely happens."

Jax resisted the urge to roll his eyes as he took a seat across from Tanner. "Knowing you, I'd say it happens all the time. That's how you get your dates."

"I do not abuse my badge," he corrected. "The woman claimed she was from Atlanta, which might explain why she was speeding through town. City folks have no respect for the small towns."

"You said she was from Atlanta?" Jax asked, figuring he knew who his cousin had pulled over.

Tanner knew Jade and Livie, so that pretty much left Melanie. She would definitely be his cousin's type. Beautiful, classy. Tanner actually preferred all types. He had a habit of dating once and being done. Settling down wasn't an option for him because he'd seen enough from Jax and Cash to be scarred for life.

Perhaps Jax should've gone along with that way of life and just dated. Marriage clearly hadn't worked for him, but had he not married, he wouldn't have Piper and he couldn't even fathom his life without her.

"Blond. I believe her name was Melanie."

Jax smiled. Looks like the tide was about to turn. "That's Livie's friend. She's staying with her."

Tanner quirked a dark brow. "Is that so?"

"Livie, Melanie, and Jade are all staying together. I don't know anything about Melanie, though. I just saw her the time I went to pick up Livie."

Cash stepped back into the room. "What are you two ladies gossiping about?"

"She asleep?" Jax asked.

Cash nodded and grabbed a bottle of water from the fridge. As a fitness trainer and coach, he was extremely particular about what he put into his body. At times he could be extreme, but Jax wasn't judging. Cash had made quite a name and a business for himself over the years. His gym was the most popular in the area and Cash's clients were constantly singing his praises on social media and around town.

"I'm thinking about asking Livie out while she's in town," Tanner stated.

Jax refused to take the bait. "Go ahead."

Cash smacked Tanner. "Shut up. You're not asking her out because you know she'll turn you down and you hate rejection."

"I don't get rejected," he retorted.

Cash circled the table and took the seat Piper had been in. "We playing poker or is it time for our girl chat?"

Jax didn't keep secrets from his cousins—they'd been through everything together from the time they were toddlers, through school, girls, sex, the military, and now as adults. He valued their advice, and though he didn't always take it, he still wanted to hear it to weigh all his options. Besides, he wasn't about to go into this little meeting with her without some type of mental backup.

"Livie approached me about renovating the airport."

Cash and Tanner stilled and stared across the table. Sliding his thumb over the condensation dripping down his bottle, he tried to still make sense of how this plan would come to life . . . if he and Livie ever got on the same page about anything other than kissing. Because they were most definitely on the same page about that.

"So she doesn't want it sold?" Cash asked. He leaned forward on his elbows and gripped his water. "What type of renovating does she want to do?"

"She mentioned turning it into a private airstrip for high-profile clients."

Jax still wasn't sure how he felt about that. This was a small town, he wanted to keep that ambiance. Granted the place could use some TLC, but changing the dynamics of the entire business was quite a bit to consider.

"She said I'd continue to fly my regular clients, and the hangars we rent would still be the same. Jade had an idea—"

"Jade's here too?" Cash asked, his brows rising. "I haven't seen her since high school."

Jax nodded. "Livie, Jade, and their friend Melanie. Ask Tanner about her."

Cash glanced over. "Melanie?"

Tanner shrugged. "I gave her a speeding ticket. That's all."

"She hot?" Cash asked.

"You could say that."

Jax laughed and got up to toss his empty bottle. "She's

blond, petite, and he gave her a ticket days ago but is still thinking about it."

"Can we get back to this talk of renovations?" Tanner asked with a frustrated tone.

"Jade said since there's a huge influx of filming going on in Georgia, it would make sense to explore this angle." Jax sank back down into his seat and leaned back, tapping his fingers on the table. "I don't know, though. I mean, that would take an exorbitant amount of money, plus the planning, and . . . hell, I don't even know what all would go into that. I'm sure some legal BS I don't want to deal with."

"So what are you going to do?" Tanner asked. "Tell her you don't want to sell or renovate? She's not just going to go away."

No, no she wasn't. Jax wasn't so sure he wanted her to go away. She intrigued him. Beneath that stuffy exterior, the polished clothes, and the defiant tip of her chin she always gave him, Jax knew the girl who had grown up here and had fallen in love with the sport of flying was still in there . . . and he was damn well going to bring her out.

"I don't know what to do," Jax admitted, blowing out a frustrated sigh. "I guess I'll let her talk and then think about it. I'm in no hurry to do anything, really. I'm not selling, so anything else she proposes will be in my court. She's going to have to go back to Atlanta at some point."

Not that he wanted her to go. He must have been a masochist because he actually enjoyed having her around. That was obviously the case considering he could still taste her kiss, feel her body pressed to his.

Jax reached for the cards. He didn't want to keep hashing this out with his friends. He needed some guy time now that Piper was asleep, and poker was the perfect solution.

"Hope you ladies brought money," he stated as he started shuffling. "I'm still saving for that new plane."

Cash snorted. "You're going to have to find a sugar mama if you want that to happen or sell everything you own and live in it as well."

Jax wasn't deterred by finances. Yes, things may have looked bleak, but he wasn't about to give up. When had he ever? It may take him until he was ready to retire, but he'd save every extra dime he had.

"So let's hear more about this Melanie." Cash reached for his cards and shot a look to Tanner.

Jax merely smiled as Tanner groaned. "Yes, let's hear more."

"What are you doing?"

Olivia stared at Jade as her friend came out the back door with trash bags. Not just the small ones from the kitchen, but the large black ones they'd had upstairs.

"Getting a move on this." Jade wrestled the bags down the steps. "There's two more if you want to go get them."

They'd only been back from their morning run for a half hour. Olivia had grabbed a quick shower and made coffee, and had just settled on the back porch to answer e-mails.

"I'll throw the stuff away when I'm ready," she argued. "Put those down."

Jade dropped the bags and propped her hands on her hips. "Trash runs tomorrow. We need to get rid of these."

"We're not paying for trash," Olivia countered. "We're not going to be here that long."

"One of your nosy neighbors said we could put it with hers. I asked."

Olivia stared down at her friend at the base of the steps. At some point, Olivia was going to have to let go. She didn't think saying good-bye to old memories and her father's things would be this difficult. She'd assumed she'd come into town, offer to help set up the sale of the airport, clean out her childhood home, and be back in Atlanta before she had to tap into any emotions.

In theory that all sounded fantastic. But reality had settled in and Olivia knew she was going to have to truly focus if she wanted to get out of here.

"Which sacks are those?" she asked Jade.

"Just the old school papers you said to toss." Jade tipped her head, her red ponytail swinging across her shoulder. "I'm doing this for you. If you can't get rid of the stuff, then I can. Melanie and I are here to help."

Olivia sat her laptop on the side table. "I know. It needs to be done. Go ahead and make sure you tell Mrs. Timmonds thanks. We'll have to make her a cake or something."

"Melanie can. I suck at baking."

Olivia laughed as Jade hauled the two sacks across the driveway toward the elderly lady's house. Glancing back to her laptop, Olivia stared at the e-mails, but reached over and closed out the screen. She grabbed her phone and went to the notes section. There were some minor repairs she needed to do to the house before she could sell it. There wasn't much reason for her to keep it since she didn't plan on staying in Haven. Even if she and Jackson came to some agreement on the plans for the airport, she had no intention of living here.

Olivia quickly typed in the issues she knew needed to be addressed. The living room and kitchen needed fresh coats of paint, the master bedroom carpet needed to be replaced, the floor in the kitchen needed to be changed out. The more Olivia added, the more she realized this was going to take a while to get done.

She'd need to call someone to come measure and give her a price on new flooring. Not exactly what she wanted to spend some of her savings on, but she'd get a return back once the house sold. There was no way she could put it on the market in the state it was now. With the town thriving, people would expect the homes to be up to the same standards.

As she was reading through her list, her cell rang. The number on the screen had her heart kicking up.

"Tom," Olivia greeted. "Good morning."

"Morning. I hope I didn't catch you at a bad time."

"No, this is perfect." As if she'd tell the CEO any different. Why was he calling? The endless possibilities made her stomach churn. "I trust you saw the marketing plan I laid out for the VanKirk Agency."

"That's why I'm calling. I have given that account over to Steve for the time being."

She'd busted her ass for this company. Her accounting degree was only a sliver of the talent she gave to this place. She'd always thought she was valued no matter what corporate hat she wore.

Olivia's heart sank, her breath caught in her throat. She came to her feet just as Jade came back around the side of the house. Whatever her friend saw in her eyes had Jade coming up the steps and standing right by Olivia.

"May I ask why?"

"I have something else in mind for you, and it's something I only trust you with."

A little part of Olivia eased, but how could the largest account just be taken from her like that? Did this mean he thought Steve was better for the job or did Tom believe Olivia was the best and he was giving her an even bigger account? Too many questions and she was in no position to second-guess her boss.

"I'm honored you trust me," she stated. "Is this a new account or an already established client?"

"I'm going to e-mail you the details shortly," Tom told her. "I wanted to let you know about the VanKirk Agency first before you followed up with them or had any more contact. I'm putting you on a delicate would-be clientele.

We're hoping to sway them our way and if you can manage that, it will be the biggest project you've ever had."

Olivia rubbed her forehead, a little worried over what was to come, but excited at the prospect of pulling in the largest account they'd ever had. Surely that would ensure her position as COO . . . right? There was no way to know what her boss was thinking, but with the promotion on the line, Olivia would do what was asked of her.

"I look forward to seeing more details," she told him honestly. "Thank you for trusting me."

"No thanks necessary," Tom replied. "On a personal note, how is the packing coming along?"

Olivia had simply told her boss she needed to settle her father's things and pack up the house before coming back. He'd been amazing by telling her to take her time because he'd lost his grandmother a year ago and had done the same.

"A little slower than expected, but nothing I can't handle."

"I never had any doubt," he stated, a smile to his voice. "Take all the time you need. So long as you're working, I'm fine with you not being in the office for now."

She knew he was sincere with that, but at the same time, she wanted to be back. She didn't know if Steve would try something sneaky with her gone and she didn't want to give him the opportunity, either.

"I hope to be back within a couple weeks. I'm working on cleaning out the house, and then there are some minor repairs that need to be done before I can list it."

"Well, like I said, if you need more time, just let me know. I'll send that e-mail within the hour."

Olivia disconnected the call and sank back into the chair. Her mind raced in all directions and she couldn't wait to get that ping from her phone and open the e-mail.

"I can't decide if you're panicking or if you're fine."

Jade sat down on the porch swing on the other side of the chair. "Was that your boss?"

Olivia nodded. "I'm fine, but panicking. He's pulled me from one account and has something else for me. He claims it's even bigger than what I was working on. I'm waiting on the details now."

"Does that mean you're out of commission until you hear from him?"

Narrowing her eyes, Olivia stared at her dearest yet sometimes sneaky friend. "What did you have in mind?"

"I just figured we could go see Jax." She offered a mega-watt smile. "All three of us."

Olivia knew precisely what her friend was doing. She was being nosy and planned on pulling Melanie in on everything as a sidekick.

Jade merely raised a brow and crossed her arms. "I can be showered and ready in twenty minutes."

"Which is another reason I hate you," Olivia grumbled, reaching over to pull up her e-mails again. "How can you look like you walked off a magazine shoot and take so little time?"

"It's the Irish genes," she explained, batting her lashes. "Now, give me just a few minutes. I'll let Mel know we're leaving soon."

As Jade literally raced past Olivia into the house, Olivia couldn't help but laugh. Whatever it took to keep her friends' minds off their own issues. If they wanted to join forces with her when she went to talk to Jackson, the more the merrier. Perhaps Jade could convince him to . . .

What? Did Olivia actually want to make this grand change to the airport? Did she want to devote all the time, energy, and funds to not only get the place up and running to a normal standard, but to make it bigger and better than ever?

Olivia stared at her e-mails as the one she'd been waiting for finally appeared in bold letters at the top. As she opened it and began reading, she realized her life may be getting more hectic than ever, but yes, she did want to make this work.

Somehow, someway, she would. Because Olivia had never backed down from a challenge and if this risky renovation was going to bring in more money in the long run, then she'd be a fool to pursue the sale like she'd initially planned.

First, she needed to reply to her boss, and then she needed to round up her girl posse and head to the hangar. She wasn't sure if Jackson was out flying or if he'd be around, but she'd be ready for him. And if she had those chaperones they'd joked about, he wouldn't try anything . . . would he?

Chapter Ten

"I need to get to the station."

Jax glanced up from the invoices and gave his cousin a nod. "Close the door behind you. I don't have any flights until later this afternoon."

"Who's getting Piper from school?"

Jax loved how his cousins were always eager to pitch in and help with his daughter. It was almost as if she had three dads. When Jax had come back from the air force, Tanner and Cash hadn't even hesitated to step up to the plate and help. They'd only bashed Carly a little, until Jax put a halt to that. While he loathed her for leaving Piper and ignoring their sweet, innocent baby, he never wanted Piper to overhear anything negative about her mother.

He'd delicately explained that she had to leave and couldn't come back. No doubt as Piper got older she'd ask more and as he saw fit, he would explain. But for now, she didn't ask about her own mother anymore . . . she was too busy hooking him up on dates with Livie.

"Cash is picking her up and taking her to the gym. I'll get her there after work. I just have to fly a couple to

Charleston. They're planning on staying a few days, so I'll head back up when they're done. It's just a quick flight there and back."

Tanner nodded and started for the door leading to the hangar. "I'll be covering a shift until eleven tonight, but text if you need anything."

Jax glanced back down to the invoice currently on the top of his pile, wondering how the hell he was going to get all of this paid on time. The flight today would bring in a good chunk since it was a little farther than most of his clients traveled. But with Piper wanting to join a karate class, he was probably going to have to pay these bills by priorities. Half now and half in a couple of weeks when the renters' checks were due.

He wished he could get more pilots to house their planes here. Not only would it generate more income, but it would also add an attraction in a positive manner toward the place he loved to call home.

Women's voices mixed with Tanner's, pulling Jax out of his thoughts. He pushed away from his desk and stepped out of his office to see Tanner standing in front of the firing squad—er, Livie, Jade, and Melanie.

"You know this guy?" Melanie was asking her friends as she pointed an accusatory finger at Tanner.

"We went to school together," Olivia stated. "How you doing, Tanner?"

Tanner looped his thumbs through his belt loops and nodded. "Doing great. Headed out to work now."

"To give more tickets to innocent people," Melanie muttered.

Tanner laughed. "If you were innocent, you wouldn't have been pulled over, and I wouldn't call speeding nearly twenty miles over the limit 'innocent.'"

Jax glanced to Livie, who looked like she was holding back her laughter as well. When she met his gaze, the slight grin on her face twisted something in his gut. He didn't know if she was smiling at him or just at the situation. Either way, he'd take it. He didn't recall seeing a genuine smile since she'd been back. Even when she lived here before and he'd been an awkward preteen, Livie had never flashed him a smile.

"Tanner." Jade stepped forward and crossed her arms over her chest. "Haven't seen you in years."

"Jade." Tanner nodded his greeting. "I never thought you'd be back in this town."

She shrugged a slender shoulder. "Hadn't planned on it, but I'm here for Olivia."

"Why are you nice to everyone but me?" Melanie grumbled.

Now Olivia did laugh. "Calm down, killer. Tanner is headed out to work and I'm sure he'll target other unsuspecting criminals."

Tanner threw Jax a glance over his shoulder. "See ya, man."

Once Tanner headed out the door, Jax turned his attention back to the small gang of women. He knew this was not just a simple social call and he was about to get bombarded with estrogen. He had no problem taking time from his day, and from the looming invoice, to see Olivia.

"I assume the three of you are not here to take me to lunch?" he asked, propping his hands on his hips.

"Not likely." Jade glanced around the hangar before turning her attention back to him. "Place hasn't changed much."

Jax could tell from her tone that she wasn't being judgmental. If anything, she was being kind because the place *had* changed. While it may have needed some minor repairs, he did most everything himself and definitely kept the place clean. Just because he was low on funds—story of his life—didn't mean he was lazy. He worked his ass off to make sure this place stayed running. As long as the planes took his clients to and from, that's really all that mattered.

"Is this where you all tell me about this grand idea to transform my airport into something on a bigger scale with fancier clients?"

"Not how we would've worded it, but sort of," Livie stated. "Should we go outside or into your office?"

Jax shrugged, not really eager to do either. He still hadn't given this a good deal of thought. Of course it had been on his mind, but he'd done a school project with Piper, then they'd baked cookies, and then he was scheduling future flights, and mulling over bills. So, the whole spending more money to make the airport "better" wasn't something he'd focused on.

"We'll go to your office," Jade chimed in. "It's hotter than Hades out there even in the shade."

Resigned to the fact he was going to have to face this firing squad, Jax led the way back into his office. He gestured toward the sofa, which still had Piper's sleeping bag spread out.

"Go ahead and sit on it," he told them. "The couch is scratchy, so we keep Piper's bedding out for when she's here and naps."

Suddenly he felt as if he were under some sort of scrutiny. Why was he explaining to them why he kept a princess sleeping bag on a ratty old plaid sofa? Maybe he liked princesses.

Once they took a seat, Jax still wanted to maintain some of the upper hand, so he propped a hip on the corner of his desk.

"Okay. Let's hear the speech you rehearsed." He held up a hand to stop them before they started. "Wait. Do you each have a part, like a play? Or are you winging it? Oh, no. Is this going to be a good cop–bad cop rendition?"

Melanie laughed. "How do you want us to deliver the message?"

Livie waved a hand. "We didn't come for dinner and a show," she stated. Her bright eyes came back to land on him, once again socking him right in the gut with arousal. "I've been thinking and Jade's idea is actually brilliant and something that is a win-win for both of us."

Crossing his arms, he made sure to look her right in the eye. She may be a corporate shark and used to negotiating, but he was a former member of the United States Air Force. He used to answer to the government. He wasn't too afraid of three women. Though they seemed to be staring at him. Were they waiting to attack or were they evaluating him?

No doubt Livie had told them about the kisses. Women liked to chatter, to get opinions, to make sure their friends were in their corner. He didn't care. If she was talking about their kissing, then that meant she was thinking about him. Jax was more than okay with that.

"And how will we be winning?" he asked. "Because the way I see it, we'd have to invest an amount of money I can't even wrap my mind around, plus hire contractors, designers. All of that renovating would disrupt the flights."

Jade held up her hands. "Wait. This can all be worked out. As far as the money goes, there are grants for this type of thing. The money isn't going to be as big of an issue as you believe."

"Grants," he muttered. "So who will draw up those proposals?"

"Actually, I'm an attorney and Olivia works with budgeting and numbers all day." Melanie offered a sweet smile and Jax immediately saw why Tanner had been so taken with the new girl in town. "Between the two of us, we'll get it done."

Her assurance seemed so genuine. He had no doubt with these three they would get the job done because Olivia and Jade were strong, independent women. He didn't know Melanie, but if she kept company with these two, then she had to be cut from the same cloth.

"Where do you fit in?" He nodded toward Jade.

"Oh, I'm the mastermind," she stated as if that should've already been known. "I've been working in business for years. I am more than capable of finding contractors and architects to draw up plans."

Jax rubbed the back of his neck. Was he supposed to make a decision now? He had six eyes on him, the room wasn't filled with tension, it was more like . . . uncertainty. How the hell was he supposed to know what the right decision was? If he knew the investment would be profitable, if they could get the funds covered, and only if his already established clients were not disrupted. Not to mention the pilots who rented from him. There were so many variables and not enough answers.

"I need time to think about this," he told them. "It's not something that I can decide in a short time. This is my livelihood. You'll plan from Atlanta where you can continue to work. I have to be with the mess, the contractors. I'd be the one on-site trying to make decisions while you're hours away."

Livie's gaze never wavered. Not once. It was as if she was daring him to keep finding reasons this wouldn't work. Her set jaw, her clasped hands over her perfectly pressed capris were all telltale signs that she wasn't going to back down from this.

Well, he'd wanted her to move on from selling, right? In his mind, though, he figured he could talk her into just leaving him alone and moving on.

But on the flip side, she'd have to stick around at least for a while to get this ball rolling . . . wouldn't she? Jax wasn't too proud to admit he wanted her. That adolescent crush had blown up into something he hadn't expected, and frankly didn't welcome. He had a young daughter and he was always careful not to bring women around. Not that he dated, but if he were to find someone, he'd have to be very careful about who he let into his life. Piper was at an age that she wouldn't understand. And with her mentioning a mother lately, he really had to watch his actions and words.

"I'd be here some," Livie informed him. "But I am going to have to get back to Atlanta soon. So we don't have a lot of time to think on this."

Jax came to his feet, propping his hands on his hips as he shook his head. "You're not giving me much choice when half of this is mine."

"Maybe Jade and I should wait outside." Melanie stood and glanced down to her friends. "This is between Livie and Jackson."

Jade came to her feet and sighed. "As much as I want to stick around and be nosy, I know Olivia will tell us anyway."

Jax watched as the two ladies left his office. Jade shot him a wink as she closed the door behind her. With a laugh, he turned his focus back to the woman on his couch.

With her hair perfectly groomed over her shoulder, the polished clothes, and manicured hands, she looked completely out of place in this dingy room. But, at the same time, she belonged here, because beneath all that perfection was the girl who used to call this hangar home.

Her eyes darted around the room. Nothing had changed since her father had passed. The same picture hung on the wall behind the desk. The picture her father had taken of him when he first purchased the Cessna that sat right outside the office door. With a wide smile on his face, Paul Daniels stood proudly in front of the plane.

Piper stared at the photo. Slowly she came to her feet and kept her eyes locked on the picture behind him. He didn't say a word, didn't want to break whatever moment she had flashing through her mind. Maybe she was recalling a time when her father taught her to fly. Perhaps she was remembering how he always used to slip her money when she came to see him. Even if it was just five dollars, he always said he wanted Livie to have everything.

At the time, Jax didn't understand why Paul would literally give the last bit of cash from his wallet, but now he realized that he only wanted Livie to love him.

As she grew older and more distant, Paul randomly reached out to her, trying to connect with her but not push too hard. Livie had always been his little girl, they shared a bond. But when the marital issues started, Jax firmly believed Livie's mother told her lies and turned her against Paul. Jax never really knew, but nothing else made sense.

He turned to keep his eyes on Livie. She stood within inches of the picture, her shoulders not as rigid as they normally were.

"You said he was sick when we left."

Her words hovered in the air between them. He knew she'd bring that topic up and he owed her some answers since he was the one who'd tapped into this to begin with.

"He didn't want you or your mother to know."

Livie threw a glance over her shoulder. "It doesn't much matter now, does it?"

Not really, but he'd been the only one Paul had confided in about his fears. Most of the people in town knew he was sick, but Paul did a good job hiding the fact. He never wanted pity, never wanted handouts. He was the most prideful man Jax had ever known.

"He had cancer."

Livie stared at him another minute before turning her attention back to the picture. "Why didn't he want anyone to know?"

"The marriage was over, you had sided with your mom and were eager to leave Haven." Jax would never forget the look of defeat on Paul's face when he realized his family was leaving for good. "He didn't want your attention or your mom's out of pity. You know how he was."

Livie nodded as she twisted around and gripped the back of his desk chair. "I know. Damn pride."

Tears shimmered in her eyes, but he wasn't going to mention it or try to console her. He may not have known the new Livie well enough, but he figured someone this determined and strong wouldn't appreciate having her weakness brought to light.

She glanced around the office once again, this time her eyes landing on the back of the door. He didn't even have to turn to know what she saw.

"They've hung there forever," he told her. "Piper loves to put them on and pretend to be my helper."

Livie's sad smile caused a tear to trickle down her cheek.

Well, hell. He couldn't exactly ignore that. Jax circled the desk and came to stand beside her.

"Don't." She held up a hand. "If you touch me, if you try to comfort me, I'll break. I'm barely holding it together."

Ignoring her request, Jax wrapped an arm around her shoulders and pulled her against his chest. Her fists hit his shoulders as she dropped her head.

She may not have wanted to accept his comfort, but he wasn't a complete jerk. No way could he stand by and watch as she was obviously hurting. He had no idea what she was going through, and he'd do well to remember that. Her life had been turned upside down too.

"I don't want to be here," she murmured.

He knew she didn't mean in his arms. Livie wanted to be back in Atlanta with her perfect life she'd created. Instead, she was here dealing with a past she'd done a pretty good job of ignoring.

"You're not upset because you're here," he told her, running his hand up and down her back. "You're angry because you have feelings. You're upset you left and never saw your dad. Maybe you feel guilt—"

Livie pushed back, swiping at her damp cheeks. "I'm not feeling guilty. I'm angry that I didn't know what was going on in his life."

"But you chose to walk away," Jax stated.

"I was eighteen," she cried.

Jax wasn't about to get into a pissing match with her over the past. They both had their own points of view on the subject . . . the only problem was, he knew the full story and she didn't.

The office door opened slightly and Melanie poked her head in. "Sorry. Um . . . we heard yelling and there's a young boy out here to see you, so—"

"We're done here." Livie wiped her face and smoothed her hair back into place—always needing to put the best image forward. "Jackson is free for his visitor."

Now wasn't the time to protest or tell her that what was happening between them, and even in her own mind with her internal battle, was much more important than any unexpected guest.

"I'll be in touch," Livie said as she started toward the door. "Make sure you know your answer when I call."

Her parting words sounded so businesslike, as if she hadn't just broken in his arms. They'd shared something whether she wanted to admit it or not. None of this was going to be as perfectly cut-and-dried as she wanted it to be. Things were going to get messy and they were both going to be tested—and they'd both see exactly what the other was made of.

Jax stepped out of his office and watched as the trio of gorgeous women exited the hangar. That sight alone would have any man giving a double take.

Pulling in a deep breath, he turned to the young boy who was checking out the Cessna. "You're here to see me?"

The young man turned around and Jax recognized him as Brock Monroe. Brock was part of the family who had opened the women-only resort and spa in Haven. He'd been a runaway, then adopted, and blended in perfectly with the family.

With Haven being a small town, and Brock being added into such a prominent family in the area, everyone knew who he was.

"I wanted to talk to you about taking lessons." The young man started across the open hangar. "I'm Brock, by the way. I should've called first."

Jax held his hand out and greeted Brock. "I know who you are."

Brock gave a lopsided grin and shrugged. "Do you give lessons? I've done some training on the Internet, the book stuff, but I wanted to try to get some hours in and I didn't really know who to talk to."

"How old are you?" Not that it mattered for flying purposes. Jax was just curious.

"Just turned nineteen."

Young and eager. Perfect pilot material. Jax loved getting the younger generation involved in this dying sport. With Brock already doing much of the training, he was going to be a great student.

"You in college?" Jax asked, shoving his hands in his pockets.

"Yeah. I help at the resort and take online classes."

"What do you want to study?"

Brock shook his head. "No idea."

That was common for someone fresh out of high school. "Thought about the military?"

A wide smile spread across Brock's face. "All the time."

Jax reached out and slapped Brock on the shoulder. "You got somewhere to be?"

"Not for a few hours. Why?"

"Let's take a ride and talk."

When Jax started heading toward the plane to do a preflight check, Brock came up beside him. "In this?"

Jax laughed. "Do you object?"

"No, man. I just . . . I didn't expect to fly today."

Jax propped his hand on the wing and stared at this young man who had his whole future ahead of him. He was at a crossroads and if Jax could help him through to the next journey, he damn well was going to. Hadn't Paul done that for him?

And now Jax found himself at his own crossroads. The only problem was, Livie was wanting to go one way, and he wanted to go another. Somehow, they were going to have to meet in the middle.

Chapter Eleven

"You can't possibly paint the kitchen something called *Yellow, Is It Me You're Looking For*."

Olivia held up the paint swatch and met Jade's horrified look. "I think it's pretty. This place is too beige."

"It's bright yellow," she reiterated.

Melanie pulled a sample from their pile on the island. "What about this one?"

"What's the name on that one?" Jade asked, examining the colored square.

"*Blonde. James Blonde.*"

Olivia laughed. "The names don't matter. It's the tone and the entire house is drab."

"Do you want to sell this house or make it about what you like?" Jade asked. She took a seat on one of the barstools and started sorting through the colors. "You need to keep things neutral because most likely whoever buys the place will put their own touch on it anyway and repaint."

"Then if they're repainting, I'm doing the bright yellow," Olivia confirmed.

Jade groaned. "Can I at least choose the color of the master bedroom?"

Olivia glanced through the shades. "As long as it's a color and not another shade of beige."

"Your condo is full of color," Jade argued. "Why are you making this house about what you like?"

Olivia shrugged. "Maybe because it's still mine for now and I want to see the change."

Quite possibly there was some deeper meaning she wasn't ready to face yet. Which was even silly to entertain considering she didn't like being back, she didn't want to be here. But she couldn't help but feel the nostalgia in each and every room. She'd have to be completely unfeeling and dead inside not to have all her emotions stirred with each picture she came across.

"I'll do this one, then." Jade pulled up a swatch. "*Shades of Summer*."

Olivia rolled her eyes. "Even the name is boring. It's a cross between tan and yellow."

"Then get bright curtains if it makes you feel better."

Dollar signs kept racking up in her mind. She knew she'd regain her investment once the house sold, but she also didn't want to get out of control with the amount she sank into this place. She truly only wanted to do the necessities. And so far, the kitchen was going to be the biggest money suck.

"Fine," Olivia conceded. "Mel, do you want to choose a room color?"

"Sure, but if you want me to paint, you should know I'd rather go see the dentist and gynecologist in the same day."

Jade's brows rose. "Well, then. We'll just count on you to fix lunches and make sure we're well supplied with drinks."

With a nod, Melanie reached for a color. "Sounds like a deal. I've been looking at this color. I think it would look nice in the living room."

"I wasn't going to paint the living room," Olivia stated.

"Honey, every room needs some love." Jade took the sample from Melanie. "*Olive-ia Newton John.* I like it."

The pale shade of green was beautiful and would look nice in the living room with the wide bay window letting in the morning sunlight. Since Olivia wasn't changing out the furniture, that color would be perfect with the dark brown leather sofa and dark tables.

"Fine," she told them. "Now that we have this done, who's going to Knobs and Knockers to pick all this up?"

Knobs and Knockers was the town hardware store now owned by the third generation. Macy Hayward Monroe had taken over her father's business, but she was now married to Liam Monroe.

Everything in this town seemed to circle back to the Monroe boys and that resort they opened. Maybe Olivia should go and chat with Macy and see if she could squeeze in some massages at Bella Vous. They'd need their muscles worked out once all the painting was done.

Well, Melanie wouldn't, but Olivia would make an appointment for her, too. She was part of this painting project by default.

"I don't mind going," Melanie volunteered. "What time do they close?"

Olivia glanced to the old clock over the window. "It's only three. She'll be open another couple hours."

They'd gone straight from the airport to Knobs and Knockers to get the samples. Her friends were wise enough not to question her when she came out with tear-stained cheeks after talking with Jax. They knew her well enough to know that if she wanted to talk, she would. Right now, though, she wanted to do something productive to make it seem like she was getting somewhere and not at a total standstill.

"I'll go get the paint," Melanie said as she grabbed her

purse and the keys off the hook by the back door. "I assume we need drop cloths, brushes, rollers, trays."

"All of that," Olivia agreed. "And paint stirrers. We won't get to all of the rooms today."

"Want to start in here?" Jade suggested.

Olivia glanced at the walls, the curtains. "Sure. I'll take this stuff down. Oh, make sure you get some painter's tape so I can protect the cabinets. Several rolls since we're doing so much."

"You might want to text me all the supplies so I don't forget something."

Jade came to her feet. "I'll ride with you. Between the two of us we'll remember."

Olivia handed over all the colors they'd agreed upon and waited until they were out the door before she started removing pictures from the walls. She piled everything onto the island, ignoring the faded outline from where things had hung for the past decade.

The ache in her chest couldn't be described. Knowing her father had been sick when she and her mother left cut so deep through her emotions. He'd spent more time at the airport in those final days before Olivia left in an attempt to hide his illness. What did that say about the marriage? Olivia was starting to see that maybe her father had stepped back when his marriage fell apart and let his daughter make her own decisions.

Part of her feared she'd made the wrong one.

Granted, the cancer hadn't taken his life and he'd come through, but Olivia wondered who had been there for him. Had he been sick long? Who helped him get to and from appointments on days he felt too bad to drive?

She climbed on the counter and started tugging at the curtain rod. It came loose and she tossed it to the floor. She stared at the brackets and realized she'd have to go to the garage and get a screwdriver. The garage was one place she dreaded tackling. What should she do with all those tools?

She swallowed the lump of guilt and hopped off the counter. Pulling her phone from her pocket, she sent off a text to Jackson. She didn't want to see him or talk to him right now, not when he'd slapped her in the face with reality and the truth. She was humiliated and angry at herself for being a selfish teen, not seeing how much her father had needed someone.

Olivia could freely admit, since this new fact had come to surface, she was angry at her mother as well. Had she seen signs her father wasn't feeling well? He'd obviously had to go through some doctor appointments and testing to get the final diagnosis. How had they not known?

Another part of her was angry at her father and his pride. Damn it. Why hadn't he reached out? Yes, she understood his concern of them staying out of guilt, but what would have been so wrong with that? At least he wouldn't have been alone.

Olivia grabbed the handle in the middle of the garage door and gave it a twist. She shoved the door up and headed inside. She didn't park her car in here because there was no room. She doubted her father ever had his car in there since she left because the one-car garage was overflowing with tools, spare parts for lawn mowers, a couple of old push mowers, and random things she'd have to classify as junk.

She had no clue what his filing system was, or even if he had one here, but she was going to have to find a screwdriver in this mess. With the sunlight pouring in, she glanced around the mayhem. At this rate, she may have been better off texting Melanie and telling her to just buy one. There was no way she'd find anything in here . . . except maybe a critter.

The thought crept into her head and sent shivers racing

through her. Olivia didn't want to stick around to see if something had chosen to take up residence.

Just as she turned, she ran directly into a hard chest.

"Easy there." Jackson's hands gripped her arms. "Where you running to?"

This was the second time today he'd grabbed her . . . and the second time her body responded instantly to his touch. The arousal that assaulted her each time he was around was only growing stronger and stronger. Denying her ache was a moot point because she constantly lived with it now.

Why did she have to find this man attractive? Wait, *attractive* was much too tame of a word to describe what she felt for Jax. He was sexy, caring, frustratingly smart, and managed to take up some serious real estate space in her mind.

There were so many red flags that popped up when her hormones attempted to take over. She was much older than him, she wasn't sticking around here, and . . . well, that's all the reasons she had. Wasn't that enough?

"I'm positive there's a rodent in there or a snake or a hairy spider." Once again, she shivered. "I was trying to find a screwdriver and . . . what are you doing here?"

"I was on my way home when I got your text." He glanced over her shoulder and surveyed the inside of the garage. "It would be a miracle if any living creature could survive in that place."

His eyes focused back on her, a naughty grin spreading across his face. "How bad do you want that screwdriver?"

Olivia narrowed her gaze. "I'm still upset with you, so keep your lips and all other body parts to yourself."

Jackson reached out and tucked her hair behind her ear, feathering his fingertips down her jawline. "You can still be upset and turned on."

Batting his hand away, she lifted her chin because *damn it* she was definitely turned on.

"I'm not any such thing," she insisted.

His laugh mocked her, but she held her ground. No way would she admit the mere sight of him did funny things to her belly. Fighting this attraction clearly wasn't working. How could she lose a battle with herself? That didn't even make sense.

"Well, then I guess that was someone else clinging and moaning when we kissed."

Before she could reply, he'd released her and headed into the garage. And he had the gall to whistle. Whistle as if he hadn't kept her on her toes since she came back. Whistle as if he hadn't a care in the world while she was more confused than ever.

She hoped a big hairy spider crawled inside his shoe and bit his toes off.

"Don't you have a daughter you need to be with?" she asked, remaining on the outside away from the unknowns inside.

"Cash has her at the gym," he replied, his back to her as he searched through the mess. "I was headed home to shower when you texted, so I have time to find a screwdriver and glance to see if there's any tools I might want."

He went back to whistling and it took everything in her not to explode. She waited while he dug around, muttered under his breath, examined various parts to machinery.

"The screwdriver," she reminded him when he seemed too enveloped in all the other things in the garage.

"I'll get to it. I'm just looking as I go."

"Well I need some brackets down so I can start painting. If you could speed up your shopping spree, I would appreciate it."

With some greasy part in hand, Jackson turned to face

her. "I have a screwdriver in my truck. Why didn't you just tell me you needed something done right now?"

He laid the part down and headed down the driveway. "I did tell you," she argued as she followed the infuriating man.

"No, you just said you needed a screwdriver. I thought you wanted one on hand for convenience."

He opened his squeaky door and reached behind the driver's seat. Pulling out a small black toolbox, he dug around and found what she needed.

When she reached for it, he shook his head. "Show me what needs done."

"I can do it myself."

He kept walking and started up with that damn whistling once again. Olivia ran ahead and stood in front of him, blocking his path.

"Why are you doing this?"

He raised his brows, but she couldn't see his eyes behind his aviator glasses. "Can't you just let people do things without questioning everything?"

"No."

Jackson laughed and darted around her. "Get used to it if you're going to be working with me."

She followed behind as he mounted the back steps and just helped himself into her house. No, her father's house. This wasn't hers other than on paper.

"What does that mean?" she demanded as the screen door slammed at her back. "You're going to do the renovations?"

"It means I'm not completely opposed to more discussions."

He stared at the brackets and leaned against the counter. When he reached up over his head to unscrew the pieces, his T-shirt came up slightly, giving her a magical glimpse of the side of his abs, and the vee disappearing into his jeans.

She really should have looked away, or replied to . . . what had he said?

"Piper has a birthday party Saturday afternoon. We can talk then. Just come by my house."

Olivia took a second to process what all he was saying. He wanted her to come by his house . . . when they'd be alone? Did that mean they wouldn't even be chaperoned by an adorable four-year-old?

"Don't you have to go to the party?" she asked.

He sat one bracket next to the sink and reached up to remove the other. "I offered, but another mom took pity on me since it's a spa theme and she didn't figure I'd want my toes painted."

Olivia laughed. "Oh, but red would be your color."

Jackson pulled the last bracket out and laughed. "Well, I've had many shades in the past several months. Piper has really taken interest in girlie things. I went to the dollar store and bought some things for her to play with. Makeup and stuff, but I don't have a clue what I'm buying. I found some sparkly tote to put it all in so that seemed to excite her even more."

Why did he have to be such a great dad? Jackson may have had a rough hand dealt to him, but he hadn't once complained, at least not that she'd heard. If anything he acted like he was the most blessed man on earth. He kept Piper and the airport at the top of his priority list. He was faithful, loyal . . . and so damn sexy she was having a difficult time finding a flaw with him.

"I hate not to go to the party, but at the same time, I know she would rather go with a woman," Jackson went on as he sat the screwdriver and last bracket down.

"She loves her best friend's mom, so she'll be fine. It's just difficult sometimes—"

"I'll take her."

Where had that come from?

Olivia didn't know who was more startled at her declaration. Jackson stared at her with his mouth wide open and Olivia rubbed her palms down her pants. She had not given herself permission to say such nonsense. Why on earth would she volunteer to do such a thing?

"You don't have to do that," he told her after an awkward moment settled between them. "She's used to tagging along with another mom at this point."

"But she shouldn't have to."

Shut up, Olivia. You have so many other things to do besides get more involved with the toddler you've fallen for.

But she couldn't let it go. Piper was the sweetest little thing with a mop of curly blond hair on the rare occasion it wasn't in crazy pigtails, and the image of her in Olivia's old bibs kept flashing through her mind.

"I could just go as a friend," she explained, realizing she truly didn't mind stepping in. "We'll just explain to Piper that you and I are friends—"

Jackson snorted. "Is that what you call it?"

She quirked her brow and continued. "Friends only and I'll tell her I need a break and a spa party sounds lovely."

Jackson narrowed those gorgeous deep brown eyes. "You're up to something."

Olivia swallowed. She didn't want to admit she knew that emptiness of having one parent being around more than the other. Granted Olivia was older, but Piper had a void in her life and try as Jackson might, he couldn't fill it completely. Not that Olivia was trying to step in as a mother, but she could be a friend to sweet Piper while she was in town.

"I don't have to," she told him, leaning against the counter. "I'm just throwing it out there."

"Are you that desperate to get out of talking to me?"

She hadn't thought of it from that angle, but being alone with Jackson wasn't smart. So, if she went to this party, it would be a win for Piper and Olivia.

"I'm doing this for your daughter."

Jackson shrugged. "I'll ask her, but I want her to understand that you're just a friend. She can't be confused about what you and I have going on."

"We don't have anything going on other than trying to figure out the airport."

That sly grin spread slowly across his face as he took a step forward and closed the distance between them. "You can keep telling yourself that, but I don't believe it any more than you do."

He didn't touch her, simply put one hand on the counter, turned his body toward hers, and put his other hand on the opposite side of her, trapping her against the counter. Her eyes widened. Perfect, she wasn't as unaffected as she kept claiming.

"You want to be angry," he murmured, his eyes darting to her mouth. "But you're not upset with me, you're upset because you have emotions you don't know what to do with."

"Stop touching me."

He leaned in within a breath of her lips. "I'm not touching you at all," he whispered. "I haven't even begun."

She closed her eyes. "I can't think when you're this close."

"Then we're on the same page."

He slid his mouth over hers. Without rushing, without pressing into her, because he wanted to get to know that touch, that taste that only Livie provided. When she opened for him, it was all Jax could do to continue to tease her. He wanted her aching, he wanted her to be just as frustrated as he was. And she was. He could tell by the way she looked at him, the way she kept trying to dodge him, but her body betrayed her when she melted against him.

Jax continued to only touch her with his mouth, but her fingertips gripped his forearms, digging in as if she were barely holding on by a thread, too. He wanted her to snap, he wanted to see her unleash that inner passion. Why did she keep it so pent up when there was obviously so much inside of her?

She whimpered slightly, arching as her hands trailed up his arms and over his shoulders. Her fingers threaded through his hair as she angled her head the opposite way.

There. She was taking the lead. The one and only time he would relinquish control with Livie would be if she wanted to show him exactly what she needed. He'd not been this stirred up by a woman in so long, he couldn't even attempt to stop this roller coaster of emotions.

"Well, I see why she wanted us to go get the paint."

Livie jerked in his arms and Jax glanced over his shoulder toward the back door where Melanie and Jade stood, both wearing huge grins. Their arms were loaded with paint cans and sacks from Knobs and Knockers.

"Ladies," he greeted, while Livie attempted to disengage herself from between his body and the counter. He wasn't quite ready to let her go, nor was he going to act like they were caught doing something wrong when it had felt so very right.

"I did not ask you to go," she corrected. "You both volunteered."

Jade sat the gallon of paint on the counter. "Looks like you took advantage of the time we were gone. We can come back later if you'd like to finish."

Jax hadn't known Jade well when she'd lived here before because he was so much younger, but he liked her sass.

Livie gave him a shove that had him stepping back. "There's nothing to finish," she argued, straightening her clothes. "Jackson stopped by to look at the tools in the garage to see if he wanted anything. Then I had him take the brackets down."

"I've never seen brackets removed that way before," Melanie replied in her sweet tone as she sat her bags on the counter.

Jax couldn't help but smile. Melanie had that perfect Southern belle appearance with her blond hair and her bright blue eyes. Her voice was like honey, sweet, soothing. But she delivered that snarky comment like a seasoned pro.

Livie let out the most unladylike growl and grabbed his screwdriver from the counter. "We're done here." She handed him the tool. "Let me know what time the party is."

"I'll text you about the party," he told her. "And keep the screwdriver. You'll need it when I come back to put the brackets back in place."

Because he just wanted to, and maybe because they had an audience, he leaned down and captured her lips one last time. Before she could protest, he stepped away and rounded the island.

"Looks like you guys are all set," he said, nodding toward the counter full of supplies. "That's my cue to go because I don't like to paint."

"What party were you two talking about?" Jade asked, eyeing him. "A private party like what we walked in on?"

A burst of laughter escaped him. "Not yet. Livie can tell you about it."

He let the screen door slam behind him as he started whistling and headed down the steps. Painting never bothered him, but there was no way in hell he was going to stick around with those questioning eyes on him. His body was still revved up from that simple, yet gut-churning kiss.

Why did every taste of her leave him even more needy than the last? Why did it have to be this woman who got him in knots? Since his wife left, he'd sworn not to get involved with another woman unless it would lead somewhere—mainly because of Piper, but also because he didn't want his heart crushed again.

Even at the bottom of the porch steps, he heard the chatter inside the house. He rounded the corner and headed down the driveway. With a glance at his watch, he realized he had just enough time to get home for Cash to drop off Piper, but not enough time for that shower. Oh well. Some things were worth a disrupted schedule and kissing Livie Daniels was certainly one of them.

Chapter Twelve

With the kitchen and living room painted, the bathrooms up next, Olivia was pleased with the progress they'd made in just a few short days. She had stopped to get flooring samples this morning, so with those taking up the trunk of her car, she focused on another project. The birthday party.

She guided her car toward Jackson's house. He'd explained that he lived in the subdivision behind the school at the end of the cul-de-sac. As she turned onto his road, she glanced to her red sundress and wondered if she'd gotten too dressed up. She'd only brought a limited supply of clothes because she hadn't planned on staying too long, so she'd had to go buy something for this toddler spa party.

What grown adult went and bought a dress for a child's birthday party? Olivia didn't know any of the people who were going to be there.

Dread curled in her belly as she realized that she most likely would know people. As Jackson's two-story house came into view, Olivia had to fight back a panic attack. Haven wasn't a large town by any means, so most likely there would be people there she went to school with. What had she gotten herself into?

She wasn't an extrovert—she lived in her office in Atlanta and cranked out killer marketing deals for companies. Her interaction with others tended to be via e-mail or social events with associates. What did she know about children?

"You can do this," she whispered to herself as she pulled into the drive.

She wasn't sure what she expected out of his home, but the porch swing and the bright flowers along the sidewalk were a pleasant surprise. His home nestled back against the woods, almost giving it a feel of being all alone and away from neighbors. Old mossy oak trees surrounded his property and for a moment, Olivia envied the quiet, peaceful setting. She didn't have plants or trees or flowers at her condo. She certainly didn't have a porch or a swing. She did have a killer view of the city, though. That was something . . . wasn't it?

Olivia pulled in a deep breath. She'd clearly been in this town too long if she was growing envious of her surroundings. She needed to remain focused on getting some concrete decisions made and getting out of Haven.

As she stepped out of her car, Piper ran onto the porch. "You're really here," she squealed. "I didn't know if you'd actually come."

The way Piper ran off the porch and raced down the drive had Olivia smiling and bracing herself. Tiny arms flew around Olivia's waist as doe-like brown eyes stared up at her.

"You're going to be the prettiest one there," she said. "I don't own a dress, but I wore my favorite new sandals."

Didn't own a dress? Because she didn't like them or Jackson just didn't buy them? She never thought too much about the dynamics of a single father raising a little girl.

Were there things she wanted and missed out on simply because he never thought of such things?

"Of course I came."

Olivia leaned over to look Piper in the eyes. She was well aware Jackson had stepped onto the porch and stood looming over them. Her heart kicked into high gear, but she ignored that automatic reaction and the curl of desire.

"I can't wait to spend the day with you," Olivia stated, surprised that she was being completely honest.

Seeing Piper's excitement was well worth the doubts and turmoil she'd experienced moments ago.

"I need to get the present." Piper raced back up onto the porch, but turned around and pointed at her father. "Don't forget my booster seat."

He laughed and gave a mock salute. "Yes, ma'am."

As Piper went inside, Olivia straightened her dress because Jackson was heading her way and she . . . well, damn it, she was fidgety.

"You look amazing," he told her as he stopped directly in front of her. "Would you get this dressed up for me if I took you out?"

The flirting, the kisses, the heavy-lidded glances were all getting to her. She was having a difficult time trying to remember why being near him was a terrible idea. Because each time he came close, she got swept up in those dark eyes, that devilish grin, and that sweeping glance he'd give her that told her he was taking in every inch of her in one swoop.

"We aren't going out," she countered, thankful her voice sounded strong.

"Maybe not," he agreed. "But let's say I asked you out. Would you wear something like this? A little dress that showed off your shape? Or would you go back to those stuffy clothes that scream CEO?"

She swallowed. "I'm not a CEO."

Jackson leaned in and whispered, "I like this Livie better."

"Olivia," she murmured.

"Not to me." He eased back. "I'm going to get the booster seat from my truck and put it in your back seat. You think about when you want to discuss the airport plans."

He walked away and Olivia turned to watch him go as if he hadn't just flirted, came within a breath of kissing her, and told her she looked beautiful. She seriously couldn't keep up with that man.

"I'm ready, Livie."

She spun around as Piper came bounding down the steps, her pigtails in perfect position today and even tied with little blue ribbons. The image of Jackson using those big strong hands to tie something so dainty and feminine did nothing to squelch her fascination and attraction.

Jackson put the booster seat in the back of Olivia's car and propped his arm on the top of the open door. "Come on, hot shot."

Piper climbed into the back of the car and sat the gift bag beside her. "Bye, Daddy. Love you."

He leaned in, fastened her belt, and kissed the top of her head. "Love you, baby girl. Have fun and be good for Livie."

When he closed the door, he turned to Olivia. "I'd tell you to have fun, but you look like you'd rather do anything else. It's not too late to back out."

Piper stared out the window, a wide grin spreading across her face. There was no way Olivia would back out. She knew exactly what it was like to be let down, to not be able to depend on someone. Even though Piper wasn't a permanent part of her life, Olivia would never purposely disappoint such a sweet child.

"I'm fine," she assured him. "I'll bring her back once the party is over."

He nodded and stepped aside. "I'll be here. Just text me if there's any problems."

She nodded and slid into the driver's seat before he could say anything else or touch her. Not that he'd do much with little eyes watching, but Olivia wanted to get the car started since it was so hot.

As she backed out of the driveway, she tried to focus on not looking at Jackson staring at her. She did give him one final wave as she headed in the opposite direction.

"Thank you for taking me," Piper said from the back seat. "I know you probably had other things to do—"

"Actually, I had nothing to do today." Olivia steered toward town where the party was at a salon owned by the birthday girl's family. "I have never been to a spa party, so I'm super excited to spend this day with you."

"Daddy said you didn't care, but he also told me I should thank you."

"Your daddy is teaching you manners." Olivia glanced into the rearview mirror and smiled. "You're lucky to have him."

"Can you fix hair?" she asked, suddenly into another subject.

"I suppose I can. I do mine every day."

"Would you do mine?" Piper asked, her eyes locked onto the mirror. "One of my friends always wears hers curly and she looks like a princess."

Olivia's heart went out to Piper. How could a four-year-old know exactly how to make the largest impact with just a few simple words?

"I'm sure I could curl your hair."

"Today?"

Olivia gripped the wheel and thought of how she should approach this. Jackson may not want Olivia spending a bunch of time with his daughter. Olivia completely understood not wanting to give the wrong impression. At the same time, Piper was only asking for some girl time and there was no way Olivia could deny her.

"Of course," Olivia answered. "How about after the party? I have some friends at my house and we could just continue spa day with them."

Olivia glanced to the mirror long enough to see Piper's eyes light up. "Really? I love you."

Emotions threatened to overtake Olivia. Were all children this expressive? Did they all have their barriers down, ready to welcome the life that surrounded them? Had Olivia ever been that innocent and ready to pull people into her life?

"I'll text your daddy to make sure it's okay first."

"He won't care. He likes you."

Okay. Definitely not something she wanted to chat about with a four-year-old, but at the same time the inner high school girl in her came out and she wanted to know exactly what he had said, the tone he used, and how often he spoke of her. That wasn't immature . . . was it?

"Your daddy is a good friend." Okay, that didn't sound convincing, but her audience was a toddler, so . . . "I like him too."

Yeah, that sounded convincing because it was completely true. He made her feel all giddy, which was ridiculous. She was a grown woman with a very prestigious position in a marketing firm. She didn't do giddy . . . or at least she hadn't before coming back to Haven.

She resisted the urge to groan. How could she even entertain the idea of getting tangled with Jackson—"just call me Jax"? He was much younger than her and . . . well, there were several other reasons. Many reasons, in fact, and she didn't have the mental stamina to list them all.

"I heard him telling Cash and Tanner that he kissed you."

Olivia completely failed at keeping her expression blank. How did she respond to that?

"They thought I was asleep," Piper went on. "They do that all the time. They come over for dinner or cards and then they tell me it's time for bed. But babies go to bed early and I'm not a baby."

"No, you're a big girl," Olivia agreed, wanting Piper to move back to the portion she overheard. "Maybe you misunderstood what your daddy said."

"I heard real good, Livie," she insisted. "Daddy said he took you in his plane and you argued, then he kissed you."

Considering that's exactly how their first kiss went down, Olivia knew Piper had heard correctly. But Olivia was more interested in the fact that he was discussing her with his cousins. That was something she'd talk to him about later. Because Olivia wanted to know exactly what he thought he was doing and where he thought all this attraction would lead.

Okay, she knew what his answer would be, but she wanted to know what he thought they'd accomplish by acting on this attraction. They still had the airport between them and it appeared they were going to move forward with renovations. Letting personal emotions and hormones interfere would surely just cause a mess in the long run.

At least, that was the only reason she could come up with to keep her distance because everything in her wanted to ignore the red flags and take what she wanted.

And she wanted Jackson.

"Can I have my hair your color?"

Piper's wide eyes zeroed in on Jade's crimson hair. Olivia had brought the eager toddler home after Jackson gave the okay. Now they were getting ready to have a hair session and some girl talk—toddler-level girl talk.

"I'm not sure your daddy would appreciate if I brought you back with colored hair," Olivia answered with a smile.

Melanie plugged in the curling iron and patted the seat to the vanity. "Come on over, Piper. Let's see about making you a princess."

They'd congregated in Olivia's old bedroom where there was still an old antique vanity with a large oval mirror. She'd loved this station when her father had found it for her. Her mother had wanted something fancier, but when her dad brought the vanity set home from a yard sale, he'd sanded on it for days, then repainted it a crisp white and added new hardware.

Those memories kept creeping up. The ones that forced her to realize that her father did love her, that he did things for her that went against her mother's wishes. But being a child and spending most of her time with her mother, Olivia hadn't seen things from his perspective.

She swallowed back her emotions. Now wasn't the time to face them, not when she had an adorable little girl waiting for this much-needed female bonding time.

"I don't just want to be a princess," Piper said as she settled onto the cushioned bench. "I want to be a pilot like my daddy."

"That sounds like a perfect goal," Jade replied as she sat on the edge of the bed. "Do you like when your daddy takes you on trips in the plane?"

Piper nodded. "Yeah, but we don't get to go many places by ourselves. We want a new plane, so we're saving money. Well, daddy says it's not brand-new but even used ones take a lot of money. I told him he could have my piggy bank. I have almost four dollars saved. I was going to buy a Play-Doh set I saw on TV, but I'd rather have a plane."

Melanie and Jade shared a look before both women turned to Olivia. She merely shrugged. She didn't know what to say—she didn't know Jackson wanted a new plane. The fact Piper was offering all her savings just proved children were so much more giving and precious than Olivia thought. There was definitely something to be learned from hanging out with a chatty toddler.

"I'm sure your daddy appreciates you offering your money." Olivia went over and sat on the floor next to the vanity, her back against the wall. "But I bet he'd rather you keep that for yourself."

"I really want the new plane," Piper whined. "He has a picture of it hanging on our fridge. It's so pretty and shiny. He said he wouldn't have to keep sinking money into the old one."

Olivia pulled in a deep breath. "It is old," she agreed. "That plane was one my daddy bought used and I learned to fly in it."

Piper's eyes widened. "You're a pilot, too? I love you so much. You're the coolest girl I know."

And that was the second time this precious girl professed her love and Olivia still wasn't sure how to respond.

"My first plane ride was with Olivia," Jade chimed in. "She's an awesome pilot."

"Will you take me?" Piper squealed. "I know Daddy won't care."

Melanie wrapped another long strand of blond hair around the barrel of the curling iron and met Olivia's gaze. She hadn't piloted since leaving Haven, but there were some things that were just engrained in you and you never forgot. She didn't know why, but she'd always renewed her pilot's license and now she was glad she had.

Olivia had to admit that being back made her want to get behind the controls again. She wanted to know that freedom, because the only place she'd ever felt that was when she was in the sky.

"I'll have to talk to him," Olivia stated, not committing to anything just yet.

"Tell me about the birthday party." Melanie sat the iron

down and parted off another section of Piper's hair. "I love that purple on your fingers and toes."

Piper held up her hands and smiled. "Purple is my favorite color. Daddy paints my nails sometimes, but it doesn't look this good. He's a boy so don't say anything."

Olivia realized she could learn quite a bit about Jackson simply by spending more time with Piper. But on the flip side of that, she didn't want to get any more involved than she already was.

"What is your friend's name who had the birthday?" Jade asked.

"Molly Ann. She's my best friend. We have cubbies next to each other and we put our cots together at nap time. We don't nap, though. That's for babies."

"Oh, I don't know." Jade shook her head and smiled. "I never turn down a nap when I get the chance."

"I hate naps," Piper insisted. "Me and Molly Ann whisper. I think the teacher saw us once, but she didn't say anything. Only the bad kids get in trouble."

"Do you like school?" Olivia asked, wrapping her arms around her legs.

"It's fun, but I miss being at the airport all the time. I don't get to go on as many trips with Daddy like I did before school."

Olivia vowed then and there to make sure this baby got on a fun flight soon. Not transporting another client, but something just for Piper. Another item she mentally added to the list of things she needed to discuss with Jackson. At this rate, she'd have to schedule a two-day conference with the man.

"Are you going to make the airport bigger?"

Piper's question caught Olivia off guard. "Excuse me?"

"Oh, that was something else I heard Daddy say when he thought I was in bed."

Her devilish grin was so rotten and adorable at the same time. Olivia wondered if Jackson knew he had a very intelligent kid on his hands.

"I'm not sure what we're doing quite yet," Olivia answered honestly. "Your dad and I are going to talk. What do you think we should do?"

"Well, he said something about movie stars." Piper's focus went back to the mirror as Melanie continued curling ringlets. "That would be the coolest thing ever if my daddy got to fly them. Maybe he'd let me ride too."

So that was the angle he'd been discussing. From a business standpoint, the idea was brilliant and other than the obvious risk, there was no good reason not to pursue the plans.

But, from a personal, emotional standpoint, there was every reason not to push forward.

"Maybe if rich people use the airport, Daddy could buy that plane." Piper's questioning gaze turned to Olivia once again. "They'd have to pay a lot of money, right? Then we could afford it."

Olivia wished she had that large chunk of money because she'd just buy the plane for Jackson and Piper. It was obvious they were a team and Piper thought the sun rose and set on her father . . . as most little girls do. Olivia had been no different at that age.

"Do you want your curly hair up or down?" Melanie asked as she fluffed up the curls.

Piper shook her head from side to side, watching in the mirror as each curl swung wildly. "Down. I always have two ponytails because that's all Daddy knows how to do. Maybe you guys could teach him something new."

"Olivia would love to show your father," Jade piped up.

Narrowing her eyes, Olivia shot a death glare to her friend. Jade winked and offered a half grin.

What was one more thing to add to the list of things she

wanted to discuss with Jackson? Perhaps she could just search some YouTube videos and send him the links. That way he could learn himself and she didn't technically have to be there.

Melanie placed the curls in just the right spot and put a light spray on Piper's hair.

"There." Melanie stood back and clasped her hands together. "You are a beautiful young lady all the time, this is just a new look for you."

Piper hopped off the bench and did a twirl. "Now I need a dress. Something that looks pretty when I spin."

Jade came to her feet. "Then let's go shopping."

Once again, Olivia looked at her friend like she'd lost her mind. "Now?"

"I have nothing else to do but paint a bathroom," Jade replied. "I'm always up for some retail therapy."

"Is there anywhere close that sells kids' clothes?" Melanie asked.

"Oh, my friend's mom has a store," Piper exclaimed. "It's called . . . hmmm . . . I don't know. But it's by the store that sells fish."

Fish? Haven didn't have a pet store that Olivia was aware of. "Do you know the name of the fish store?" she asked.

Piper shook her head, sending the curls flying. "No, but it's by the place that has stamps."

Okay, so this new store was near the post office. That shouldn't be too difficult to figure out.

"I better text your daddy again and see if he cares."

Olivia pulled out her phone and sent off a message. She was shocked to see how much time had passed since she'd first picked Piper up. She was the sweetest little girl and it was obvious she was thoroughly enjoying her girl time and in all honesty, Olivia was, too. Jackson had raised one very special girl and he was doing his best as a single dad, but sometimes a girl just needed another female . . . no matter how old.

Her phone chimed with his reply.

"Your dad says you can go."

Piper squealed and started dancing around the bedroom. "I've been wanting to go to this place, but I didn't think Daddy would like it so I never asked. Can you take me by my house first?"

"For what?" Olivia asked.

"I want to get my piggy bank. If Daddy doesn't need it for the plane, then I can use it for a new dress."

Olivia's heart lurched. There was no other way to describe the strong emotions she felt right at this moment. The girl didn't ask for anything except love and affection. She just wanted to be with women, to be shown what it was like to have some girl time and do all the things her father wasn't quite sure about. He was a remarkable man, an impressive father, but understandably he couldn't make up for the absence of a woman in her life.

"I'll buy you any dress you want," Melanie stated. "You keep saving for that Play-Doh set."

Piper's brows drew in. "Are you sure? I don't mind giving you my four dollars."

Melanie leaned down and gave her a hug. "I'm positive. But there's one condition. You have to let me approve of it, so that means you're going to need to try it on and model it for us."

Piper clapped her hands wildly. "I will, I will. Let's go."

She raced out of the room, leaving everyone behind. Jade glanced to Olivia. "We've been with her such a short time and I'm already in love."

Melanie nodded her agreement and Olivia blew out a sigh. "Yeah. She's impossible not to love."

"It's going to make that attraction with Jax all the more difficult to fight," Jade added.

"She wasn't fighting it the other day," Melanie stated with a grin. "Sorry, I couldn't resist."

Olivia smacked her friend's shoulder. "Hush. I'm confused, that's all."

"All the more reason to get out of the house and have some fun." Jade slid her sandals on and headed out of the room.

"When are you going to talk to Jax about the airport?" Melanie asked as she unplugged the hot curling iron.

Olivia shook her head. "I don't know. I guess today when I take Piper home. We can't keep dancing around the doubts and worries. We need to make a final decision."

"Need us to come with you?" Melanie offered.

"I'll be fine." Olivia crossed the room, but glanced over her shoulder. "It's not the airport I'm worried about when I'm with him."

Chapter Thirteen

Jax stared at the sacks of clothes and rubbed his forehead. When Livie had picked up Piper this morning, Jax never dreamed his daughter would come home with purple nails, curly hair like he'd never seen, and wearing a new dress . . . not to mention the six other shopping bags that held who knew what.

"Maybe I should've just taken her to the party," he mumbled as he glanced from the sacks to Livie.

Oblivious to life around her, Piper twirled in her new dress. She spun one way, then the other, all while staring down at the rippling skirt.

"We may have gone a little overboard," Livie agreed. "But three women who don't have kids took an adorable little girl to a new boutique. I'm impressed we held back."

Jax stared at her, stunned she thought this was held back. "You're kidding, right?"

Livie shrugged. "Shop local. I'm just helping the economy in Haven."

"Do you love this, Daddy?"

He turned to Piper, who stood across the room holding her skirt out for him to see the glittery pattern. "You look like my little angel. Why don't you take your things to your room and play? I need to talk to Livie for a bit."

"Oh, about the fancy new airport?" Piper exclaimed jumping up and down.

"How do you know about that?" he asked. He'd never said a word to her about this newfound idea Livie had presented.

Piper's eyes widened. "Never mind."

She grabbed her sacks and raced up the stairs to her bedroom. Jax immediately focused his attention back on Livie.

"Did you tell her?"

Livie held her hands up. "Don't look at me. She overheard you talking with your cousins. She also heard you talking about our kiss. Care to unpack that conversation with me?"

Jax shrugged. "Like you didn't tell Jade and Melanie about how much you liked kissing me."

With an unladylike snort, Livie shifted toward the door. "Forget it. I'm done here."

"We still need to talk."

Livie put her hand on the knob and glanced over her shoulder. "About the airport? It's simple. You're either on board or you're not."

"Are you one hundred percent committed?" he countered, crossing the space between them. "Are you ready to work one-on-one with me to get this figured out? Because this will be daunting and it won't be easy. I know you have a life in Atlanta, but you can't forget this is my life here and I won't have you screwing it up."

Livie spun completely to face him, her eyes narrowing. "You think if we moved forward on this that I don't have just as much to lose if we fail? I own half of this as well, Jackson. Don't forget that."

"As if you'd let me."

He realized he'd come to stand so close, he could easily see the variation of blue in her eyes and the navy flecks. Her eyes seemed brighter today, whether from having a relaxing day or from being angry with him, he didn't know, but she looked too damn good to resist.

"Don't leave," he commanded.

Her eyes widened. "I'm not staying—"

"You are." He took her hands, holding them up between their bodies. "We're going to talk. Piper will go to bed soon and then you and I can get this ironed out so we can take the next step. I'm done dancing around the topic and I know you want to have some finality."

She stared at him, worrying her bottom lip between her teeth. Her unpainted lips begged to be touched, but he wouldn't do anything to confuse Piper further. If she'd already heard him talking with Tanner and Cash, then he needed to talk with her so she wasn't led astray. He didn't want her to think anything was going on here, because it wasn't. Well, other than the business arrangement and the flirting and his all-consuming need to have her.

Maybe it would be best if they hashed out all the details and she left. Maybe then he could get his mind back on his priorities and stop living with this real-life fantasy always in his personal space.

"I don't think it's a good idea if I stay," she countered. "Maybe we could just talk on the phone."

Jax laughed. "Careful, Liv. Your fear is showing."

Piper chose that moment to bound back down the stairs and Jax reluctantly let go of Livie's hands.

"Can we have popcorn and a movie?" Piper asked as she stepped between Jax and Livie.

Those bright eyes stared up at him and he had such a difficult time when she was being sweet. It was nearly bedtime, but he figured a movie wouldn't hurt.

"Sure."

Piper's smile widened as she turned to Livie. "You'll stay, right? I'll share my popcorn with you and you can even pick from my movies."

Livie glanced up to him, but Jax gave no indication that he wanted her to stay—and he did. But he wanted her to decide. He wasn't going to beg.

"Please," Piper added when the silence stretched too long.

"I'd love to," Livie finally said. "I can never turn down popcorn. It's my favorite snack."

"I like chocolate kisses, but Daddy won't let me have those this close to bedtime."

Livie laughed. "Probably because he wants you to get a good night's sleep."

Piper ran toward the television and started digging through her basket of movies. He did a double take at her pajamas.

"Did you buy those, too?" he asked.

Livie patted his shoulder as she eased around him. "A little girl always needs one satin gown." She took a seat on the floor next to Piper as if she belonged here. "That was the very first thing she asked for when we got to the store."

Jax listened to her defense, but he couldn't get over the way she looked almost at ease here in his home. She smoothed the skirt of her dress around her legs and started chatting movies with his daughter. No woman had ever been in his home, let alone cozied up with Piper ready for movie night. There was so much wrong with this moment, so many reasons he needed to guard his heart and his family, but all he could think of was the kernel of something deep within him that said this wasn't wrong at all.

Livie tossed a glance over her shoulder and grinned. A genuine grin that clenched his heart and made him want to know what the hell he was thinking letting her infiltrate every aspect of his life. The airport he didn't have much control over since half was legally hers. But he'd voluntarily let her into his personal life, into the life of Piper.

"We've got this," Livie stated, still smiling. "Why don't you go start that popcorn."

Right. Popcorn. For the movie night. A simple evening that should be relaxing, but seemed more like a family night in . . . and that hit very close to his scarred heart.

As he headed to the kitchen all he could think about was the last woman he'd let into his personal space. She'd been beautiful and charming, she'd stolen his breath with just one look and she'd vowed to love him forever.

He couldn't risk letting down his guard again, not when he had a precious, impressionable daughter who needed stability. There was nothing wrong with the obvious friendship Piper and Livie had formed today, but there was something terribly wrong with the way his heart kept tugging at the image of them laughing and chatting.

Jax rested his palms on the center island and hung his head between his shoulders. He was barely hanging on to this slippery slope and if he wasn't careful, he'd lose his grip and find himself in the exact position he'd been in once before.

By the time they reached the middle of the movie, Piper had curled up in Olivia's lap, laid her head on her shoulder, and promptly gone fast to sleep. Darkness had fallen outside and the only light in the living room came from one lamp on the side table and the rolling credits on the television.

Olivia had never thought about having children before, had always been too focused on the next rung on the corporate ladder, but after spending the day with Piper, there was a definite possibility. Having someone who trusted you with everything, who encouraged you to not only have fun but to thrive in the moment, it was all so much to take in.

She hadn't been sure how today would go with attending a toddler birthday party, but it was an absolutely perfect day.

Piper had her little purple painted fingers resting on Olivia's arm, her knees tucked up under her satin gown, and her curls spiraling over her shoulder.

"I can carry her up to bed." Jackson came to his feet and reached for Piper. "Give me just a minute."

Olivia hated letting go. Her lap and arms instantly grew colder without the weight of the precious child. Piper stirred a little, but settled back in with her head on Jackson's shoulder. There was a niggle of something she didn't recognize deep in her heart as she watched them disappear when they rounded the landing.

She shouldn't be getting this cozy, this comfortable with Jackson, Piper . . . with this town. There was nothing here for her other than an airport she'd inherited and was now going to sink money into in the hopes of making a return profit.

Olivia came to her feet and picked the empty popcorn bowls up off the coffee table. She took them into the kitchen and sat them in the sink. The more she saw of Jackson's house, the more she was impressed with just how homey and cozy it was. If she'd had to guess before, she'd say it was a typical bachelor pad, but that was far from the truth. This was definitely a single-father-raising-a-little-girl type place.

Jackson's large, scuffed work boots sat by the back door, next to a dainty pair of purple sparkly flip-flops. This adorable relationship touched Olivia's heart in ways she couldn't explain. Jackson put his daughter first. When it would've been easy for him not to give up everything he'd ever wanted and let grandparents raise her, he'd come home. He'd come home instantly and taken the role of both parents.

And little Piper was so sweet and caring and such a joy to be around. Olivia didn't know how it happened, but Piper had worked her way into Olivia's heart. Maybe it was the second she'd seen her in those old bibs, perhaps it was during the party, or maybe it was when she'd twirled around the fitting room earlier today. All Olivia knew was that there was something special happening and she had no control over the outcome.

"You didn't have to pick up."

Olivia spun around, her hand on her chest. "I didn't hear you come back down."

Jackson stood in the doorway between the kitchen and living room. That piercing gaze of his had her frozen in place. Why did he always manage to look at her like he could see into her soul?

Wiping her hands down her dress, she forced herself not to fidget too much. Just because she was alone with Jackson, just because she'd gotten cozy like a family this evening, and just because he was now stalking across the kitchen with his eyes never wavering, didn't mean she needed to be nervous.

But she was. She'd never been jittery around a man before. Everything about Jackson made her on edge, made her daydream more than she ever had in her life.

"So, do you want to hear my ideas for the airport?" she asked.

A slow grin spread across his face as he came to stand directly in front of her. "We'll get to that."

Her heart beat faster in her chest, she licked her dry lips, drawing his attention to her mouth, which was absolutely not her intent.

"Thanks for all you did with Piper today."

"Oh, you're welcome. She's fun to be with."

Jackson's hand came up and her breath caught in her throat. He tucked her hair behind her ear, leaving his hand on the side of her face, his thumb stroking her jawbone.

"Not many people would do what you did," he added. "Makes me look at you like . . ."

"What?" Why did her voice sound breathless? Oh, yeah. She was having a difficult time breathing when he stood this close, when he was touching her.

"Maybe you're not the woman I thought you were when you first came back to town."

Olivia leaned her head slightly, seeking more of his touch even though her mind told her this wasn't smart. They had important things to discuss. What things, though, she couldn't quite remember.

"I'm the same woman," she replied, grateful her voice sounded a little stronger.

"Maybe so, but you're not who I thought you were."

Because she wanted him to keep touching her, she moved away. Giving in to her desires was not what she came here for. Having Jackson and his charms so in her face, literally, wasn't going to solve this issue.

"We really need to talk," she said, moving to the kitchen table. "Jade gave me some great ideas, but I want to hear what you have to say."

Olivia took a seat as he leaned back against the counter and crossed his arms over his chest. "Do you really think you can distract me with airport talk? I mean, I'm all for work and discussing what I love, but you've been here all night wearing that sexy dress. You can't possibly be immune to this tension."

Olivia wasn't immune to anything when it came to this man. "I just think it's best if we ignore it."

His bark of laughter filled the space. "Do you now?

Because the way I see it, we should act on it and ignore the warning signs."

"That's not going to get us anywhere."

He crossed the room, loomed over her, and rested one hand on the table, one hand on the back of her chair. "On the contrary. It will get us right where we both want to be."

"Jackson—"

"So proper. Nobody calls me Jackson."

She blinked up at him, trying to catch her bearings even though she was sitting down.

"Jax," he commanded. "Just say it once."

She swallowed. "Jax."

"What else can I do to make you relax and have you put your CEO side away for a while?"

He was all-consuming, right in her face, leaving her no choice but to inhale his masculine scent, stare into those navy eyes, and try not to focus on the stubble running along his jawline, over his chin, and circling his kissable mouth.

"I'm not a CEO," she reminded him, though there wasn't much heat to her defense.

"Might as well be." He reached behind her, gripped her hair in his hand, and tipped her head back. "Tell me, do the guys you date wear ties to dinner? Cuff links? Have a perfect part in their hair? I bet they have all the proper manners and don't do anything to offend you."

He was exactly right, and that was the few times she actually dated. Because if she went out, it was with someone in the same field as her or someone she'd met through work, so of course they wore ties because most of the time they'd just left work and met somewhere.

Which may explain why she'd never felt that jitter, had that curling need spiraling through her.

"Do they do anything to shock you?" he went on, leaning in to nip at her lips. "Or do they politely walk you to your door and go home?"

"Actually, we meet and drive separate," she muttered between his kisses.

Jackson's lips trailed along her jaw and up to that sensitive spot behind her ear. "No wonder you tremble with my touch. Has anyone ever made you shiver, Livie? Has anyone ever made you ache the way you are right now?"

Never.

"Jax—"

"That's better," he whispered into her ear.

A second later, his lips covered hers as he hauled her to her feet. Instinctively, she gripped his arms and let the assault on her mouth take over. She didn't care about why this wasn't a good idea, they were well past that at this point. Every time his lips made contact with her, she wanted more and she didn't even care that she was letting him completely take over.

"Stay," he muttered against her lips. "Stay with me."

The impact of his words hit her hard . . . and for about a half second she had a valid argument. Then she didn't know what the hell she was fighting. Hadn't they been dancing toward this moment since the first flirtatious encounter?

Olivia didn't answer with words, she merely threaded her fingers through his hair and pulled his mouth back to hers. Jax lifted her off the ground and started walking.

"Wait," she panted. "Piper . . ."

"She's sound asleep and there's a lock on my door."

Olivia made a quick mental note to be gone by morning. Beyond the fact she didn't want Piper to see her still here, Olivia sure as hell didn't want to hear Jade and Melanie mock her for the walk of shame.

But right now she'd give anything to be rid of these clothes and get behind that promised locked door.

Olivia wrapped her arms around Jax and let him carry her from the room. She locked her ankles behind his back and clung to him, anticipation spiraling through her faster than she could even comprehend. Everything about this moment was so out of character, so opposite of anything she'd ever do, but nothing had ever felt so perfect. It may not have been right, but for this night, she didn't care about right or wrong. She cared about Jax and how he made her feel.

"Wait." She stopped him just before he started up the steps. "I'm too heavy for you to—"

"Shut up, Livie."

She smiled as she rested her forehead against the side of his neck. He carried her up with ease. He wasn't breathing hard, he wasn't straining, and that strength shot even more arousal through her.

He headed down the hallway and Olivia didn't even glance up, didn't need to know any more about this house. All she needed to know was how amazing she felt right at this minute, focusing on the fact she hadn't been this turned on, this anxious to be with a man in . . . well, ever.

She'd taken lovers over the years, but never one as bold, as exhilarating as Jackson—"just call me Jax." He demanded she face her feelings and as he rounded the corner to his bedroom, she was thrilled for once in her life that she'd been forced out of her comfort zone.

Her return to Haven should've been easy, should've been an in and out. A romantic involvement, no matter how temporary or shallow, never entered her mind. When did it ever? Work consumed her, she had no time for a social life, especially when vying for a top position within her firm.

"Turn it off," Jackson growled. "Whatever it is that just had you tensing up, it has no place between us."

How this man was so in tune with her and her thoughts was simply astounding. She didn't want to dive into all the reasons why he had this ability, or what this meant to the level they were about to take this relationship to.

Because whether or not she wanted to face it, they were in a relationship. It may be just business with a side of physical intimacy and nothing more, but the label was there. She'd figure out the logistics later.

Jackson sat her on her feet and before she could get her balance, he had her dress lifted and jerked over her head. Instinct had her crossing her arms over her body. Not that she was self-conscious, but she hadn't been naked in front of a man for a while and she certainly hadn't prepared to be seen in her boring bra and panty set when she'd dressed this morning.

"Don't try being modest now," he demanded, pulling her hands away. "It doesn't suit you."

"I didn't know we'd just jump into it when we got in here."

He framed her face between his hands and tipped her head so she had no choice but to meet his gaze. "Baby, we've been dancing around this for days. We didn't jump into anything."

The way his warm breath washed over her, the strength of his body pressing against hers, there was something so primal about the fact he was still fully clothed and she only had the barest of necessities . . . no matter how dull.

With a quick, yet toe-curling kiss, he released her to cross the room. He closed the door, the click of the lock echoing. The reality of the moment settled deep in her belly and she knew he was absolutely right. They'd been dancing around this for days, she'd been fantasizing about it, eagerly working herself up to this moment.

Jackson whipped his shirt off, tossing it aside, never taking his eyes off hers. The hunger staring back at her was so thrilling.

"Do you practice that look in the mirror?"

"What's that?" he asked, stalking across the room toward her.

"That predator-to-prey look."

That naughty grin she'd come to appreciate from him spread across his face. "I have no idea what you mean."

Like hell he didn't. Jax knew exactly what he was doing, exactly how he affected her, and damn if she wasn't enjoying every single moment of it.

Olivia raked her eyes over his chest, that glorious, rippled, tattooed chest sprinkled with dark hair. She stared at the ink, trying to decipher what they all were with the dim lighting.

"I'd say you have that look down yourself," he replied.

Her eyes darted back up to his. "I'm just taking all this in."

Throwing his arms out wide, he said, "Do what you want. Having your eyes on me is one of the sexiest things I've seen in a long time."

There was something about that ego she found so attractive. Maybe it was the playful way he delivered such comments, or perhaps it was just the man himself. Either way, she wanted her hands on him. Now.

Done letting him have the lead, Olivia stepped forward and curled her hand inside the top of his jeans. Those ab muscles clenched beneath her touch.

"These pants are in the way."

"Take them off," he commanded.

Olivia jerked the snap, carefully lowering the zipper. Jackson took over and slid his jeans off, kicking them aside. As he stood before her in black boxer briefs, she took a moment to admire the man before her. She couldn't believe this was the same young boy who seemed so awkward, so scrawny. Lucky for her, he grew up.

Jackson reached behind her and made quick work of removing her bra. Then they were both frantic to remove that last item of clothing. The moment their clothes were gone, Jackson lifted her up and followed her down onto the bed. His weight pressing her into the mattress had her spreading her legs to accommodate him. He was much broader than she'd originally thought.

The instant his lips covered hers, Olivia threaded her fingers through his hair, locking her fingers behind his back. Olivia arched into him, needing more, ready for him to consume her and put an end to this achiness she'd had for days.

Or this could totally backfire and she'd be craving more, but she couldn't worry about that now. There were much more important matters to be addressed.

"Tell me you have protection," she murmured against his lips.

Jax rested his forehead against hers. "You'll always be protected with me, Livie."

There was so much to that statement. The promise, the way he seemed to believe this would happen again . . . would it?

He left her long enough to shuffle around in the bed-side table. Olivia didn't stare at him, she waited for him to join her again. Those few seconds his body wasn't on her had a chill settling over her skin and she was shocked that she missed the weight of this man. Something about him seemed almost familiar, yet so foreign because these unwanted feelings were all too new.

Jax settled one hand on either side of her head, the muscles in his shoulders and biceps strained as he held himself above her.

"You're sure?" he asked.

Olivia nearly groaned in frustration. "Jax . . ."

His soft laugh washed over her. "Finally. You called me Jax without being told."

"Are we seriously going to discuss—"

He slid into her, completely shutting off any thought she had. Olivia curled her fingers into his shoulders as he remained perfectly, agonizingly still.

Olivia tilted her hips, once again arching into him.

"I've waited for this," he murmured, still staring down at her. "Here you are in a hurry."

"You have about two seconds to move. It's been too long for me."

"Is that a demand?"

She jerked her hips, pleased when his lids lowered as he let out a low growl. There. If he wanted to play dirty, in the most glorious of ways, she'd match him. They both knew she really held the power here.

As if some sort of dam broke, Jax thrust his hips and Olivia was completely and utterly lost. Maybe she was just fooling herself thinking she held all the power because right now, Jax was all-consuming, demanding her body give just as much as he wanted.

Her body heated as he captured her lips once again. They were connected in every way imaginable and still she wanted more. How did this happen? How—

Oh, hell. She didn't even care. Nothing had ever felt this amazing, this—dare she say . . . right?

His lips traveled down over her chin, along the column of her throat as she tipped her head back. Never once did he lose that hip rhythm that was driving her out of her ever-loving mind. When his mouth closed over her breast, she completely lost control. Her body trembled, she shattered in his arms, and he showed no mercy as he continued to steal every shred of sense and calm she possessed. Her body thrashed, she groaned, but the moment a sound escaped her, he covered her mouth with his.

Olivia's body had barely come down from the high when his tightened all around her. He pumped his hips, framed her face, and continued to kiss her as if she were his lifeline to air. There was something so sexy about having a man this needy and wanting all of her. There was something so empowering about the size of Jax, especially compared to her petite frame, that made her want to lie right here, and stay connected with him.

Jax's body stilled as he gentled his kiss. Easing back, he smoothed her hair away from her face.

"Stay," he whispered. "Just for a minute."

A minute. The way her body still felt as if she were floating, she wasn't sure if she could move in an hour. But there was no way she could stay here. Aside from the fact that she would be an emotional wreck if she looked at this as something more than just physical, there was a little girl sleeping down the hall who would be confused at her father's sleepover guest.

All the reasons mounted inside her mind, but no words came out and she didn't make the slightest motion to move.

"Jackson—"

"Let's not work backward," he murmured against her mouth. "After all I did to get you to call me Jax."

She smiled, unable to stop herself and she realized this was the first time since her father had passed away and she'd known she was going to have to deal with Haven and the airport that she truly felt . . . at peace. Maybe lying naked with a younger man who had just lit her boring little world on fire had something to do with the thrill she still felt.

"Fine," she conceded. "Jax. I can't stay. What if Piper wakes, what if I fall asleep?"

He ran his hand down her side, gripping the back of her leg. "You won't sleep if you stay."

Oh, those words he delivered with such a firm conviction while dripping with promise had her shivering all over again. She trailed her fingertips over his back, up and down, up and down. The ripples of his muscles were glorious beneath her touch. She could get used to this . . . but she shouldn't.

"We need to be realistic," she argued, though her tone sounded weak even to her. "I can't stay and we can't do this again."

Jax rose slightly, his dark brows drawn in. "Regrets already? And here I thought you wouldn't have those until morning."

She hated that he assumed she'd be regretting this. Did he always think the worst when it came to her?

"I don't have regrets," she retorted. "This was amazing, but I'm not looking to dive into an affair. We have things to discuss, plans to make."

He jerked her leg higher as he started to nuzzle her neck. "So go ahead and discuss. I promise, you have my undivided attention."

She swatted him. "I'm serious. I can't talk about the airport with you doing . . . that."

"What? Seducing you again? I may be younger, but even I need time to recover. I just like how you feel beneath me." He stared down at her, his eyes dropping to her mouth before coming back up to meet her gaze. "I like you in my bed."

She couldn't reply because she prided herself on honesty and there was no way she could tell him that she liked it here, too . . . more than she had a right to.

Chapter Fourteen

"Livie."

Jax shook her shoulder as she rolled over and settled deeper into his bed. After his promise of not letting her sleep, they'd made love once again and then he promised to just hold her . . . he hadn't been ready to let her go.

Yet here they were at six in the morning. He needed to get her up and out before Piper woke because his girl was an early bird.

When Livie didn't wake, he stood straight up and stared down at how perfectly placed she appeared. Her honey-colored hair fanning all over his navy sheets, her bare shoulder peeking out from beneath the quilt, her fingertips resting on his pillow.

Yeah, there was so much about this scene that he could get used to, but then there was that whole side of him that needed to keep his guard up. There was so much he'd gotten over from his past that he'd promised himself never to go back to.

It wasn't exactly fair for him to compare Livie and Carly, but in his defense, he couldn't help putting them against each other in his mind. There were so many similarities, yet the more he got to know Livie, he saw just how different she was from his ex-wife.

Ultimately, though, in the end Livie would leave . . . just like Carly.

Jax shoved aside the welling of emotions. He was stronger than this, damn it. He'd seen it all overseas in the air force, he'd been blindsided by a woman who claimed to not love him anymore and left him with an infant, and he'd faced the death of his mentor—a man who'd been like a father.

Yet he couldn't bring himself to get this woman out of his bed. Perhaps he wasn't as strong as he claimed.

Little footsteps sounded down the hallway and Jax sprang into action. Racing toward the door, he flicked the lock and stepped out.

Piper's hair was all in disarray. She rubbed her eyes, then smiled up at him. Her rotten little grin always melted his heart.

"Waffles?"

Jax laughed. He'd created a monster. He found a waffle maker at a yard sale and since that day three months ago, Piper wanted waffles every Saturday morning. But first he had to figure out how to get Livie out of his bed, out of the house, and not alert Piper to the overnight guest.

"Why don't you go down and pick out a movie," he suggested. "We'll have a carpet picnic with our waffles. I got some strawberries yesterday too."

Piper jumped up in the air and squealed. "This is the best day ever."

She turned and raced down the stairs. Jax raked his hands over his face, his stubble bristling beneath his palms. Now he had to get Livie up and dressed, keep Piper distracted, and slip his guest out the door. He couldn't help but smile at the look on Livie's face when she discovered she'd indeed fallen asleep in his bed and it was now morning.

He turned and slipped into his room, but the moment he closed the door at his back, something smacked him in the face.

"How dare you?"

Blinking, he noticed a very angry, very *un*dressed Livie. She didn't seem so shy about her body now and he couldn't help but rake his eyes over every inch of her. Granted she was walking around the room gathering her clothes, but he wasn't about to look elsewhere.

"You let me sleep," she scolded as she scooped up her shirt. "I didn't want to wake up here. I never stay, ever. This wasn't supposed to happen."

Jax bent down to retrieve her bra. Dangling it off one finger, he merely raised his brows. "I'm assuming you're angrier with yourself than with the fact you spent the night."

"Why didn't you wake me?" She hopped into her panties and yanked them up. "You—"

"Listen." He stalked across the room and handed over the bra, which she jerked from his hold. "Neither of us planned on you staying here, but right now we have to work together to get you out because Piper is downstairs waiting on waffles."

Fisting her dress in her hands, Livie groaned. "I can't do the walk of shame in front of her, she won't understand."

The fact Livie worried more about what Piper would think than her own embarrassment warmed something in him. She wasn't that selfish, stuck-up city girl he'd believed she was when she first stepped into his hangar. Livie cared, and seeing just how deep her concern was for his daughter now put him in a whole new level of frustration because he didn't want to like her . . . at least not the type of like that would involve his heart.

Jax desperately feared his heart was already involved. Damn it. Now what? He'd spent the night with her and now she stood in his room wearing nothing but the bare essentials while his daughter waited on her breakfast.

If this weren't awkward, this could be some sort of family moment . . . a moment he'd never had before. Even when he was married there were no situations like this. He was out of his element from every angle and at this point, he needed to take a step back and seriously think about what the hell he was doing. Because sex was one thing, but dragging his life and his daughter's life into the mix wasn't acceptable.

Livie pulled her dress over her head and smoothed her hair away from her face. As she started looking for her shoes, Jax realized she hadn't once looked at him. Regrets? Already?

"Livie." He put more force into his tone, one he'd used when he'd been a ranking officer in the air force. "Look at me."

"I've got to get out of here."

She muttered the statement as her eyes continued to search for her shoes. Jax closed the distance between them and grabbed her arms, hauling her against his chest. When she didn't look up, he slid his finger beneath her chin and tipped her head.

"Relax. We're adults."

The flush to her cheeks, the moisture gathering in her eyes had his heart clenching. Yeah, whatever internal battle she faced had nothing to do with him. Jax knew he was just a minor component in her struggle, but he damn sure wasn't going to let her sneak out of here like they'd done something wrong or dirty.

He wasn't sorry she'd fallen asleep in his bed. For the first time in years, he wasn't sorry he'd taken a woman to bed and had her by his side when he woke. He hadn't done that since his marriage, mostly because he was busy being a single father and didn't want to give Piper the wrong impression.

"No regrets, Livie."

She chewed her bottom lip as her chin quivered. "This isn't supposed to happen," she whispered. "I'm not supposed to want this."

A sliver of light cracked open that scar on his heart. "Neither of us wanted this," he agreed, framing her face with his hands. "But here we are and I'm not sorry. I won't let you be sorry either."

Livie closed her eyes and blew out a sigh. "I can't deal with these emotions right now. I need to find my shoes and figure out how to get out of here."

He'd let her go, for now, but only because he had a toddler waiting on him who would be coming back up any minute if he didn't get downstairs.

"Okay. I'm going to head downstairs. I will keep Piper in the kitchen mixing up the batter." Reluctantly, Jax released her and stepped back. "Check the living room for your shoes and just head out the front door. Try not to make the knob click. Better yet, just leave the door slightly cracked. I'll close it."

She nodded. "Okay. Um . . . thanks?"

The fact this strong, independent woman felt awkward and out of her element gave him a bit of hope. He wanted her to be just as confused as he was because he had no clue where this was going or what the hell to do next.

But she was right. They could deal with the feelings later.

"No need for a thanks," he replied. "I plan on doing this again."

Her eyes widened as he leaned in for a quick kiss. He turned and left the room, leaving her with her mouth agape and speechless. Perfect, just how he wanted her. Let her think about that for a bit. Because, yes, he had no clue what they were doing, but he knew for certain that he wanted to do this again. He wanted *her* again.

As he bounded down the stairs, Jax figured he'd give Livie a day to come to terms with how she felt. Most likely she'd try to go back to being all business and focus on the plans for the airport . . . which they didn't get around to discussing.

Well, she may try to get back to her CEO form, but he wasn't having that. They'd crossed a line and he'd be damned if he'd let her go back.

Still barefoot, Olivia stepped into her back door. Two sets of eyes turned to look her way.

"Not one word," she warned, closing the door at her back.

Melanie sipped on her green smoothie and Jade sank onto a barstool with her own glass of greens. Both were in their running gear, so Olivia had apparently missed out on their morning routine. Seemed to be a habit as of late. This entire town was messing with her life.

"You do the walk of shame, barefoot no less, and not expect us to say something?" Jade asked with a laugh. "It's like you don't know us at all."

Olivia sat her purse on the counter and collapsed onto the barstool next to Jade.

"That must've been some kid party," Melanie stated, a snarky smile on her face.

"I don't even remember the party," Olivia moaned. Had that only been yesterday afternoon? "So much happened since then."

"We can be supportive and nosy at the same time." Jade swirled the contents of her glass before tipping it back for a drink. "So, you went to the party, then we all went shopping and had a girl day. Fill in from after that until just now and where the hell are your shoes?"

"Probably under Jax's couch," she mumbled. "I'm going to need something stronger than a smoothie to get through this. Can someone get me a mimosa?"

Jade threw a glance to Melanie. "Heavy on the champagne."

"What has happened to me?" Olivia muttered as she dropped her head into the pillow of her crossed arms. "I don't do one-night stands."

"Was this a one-time thing?" Melanie asked.

Jax's parting words led her to believe this was just the beginning. But how could they continue? Wasn't that just asking for a disaster neither of them had time for? What good would come out of an affair?

Her body still tingled, though. Spending the night in Jax's bed had been . . . well, glorious. He wasn't the cocky, egotistical man she'd first thought. He'd been attentive, giving, and oh so thorough.

The clink of the glass by her head had Olivia lifting herself up and reaching for the breakfast drink—because orange juice with anything was considered breakfast.

Olivia took a hefty drink, welcoming the cool, refreshing liquid. She gripped the glass with two hands as she sat it on the counter and stared at her manicured fingers.

"We ended up watching a movie and having popcorn with Piper."

Melanie's gasp echoed in the tiny kitchen. "That's very . . . family-like."

Olivia nodded in agreement. The whole family atmosphere had awakened something inside her, something she didn't even know had been lurking.

There was something so therapeutic about watching a kid movie with a bowl of buttery popcorn and not worrying about e-mails or conference calls—

"Oh, damn it." Olivia jumped to her feet. "I have a conference call this morning." Panic settled in as she glanced to the clock above the sink and groaned. "I'm so screwed."

She'd missed the conference call by thirty minutes. Thirty minutes ago she was still trying to figure out how to slink out of Jax's house without Piper seeing when she should've been more concerned with her career and the promotion she'd hoped to receive.

Her boss had handed her an even bigger client, or one they hoped to sign. She'd been entrusted with this potential new client, something far better than the load that had shifted from her to Steve. Damn it.

Now she'd have to do some major ass kissing. Not to mention damage control, because there wasn't a doubt in her mind that Steve was in on that call and had gotten his subtle jab in as to his thoughts on her not participating.

She wasn't keen on lying, was adamantly against it actually, but she couldn't be totally honest with her boss. She didn't figure "I'm sorry I was sleeping off the morning after" was a valid reason.

"We'll think of a good excuse," Jade told her, patting her shoulder. "First, we need to get everything else straightened out and then you can call your boss. He's on the other call anyway right now so just calm down."

"Easy for you to say. Your ass isn't on the line."

Melanie pulled the juice and champagne back out and

topped off Olivia's glass. "This is an easy fix. All you have to do is explain you were in the middle of an emergency regarding your father's estate. That's all. They don't need any more than that. They already know why you're not at work, so I'm sure they'll understand."

Olivia listened to Melanie's simple fix. It sounded easy enough, but this wasn't how Olivia worked. Ever. She was always punctual, always efficient, and always prepared for every meeting whether it be in a boardroom or on a telephone.

"You've never missed before, have you?" Jade asked.

Swiping the cool glass with her thumb, Olivia shook her head. "Never."

"Then there you go. You're grieving and overwhelmed here." Jade drained her glass of greens and sat it back down as she let out a sigh. "Okay, that was easy. So fill us in about Jax. Please, tell me you didn't act weird this morning."

Olivia shot her a glare.

"Oh, well, aside from the fact you left without shoes," Jade amended. "You didn't act like you regretted it, did you?"

Shoving her hair away from her face, Olivia smoothed it over her shoulder and concentrated on the ends. Perhaps she should get a trim while she was here. Surely there was someplace that wouldn't botch up her cut too much.

"Your silence is telling," Jade grumbled. "Why the regrets?"

Olivia glanced to Melanie, who seemed to be offering a sympathetic smile, but at the same time waiting for an answer.

"I don't know what I feel," Olivia answered honestly. "I mean, I'm glad that tension isn't there anymore, but at the same time that probably wasn't the smartest thing to do if we're going to be working together."

"What did he say this morning?" Mel asked, leaning across the island on her forearms.

"Well, we only had a minute to talk because he was sneaking me out of the house while Piper wasn't looking."

Jade made some humming sound under her breath as she and Melanie exchanged a look.

"What?" Olivia demanded. "You guys can't do that secret code thing with me in the room."

"Did he try to rush you out?" Melanie asked.

"No. He tried to get me to tell him what I was thinking, but I had no clue." She released her hair and rubbed her forehead. "I still don't know."

"I'd say he cares for you."

Olivia stared across the scarred island to Melanie. Her friend merely shrugged. "I'm just telling you how I see it," Mel defended.

There was no doubt Jax cared. She knew by the way he'd treated her, from the little he'd told her about his past. He wasn't the type of guy to have a track record of sneaking women out before his daughter woke. Jax was a man of integrity, he was honest and loyal . . . and damn it, she was liking him more than she had right to.

She wasn't going to be in Haven forever, so why was she allowing her mind to get swept up into this fairy tale she'd just recently realized she wanted?

"I need a shower." She came to her feet, taking her glass with her. "Then I'm going to call and give some veiled, lame excuse to my boss and hope it's not a black mark against me for the promotion or this new client he's trusting me with."

She only hoped he remembered that he'd been grieving recently too. She had to play on that aspect.

"When you're done, we have a few things we need to run

by you," Melanie stated. "I started the process for a grant for the airport. We just need some information from you."

Olivia nodded as she headed from the room. "Later," she called back, waving her hand in the air. "Much later."

Right now, she couldn't think about grants or anything related to the airport because that would inevitably circle back to Jax. And right now, she needed to think about work. That was the only constant in her life. Whatever she had with Jax was temporary, so there was no room for a man and a promotion.

Chapter Fifteen

She wasn't answering her texts. Not that he expected her to, but he also didn't like being brushed off, either.

Jax pulled into her drive and stared up at the big, two-story house. Paul Daniels would love knowing Livie was living here again, even if it was temporary. He'd wanted her to come home for so long, and here she was.

"Do you think they're going to like these cookies?" Piper asked from the passenger seat. She held the tin of homemade snickerdoodles in her lap and looked at him with wide eyes.

"Of course they will," he assured her as he turned off the truck. "I bet nobody has made them cookies since they've been here."

"Then it's a good thing you thought about it."

He may have had ulterior motives when it came to the treats. One, Piper loved baking so that was some bonding time they got in. Two, he could thank the women for taking his daughter shopping. But the main reason was to see Livie and force her to stop hiding. When she'd left his house the other morning, he'd never dreamed he'd miss her, but he had. That in itself was a major warning sign he was getting in deep here.

"Can I ring the doorbell?" Piper asked.

"Sure."

He reached over and took the tin from her hands as she unbuckled her belt. Jax got out of the truck and circled the front as he came around to help Piper out of the booster and down onto the driveway. She promptly ran up onto the front porch and rang the doorbell . . . multiple times.

"I think that's good," he called as he headed down the sidewalk.

The front door swung open just as Jax mounted the steps. He glanced up to a smiling Melanie.

"Hope this isn't a bad time," he stated.

"We made cookies." Piper bounced up and down, her lopsided ponytails flopping.

Jax held up the tin. "We wanted to thank you for shopping and pampering Piper the other day."

"Oh, that was no problem at all. She's such a sweet girl." Melanie opened the door wider and took a step back. "Come in. Jade is out, but Olivia is here."

Perfect. Never say he wasn't one to take advantage of the situation.

"I hope you like snickerdoodles," Piper exclaimed as she passed Melanie. "They're my favorite."

"I don't remember the last time I had a snickerdoodle." Melanie closed the door and reached for the tin. "You can go into the living room. I'll put these in the kitchen."

Jax knew the layout of the house. He couldn't count the number of times he'd come here as a teenager and again when he'd returned from the air force.

As he stepped into the living room, he couldn't help but be drawn to the mantel and the emptiness. Paul had always kept pictures of Olivia on display. Most were of her when she'd been a young girl, but now there were no images. As he glanced around he realized there was nothing on the walls, either . . . the newly painted walls.

There was a punch to the gut he hadn't expected. Apparently, Olivia was sprucing up the place, no doubt to sell. He should've thought of that, should've seen it coming, but he'd been too preoccupied with fighting his emotions and ultimately giving in.

He'd known from the start that Olivia wasn't staying, so why would she need a house? He should be thankful they'd come to some sort of agreement on the airport—terms they'd yet to discuss.

Piper wrapped her arm around his leg and leaned into him. "I miss Papaw Paul."

Yeah, his little girl had also gotten to know the love of one of the greatest men. Jax leaned down and picked her up.

"It's okay to be sad. I miss him too." The void was more than he wanted to admit to his toddler. He chose to remain strong for her. "He sure loved you, so he'd be very proud that you are friends with his little girl."

Not that Livie was a little girl anymore, but for Piper's sake, he opted to keep his lingo simple.

"Jackson."

He turned, keeping his arms banded around Piper. Livie stood in the doorway wearing a pair of capris and a crisp, button-up sleeveless shirt the color of strawberries.

They were back to square one if the look in her eyes and the way she used his full name meant anything at all. She was too reserved, too . . . emotionless.

Maybe him giving her this time apart wasn't the smartest move, but he'd wanted her to think about him because he sure as hell was thinking about her.

"We made cookies," Piper stated, her arms wrapped around Jax's neck. "But I ate two on the way over."

Jax patted her back. "You weren't supposed to tell that part."

Livie glanced to Piper and her entire face softened. "It's difficult to resist cookies. I understand."

Melanie came back through the foyer and stepped in behind Livie. "Why don't I take Piper in the kitchen for milk and cookies and you two can talk?"

"Oh, you don't—"

"That would be great," Jax stated, cutting Livie off. "She's had two already so maybe just one more."

He let Piper down and she scurried across the room to Melanie's outstretched hand. Once he and Livie were alone, she remained in the wide doorway as if she was afraid to step into the same room as him.

They'd definitely taken a leap backward.

"We didn't get around to talking about the airport the other night," he told her, remaining by the fireplace.

She crossed her arms over her chest. "Is that why you're here?"

"Not really, but I was giving you an easier topic than what I really want to discuss."

She glanced over her shoulder toward the laughing and chatter from the kitchen. Then she moved farther into the room. Jax held his ground and waited for her to come to him. He wasn't going to beg and he sure as hell wasn't going to make this easy because he was turned inside out . . . she may as well be suffering, too.

"Would you rather start with why you're ignoring my texts?"

Without looking at him, she leaned against the window frame and stared out into the evening. "What do you want me to say?"

"I want you to acknowledge that you're just as torn up as I am." He pushed his hands into his pockets and decided to be brutally honest. "I know this complicates the hell out of things, but you can't just ignore me."

"I was doing a good job of it until you showed up."

Laughing, Jax closed the space between them. She looked too damn rigid and fearful. He was glad she could at least attempt humor.

"You didn't honestly think I'd let you off that easy, did you?"

Her hair waved down over her shoulder and he smoothed it away with the tip of his finger. She trembled, only proving she wasn't as immune as she pretended to be.

"Maybe we should talk about the plans for the airport." She turned to glance over her shoulder, those pale pink lips begging for his touch.

Without thinking twice, he leaned in and captured her mouth. He didn't touch her anywhere else, but just that simple kiss was already so familiar, so right, he lingered a little longer than was smart.

When he eased back, her lids fluttered open. "You can't do that."

"I just did and I plan on doing it again," he assured her. "I did come to discuss plans, but I also want you to be fully aware that just because I'm a guy, doesn't mean I take this lightly. Something is going on between us and I'm not going to let you scare yourself away simply because it's not what you wanted."

She glanced back out the window and nodded. "You know nothing can come from this. I'm not staying long."

So she'd reminded him a few dozen times. At this point Jax wasn't sure if she was trying to convince him or herself, because he was starting to see a little crack in her defensive barrier. She didn't want to like Haven, she didn't want to stay here longer than necessary, and she didn't want to like him. Yet here she was . . . doing all three.

He glanced around the room. "Looks like you're gearing up to sell."

"I can't keep this house," she told him as she turned to fully face him. "I have no need for a house in Haven, especially one this size. I think once I do some minor touch-ups, it will sell pretty quick, but painting one space has turned into working in every single room."

There was no doubt the home would sell fast. The location was close to town yet still out where there was a little land, the neighborhood was great, and Haven was thriving and a hot spot for those wanting to be close to Savannah.

Livie's childhood home was just outside the main part of town. It had a huge yard for children, five bedrooms, two staircases leading from the kitchen and the foyer up to the second floor. The old Georgian charm was everywhere you looked, from the built-ins to the original crown moldings to the curved staircase just inside the front door. The gleaming hardwood floors in some of the home were original and he'd bet there was more beneath the old carpet.

This house was a thing of beauty and he'd hate to see it go. Paul had loved this house. Even when he'd been alone and sick, for a time all he'd say was how many great memories he'd had here and he wouldn't trade it for anything.

"I was going to ask you first if you were interested."

Her quiet statement caught him off guard. He hadn't thought about buying it for himself. Hell, he doubted he could afford it. This house was more than double the size of his cottage. It wasn't like he and Piper needed a ton of space, but this yard was so much nicer and it was actually on the side of town where the airport was.

"I doubt that would be possible."

She tipped her head. "If you're referring to finances, I can—"

"No." Like hell he'd let her lower the price. Couldn't a man have some pride? "Piper and I are fine where we are. We love this house, we loved Paul, but you need the closure and if selling is how you're going to do it, then so be it."

She opened her mouth as if she wanted to argue, but closed it and nodded. "Okay, then. Why don't you sit and we'll discuss the plans? Jade and Melanie have already put the ball into motion for a grant."

When Livie sank into the leather chair, he smiled. Obviously, getting cozy on the couch together wasn't an option. He was fine with that, but he meant what he said. He'd have her again. That simple kiss moments ago only whetted his appetite for more.

"How soon will we know about that?" he asked, sinking onto the old leather sofa.

"Could be anywhere between a week to a few months. If they need more information, they'll let us know. If not, they'll just come back with an answer."

He didn't know which scared him more, the possibility they'd be denied or if they'd get the funds and move forward with completely renovating the small-town airport.

"I think we have a pretty good shot," she went on. "We have so many ideas regarding how to expand and how to pull in more clients, especially with the film industry booming in Georgia. But we don't want to get ahead of ourselves and spend too much time on it if it's not going to happen."

Because they all had other jobs. It was understandable, but the airport and the current clients were his job—they were his life.

"And if the grants don't go through, then what?" he asked.

More laughter filtered in from the kitchen. There was something so heartwarming about hearing his daughter bond with another woman. There were only so many things he could give her and a female's perspective certainly wasn't one of them.

"I'll think of a way." She let out a sigh and propped her feet on the coffee table, crossing her ankles and relaxing somewhat. "When I want something, I make sure I get it."

Oh, the opening was just too good.

He stared across the space between them and met her gaze. "So do I."

"You already had me, so stop looking like that."

He couldn't help but smile at her bold command. "I may have had you, but I'm not finished and neither are you. You're scared, that's why you didn't answer my messages. If we're going to go full in on this project, there will be no dodging me."

"I'm not dodging," she insisted, complete with a tilt of her defiant chin.

Wasn't that adorable that she was trying to convince herself? But he wasn't into playing games.

"You are," he countered. "But I'm not going to let you."

She opened her mouth to say something else when his cell chimed from his pocket. He kept his eyes on hers as he reached in and pulled the phone out. A quick glance and he knew he couldn't just let it go to voice mail. They needed all the business that came their way.

"Hello," he answered as he came to his feet.

"Hey, man. It's Brock. You said to call when I got my online work done and it's officially complete. I'm ready to get my hours in."

Jax was always eager to show new pilots the ropes. There was nothing more rewarding as far as he was concerned.

"What's your schedule like with work and college?"

"I'm pretty flexible," Brock replied. "I'm still working for my aunt at Knobs and Knockers and my classes are all online. I can work around your schedule."

Jax turned back around as Piper came running through the house, cookie in hand. She saw him on the phone and came to a halt.

"How about you come to the hangar in the morning about nine?" Jax suggested. "Can you spare about three hours?"

"Oh, man. I would love to. Thanks."

Jax recalled being a nineteen-year-old boy and eager to discover more. Then the military had shown him so much more than he'd ever dreamed. He'd traveled, met people who would stick with him forever, and ended up heart-broken and a single father. Life never went the way you planned when you were a teenager.

"See you then."

He disconnected the call and slid the cell back into his pocket before turning his attention fully to Piper.

"I'm pretty sure you've had enough cookies."

She flashed him that sweet smile that too often had him turning all soft and giving in. If only his air force buddies could see him, they'd be stunned that someone so little and innocent could turn him into a pile of mush. But Piper was his world and while he often disciplined, he also knew to give in and choose his battles wisely.

"Why don't you give that one to Livie?" he suggested. "Unless you've licked it."

She glanced to the cookie in hand and smiled wider. "Maybe."

Jax laughed. He couldn't help it. "I guess it's yours then. Why don't you go into the kitchen and get her one? We're almost done here."

She popped the cookie in her mouth and scurried off. Shaking his head, Jax turned his attention back to Livie.

"Come over for dinner tonight."

Livie's eyes widened. "Are you telling me or asking?"

"Which one will get you there?" he joked.

Livie stood and crossed the room to stare out the narrow, floor-to-ceiling window. "You're making this impossible."

As much as he wanted to go to her, to touch her, he kept his distance and let her battle with herself. She'd come around to finally realizing she couldn't keep him at a distance forever.

"I'm actually making this simple," he corrected.

She rubbed her forehead and let out a sigh. Oh, how sweet this was to get Miss Prim and Proper tied up in knots. The front door opened and closed just as Piper came rushing back through.

Jax turned toward the foyer to see Jade nearly get mauled by a toddler.

"Oh, cookies for me?" Jade asked.

"This is for Livie," Piper stated as she ran into the living room. "But I'll grab you one."

She handed Livie the snickerdoodle and off she went again just as fast. Jade laughed. "I wish I had that energy."

"I'm sorry she's running in your house. She's excited to share her homemade treats with you guys, plus she's had a few too many."

Jade set her keys and her purse on the entryway table and stepped into the living room. "So, did you come just to share cookies or are you returning Olivia's shoes?"

"Jade," Melanie scolded as she came in behind her friend.

With a shrug, Jade smirked and continued to stare at Jax just as Piper came back and handed over the treat.

"It was a legitimate question," Jade defended.

Piper paid no attention to the adult conversation as she sat down on the floor and attempted to tie her shoe. Apparently, it had come undone in all her sprints, but she was still learning so she would be occupied for a bit.

"I'm actually keeping the shoes and the stained suit until she comes to dinner."

Livie muttered something behind him, something akin to "jerk" and "impossible." She was crazy about him.

"What are you making?" Jade asked.

"Would you shut up," Livie exclaimed. "You're not helping."

Jax caught Jade's wink. "Oh, I think I'm being very helpful. A hunky guy is offering dinner and he's holding your things hostage. What's there to think about?"

"We'll watch Piper for the evening," Melanie contributed with a naughty grin. Who knew the shy, quiet one of the bunch could be an instigator? Jax loved these friends.

"A sleepover?" Piper squealed.

"No." Livie stepped forward, her hands up. "No sleepovers. I'll do dinner—"

"And dessert," Jax supplied.

"Can I pack my new sleeping bag, Daddy? Oh, and my pony pajamas?"

Livie groaned and it was all he could do not to burst out laughing. "Pack whatever you want," he told Piper.

"I'll be home by nine," Livie promised. "But she's more than welcome to stay all night."

Jax leaned over to whisper in Livie's ear. "Nine in the morning, maybe . . . if I let you go that soon."

Her sharp elbow hit him in the side. Oh, this was going to be a fun evening.

"Come on, squirt." Jax leaned down and hoisted Piper up into his arms. "Daddy has some things to do before his dinner guest arrives."

"Can I help you cook?" she asked, her wide brown eyes searching his.

"Of course, but first you have to help me grocery shop."

She clapped her hands. "I push the cart."

"I'll bring her back around five," he told Jade and Melanie, who hadn't stopped smiling since they'd ambushed their friend. "And pick Livie up then, too."

"I can drive."

"What kind of gentleman would I be if I let you drive to our date?" He ignored her growl and headed to the door. "See you later, ladies."

What he wouldn't give to hear those three women chattering once he was gone. But he had plans to make and he was pulling out all the stops.

As he put Piper in her booster, he recalled he was due at the hangar at nine in the morning to meet with Brock. Nothing he couldn't push back for an hour or so, because Jax had a feeling he would be preoccupied come morning.

Chapter Sixteen

"You're playing with fire."

Jax snorted and put the casserole in the oven before turning back to Cash. "I sure as hell hope so. It's been too long since I wanted a woman and I'm damn sure going to enjoy this."

"You better make sure this doesn't blow up in your face and affect the airport renovations."

Jax stared out the kitchen window over the sink and watched Piper as she swung on the old tire swing. With a fenced yard, he wasn't worried about her outside alone, but he always kept an eye on her. She'd made the dough and now it was in a bowl with a towel over it waiting to rise.

"I won't let anything stop those renovations from going through," Jax vowed. He turned around and rested against the counter. "They've come up with some great ideas, so I really think it's on the right track. With those three women and all their business sense added with my determination, we'll be fine."

"I hear you're getting ready to teach Brock Monroe."

Jax nodded and crossed his arms. "He's an impressive kid."

"He and Zach were in the gym the other night talking about it." Cash reached for his bottle of water and toyed with the label. "The women's resort they have is really booming. You may want to consider working on a plan with them as well when the renovations are done. Maybe some package for travelers coming into the area."

That was actually brilliant. "I'm impressed," Jax stated.

His cousin flipped him the finger. "Just because I run a gym, doesn't mean I don't understand business in general. You always have to be thinking of ways to expand and grow."

Jax and Tanner often teased Cash that swinging kettlebells and flipping tires wasn't a job, but Cash always threw everything back in their faces with some snarky remark. If they didn't tease and crack on one another, there would be something wrong. They'd been through it all together and this next chapter in Jax's life was just another step he'd take with his favorite guys backing him.

"I'll discuss it with Livie," he promised.

"Could you discuss before you two hit the dessert course?"

Piper burst in through the back door crying. Jax instantly crossed the room and crouched down to her. "What is it?"

She pointed to her knee while she wailed. "I broke it."

Cash stood at his side as Jax examined the injury. A skinned-up knee, typical of summertime and playing outside. But he recalled being a kid and skinning his knees, usually while riding his bike downhill and falling off, so he knew how much this stung.

"I don't think it's broken, but we need to clean it up."

She continued to cry, and Jax picked her up and carried her over to the center island and sat her down. "Cash, grab the first aid kit from under the sink in my master bath."

He blew on her knee to take away some of the sting while he waited on Cash to get back. "How did you do this?"

Piper sniffed. "When I pushed off the tree, my foot slipped and I hitted my knee."

Cash came back in and sat the kit next to Piper. While Jax carefully cleaned the area, Cash stepped up and started distracting Piper with his ridiculous, toddler-friendly knock-knock jokes.

Jax was thankful to have someone else here because it was times like this he needed the backup. Being a single father wasn't the easiest, but it was definitely the most important job he'd ever have. Having Cash here, no matter how annoying the jokes were, was a blessing. Piper loved Cash and Tanner just as much as he did and in a way, they were one big happy family.

"There you go," he told her as he placed the bright blue Band-Aid over her knee. "Good as new."

Jax swiped her tears and picked her up, giving her a bear hug. "You want to help finish the bread or would you rather go watch a movie?"

Those little arms around his neck meant everything and he wished he could prevent her from ever crying. Tears absolutely gutted him.

"I'll watch a movie with Cash," she sniffed again.

Jax eyed his cousin over Piper's head. Cash nodded.

"That's fine, but we have to leave in an hour to take you to Livie's house, so you won't be able to watch the whole thing."

Cash raised his brows. No need to tell him about the whole ambush sleepover. He didn't need more attention on the topic of Livie Daniels.

"Come on, little one." Cash rounded the island and took Piper from Jax's arms. "You go in and pick out the movie and I'll bring in some snacks."

"I'm not allowed to have more cookies today," she told him.

Cash nodded. "I'll make sure we're cookie-free."

He sat Piper down and she raced toward the living room . . . apparently snacks, a movie, and a Band-Aid were a cure-all.

"There's some fruit cut up in the fridge or you can make popcorn."

Cash went about getting snacks while Jax checked the casserole.

"So if Piper is going for a sleepover at Livie's house, but Livie will be here . . ."

Jax moved to the covered bowl with the rising dough. "Shut up."

"Awww . . . is this your first slumber party since the divorce?"

Jax pulled the dough out and onto the counter. "Kiss my ass."

Cash's laughter mocked Jax. "This is all just too easy, man. Don't tell me you wouldn't annoy the hell out of me if the situation was reversed."

He pounded the dough, ready to get his nosy cousin out of here. "You were never married, so this isn't the same. And I'm not looking for a wife, Cash. I like Livie and we're going to be working together. No reason we can't enjoy each other's company while she's here."

"Keep telling yourself that."

Cash whistled as he headed into the living room. Jax wasn't getting caught in that bait. No way. It was bad enough Cash knew about Livie coming over and potentially staying for breakfast, but that would be her decision. He wasn't going to press her or persuade her. As much as he wanted to go full-on seduction mode, he also wanted her to have this same need and ache he had. And she did, but getting her to admit it to herself was the frustrating part.

Jax readied the bread and put it in the loaf pan. He'd learned flying from Paul Daniels, but his kitchen skills were all from his grandfather. The grandfather who'd had to take over when Jax's parents had been killed in a car wreck when Jax had been only ten. That time had been the darkest, scariest of his life, but his grandfather had done the best he could. They'd mourned together and healed together.

And once Jax's grandfather had taken him on that first "for fun" plane ride, Jax had been completely and utterly hooked. Even though his grandfather had been older and weak at times, he'd made sure to make the most out of the days he was feeling good.

From the moment that first plane ride was over, Jax read anything he could on aviation and becoming a pilot. He'd learned a great deal from his grandfather, who had also been in the air force. Between those two powerful men, Jax was destined for the sky. He couldn't wait to pass the love down to Piper, who already showed so much interest.

As he finished everything up, he listened to Piper's giggles from the living room. Having Cash and Tanner as role models in his daughter's life was priceless. Jax had been worried how he'd ever handle raising a child on his own, but he was raising such a remarkable, well-rounded little girl.

He turned off the oven and left the bread and the casserole in there to stay warm. Now all he had to do was kick Cash out the door and take Piper to her sleepover.

There was part of him that knew this was more than physical. He'd already let Piper into the lives of not only Livie, but also her friends. Whatever was happening between them went far beyond sex . . . and perhaps that's what had Livie so afraid.

Well, that made two of them because he had no idea what the hell he was doing. The red flags were in place, but he forged beyond each one in his pursuit. He wanted Livie . . . and he damn well planned on having her.

"I'm impressed." Olivia stared at the spread on the kitchen table. "Who knew you were such a good cook?"

Jax sat two glasses of sweet tea on the table. "You haven't even tried it."

Gripping the back of the wooden chair, Olivia shrugged. "The fact you have all of this is impressive enough."

When he'd come to pick her up, she'd wanted to protest and stay home. But there was that part of her, the very feminine part, that wanted to come. She was a fool for even trying to pretend she didn't want this, didn't want him.

What was she supposed to do when she fell for this man? Because she was seriously heading in that direction. Honestly though, what had she done to stop it? She'd already spent the night with him and loved every glorious moment. Now she was ready for round two—but she was going to hold out. Maybe if she could resist him, maybe if she could keep this evening focused on the airport and not the fact he'd made a great dinner and he looked so sexy in his fitted jeans and T-shirt that stretched across—

Yeah. She was doomed. There was no hope at this point. Everything he did, from the way he looked, to the way he was with Piper, to the way he made her feel things she'd never known . . . it was a lethal combination for her heart.

"You're thinking way too hard." He circled the table and came to stand directly beside her. "It's dinner, Livie. I won't strip your clothes off until we've at least had salads."

No doubt he intended to take the edge off with his sarcasm . . . and it totally worked. She shifted to face him and smiled.

"Well, I wore the ugliest bra and panties I had so I would leave my clothes on."

Jax circled her waist and tugged her against his firm chest. Instantly she recalled exactly how he'd felt against her when there had been no barriers between them.

"I'll rip them off anyway," he growled as his eyes held hers. "You wasted your time putting anything on."

Oh, that promise had her shivering all over.

"One night was fine, but how long are we going to keep this going?" she asked, forcing herself not to reach up to grab hold of him.

"I plan on enjoying you as long as you're here. Do you see a problem with that?"

Olivia couldn't help the laugh that escaped her. "I see so many problems, I don't know where to start."

He kissed the tip of her nose—how freakin' adorable was he?—and pulled out her chair.

"Let's start with a salad and move on from there."

He left her standing there wondering how he could be so casual, while he dished out their food. She knew Jax wasn't one to bring women into his home, not with Piper around. He wasn't that type of man. Yet he'd been adamant she come here; he'd steamrolled her into it, actually, and now he was pretending this didn't faze him in the least.

That man was one outstanding liar.

Olivia took a seat and sipped on her tea. There was nothing like good sweet tea. She hadn't had it for a while because she opted for water or wine.

"So, you do casseroles?" she joked.

Jax took a seat across from her. "I live in the South, Livie. Casseroles and sweet tea are staples. And fried chicken. Besides, my grandfather was a pretty good cook. I learned from him. Piper is a picky eater, though, so I've had to hone my skills."

While they ate, Olivia kept the topic neutral. The airport

was the common thread that held them together, so she wanted to hash out more details.

"Melanie believes we'll hear soon about the grants." Stuffed, Olivia leaned back in her seat and set her napkin on the table. "We've already gotten a list of contractors we'd be interested in getting an estimate from for the renovations."

"Zach Monroe." Jax set his fork down and eyed her across the table. "I won't argue with you on most of this, but Zach is local, he's good, and he's a friend of mine."

Olivia wasn't surprised at Jax's loyalty to his friends or that he would be so passionate about the process. This was going to be his long after she went back to Atlanta to continue her work. She would be more of a silent partner, whereas Jax would be here day in and day out.

"Actually, Zach is the first name on our list," she explained. "We have two others that aren't local, but—"

"Zach is the one who will do it."

Olivia wanted to argue simply for spite because she hated being told what to do, but she also knew Zach from school and had met up with him again when she and her friends stayed at Bella Vous a few months ago. Zach and his brothers had truly tapped into a gold mine, so she was comfortable with him doing the work.

"That's fine," she conceded. "Anything else you won't budge on?"

Jax shook his head. "Not that I can think of. But I'm sure there will be something along the way that we clash over."

"I have no doubt."

Her cell starting chiming from her purse, which she'd left in the living room. Olivia came to her feet with a sigh.

"Can't you let it go to voice mail?" he asked.

"Never," she replied as she headed to the front of the house. "Work is always needing something."

Now more than ever she wasn't letting her phone go to

voice mail. After that slipup the other morning she had to be on her toes.

The shrill ring kept echoing through the house as she grabbed her purse and pulled the phone out.

"Hello?"

"Olivia, I hope this isn't a bad time."

Oh, no. Just the tone of Steve's voice coming over the line made her cringe. What on earth did he want and why was he calling her so late?

She glanced to the large clock overtop Jax's mantel and realized it wasn't late at all. If she were in Atlanta, she'd still be in the office . . . even on a Saturday.

"Actually, I am a little busy," she replied. If this had been her boss, she would've lied, but since her nemesis was asking, she opted for honesty. "What can I do for you?"

"I was put in charge of the budget meeting for next Friday and I wanted to know if we could count on you to be there."

Olivia stilled. Steve was put in charge of the meeting? Nobody but the COO was ever put in charge of that. Surely, he hadn't already been named. Maybe this was just one way they were continuing the interviewing process? How long was this going to take, because her nerves were about shot.

"I can be there," she told him. No way in hell would she miss that meeting and let him gloat all over himself. She was fighting to the death when it came to this promotion.

"Fantastic." His tone told her he felt quite the opposite. "The meeting will start promptly at eight. I hope you don't miss this one."

That jab referring to the last meeting wasn't worth getting worked up about. Steve was a jerk and she refused to let him goad her into a verbal sparring match. She'd show him who was the best man, or woman, for the job.

Besides, she didn't care what he thought. All she cared

about was her boss and his opinion. He'd actually been understanding the other day when she'd missed the conference call, and a sliver of her felt guilty for lying about her absence.

Steve was nothing but an annoyance and he better start treating her with respect . . . considering she'd be one of his bosses soon.

Olivia hung up without telling him bye. All manners and common sense went out the window when she had to talk to Steve. He was a smarmy jerk. There simply weren't enough negative adjectives to describe him. It wasn't that he was bad at his job—he wasn't a terrible accountant. But his inability to play well with others made her want to pull her hair out at times.

"Everything okay?"

Olivia realized she'd been clutching her phone and staring at the clock. She pulled in a breath, but that did nothing to calm her nerves. She wanted to be in Atlanta right now. She wanted to march into the office and . . . damn it, do something. Anything to make her boss realize that she could handle her personal life and the promotion.

She spun around and the look on Jax's face stopped her. With his dark brows drawn in, his square jaw set, he looked so serious, so . . . concerned. It was unusual to have someone other than Melanie or Jade look at her in such a way. Olivia wasn't quite sure what to do because when she was upset or angry, her friends either made her a drink or they went on a run to pound out frustrations.

"That wasn't work on a Saturday," he stated, clearly knowing it was. "You realize that's not normal."

Livie brushed her hair back from her face and gripped her phone at her side. "I'm in the middle of a promotion process and I'm clawing my way to the top. Nothing about this is normal, but apparently, I have to be at a meeting next week so my archrival doesn't steal this out from under me. It's mine."

Jax had the audacity to smirk. "He doesn't know who he's dealing with."

"Oh, he knows." Olivia turned to put her phone back in her purse. When she faced Jax once again, he was full-on smiling. "But he's about to realize that I can fight just as dirty."

"Did you know you sound even sexier when you're fired up?" He took one step toward her, then another, all while keeping his eyes on her. "Just like that day you came barging into the hangar angry over the fact I wasn't going to bow down and just sell the place."

"I didn't march," she corrected, tipping her head back as he closed the gap between them. "If I recall, you came out to me and put your hands all over my ass."

"You started to fall."

That naughty grin nearly melted the clothes right off her body. "No, you made me lose my balance, then you put your greasy hands on me. By the way, where's my suit?"

"It's here." He reached up, smoothing his knuckles over her cheek before gliding his thumb over her bottom lip. "Your shoes are here, too. Makes me wonder what you'll leave for me tonight."

Every breath she took, she simply inhaled more of that masculine scent she'd come to appreciate. The stubble on his jaw used to irritate her because she was so used to cleanly shaven men in suits. But there was something to be said for a man with a little scruff and a well-worn pair of jeans.

"Who said I was staying?" she countered, her voice betraying her as she got all breathy.

Why was it when she was with him she didn't recognize herself? Jax made her turn into a completely different woman. When they were together, she wanted to see him succeed with the airport, she wanted to learn more about his life, she forgot about work—unless she received untimely calls—and she craved like never before. Craved his touch, his sultry glances, his snarky comments.

Damn it. She should've worn her nice underwear.

"I'm not even answering that rhetorical question." Jax took a step back and sighed. "You ready for dessert?"

Olivia narrowed her eyes and tipped her head. "Dessert that you made?"

His rich laughter filled the living room. "Yes, dessert I made. I tried something new, but it has chocolate so I figure you'd be happy."

"You're speaking my language." Olivia gestured toward the kitchen. "Let's go."

When she started to head that way, Jax stepped in her path. Without touching her anywhere else, he leaned down and captured her lips. He completely consumed her, causing her toes to curl in her kitten heels and tingles to shoot through her from head to toe. And he only touched her mouth.

Perhaps she was so affected because she knew exactly what he could do with those hands once they got on her body. A moan escaped her, but just as she was about to give in and wrap her arms around him, Jax released her lips and turned toward the kitchen.

And he whistled.

Seriously? He could kiss her in a way that made her achy all over and simply walk away so nonchalantly?

That whistle, though. He often did that when he was finished and now it was getting on her nerves. He was revving her up, ready to feed her chocolate, and acted as if nothing had happened.

A man didn't go to this much trouble if he didn't care. Which made things even more difficult for Olivia to grasp or make sense of. If he cared, and she was starting to care, where did that leave them?

Was this a relationship? What on earth would happen if they fell for each other? He would never leave Haven and she'd worked too hard in Atlanta to be pulled away.

Olivia rubbed her forehead and closed her eyes. There was no reason to try to hash all of this out in her mind. All she could do was live in the moment and just enjoy what they had going on . . . even if she was terrified of the outcome.

Jax poked the stick through another marshmallow and extended it over the fire.

"You're going to make me fat," Livie complained. "First dinner, which was amazing, then that Death by Chocolate Layer Cake, now s'mores."

He watched the flames lick the edge of the marshmallow as he rotated the stick. "Dessert was hours ago and you're not going to get fat. You're sexy no matter what."

What was it with her and weight? Did she really worry that much about appearance? As far as he was concerned, she looked better now than when she'd been eighteen and slenderer. Now she was all woman with curves in exactly the right places. He could definitely verify how much he appreciated those curves now that he'd had hands-on experience.

A raindrop hit the back of his hand, then another. Within seconds, rain poured from the sky, drenching them both. Jax dropped the stick and grabbed the sack with the candy bars, crackers, and marshmallows. When he glanced to Livie, he was stunned to see her with her head tipped back, arms wide, getting absolutely soaked.

"Come on," he yelled over the instant downpour.

"I love the rain." She turned in a circle. "It's so refreshing."

Refreshing? He was drenched and only getting more so by the second. How did someone so structured and refined and . . . well, uptight, get so excited about becoming the proverbial drowned rat?

A rumble of thunder and flash of lightning in the distance had him grabbing her outstretched arm and heading toward the back door. He ushered her in ahead of him and quickly closed the door behind him.

Jax dropped the dripping sack onto the bench of the utility room. "Get your clothes off."

She swiped at her damp face and stared at him. "Is that your foreplay?"

Jax peeled his wet shirt over his head and dropped it with a sloppy smack onto the bench. "Yeah, it is. Get them off."

Her eyes zeroed in on his chest. Arousal speared through him at the hunger in her eyes. Added to that, she looked like some sort of wet goddess with her hair slicked back from her face, her white sleeveless button-up molded to her breasts. The "ugly" bra she'd claimed she had on didn't look so boring right now. The white outline only alluded to what lay beneath . . . and he knew exactly what she was hiding behind her clothes.

"You've got one second before I remove them myself."

That damn defiant chin tipped up as she propped her hands on her hips. "Maybe that's what I'm waiting for."

She was going to be the death of him. Jax took a step forward, keeping his eyes locked on hers. Droplets settled on her dark lashes, making her seem like some sort of magical vixen and making him crazy with desire and wanting to wax some poetry . . . if he knew how. That wasn't him, but Livie didn't seem too concerned with pretty words at this point.

He gripped the vee of her shirt and ripped it apart, sending buttons flying all over the small room.

"That's a shirt and a suit you owe me," she laughed. "I'm expensive."

"I'll give you my credit card."

Jax jerked her pants down, taking her plain white panties with it. As she stepped out of her wet clothes, he made work of wrestling his jeans down. As she stood before him completely naked, he truly wished he had the willpower to take his time and enjoy the moment . . . later, he vowed. Right now, he wanted her. It was that simple and that urgent.

There was no time to move to a horizontal surface. Jax gripped her around the waist and spun her until her back hit the wall just beside the door. Her legs instantly circled his waist, her ankles locking behind his back.

"I'm clean," he muttered against her neck. Damn, she smelled so amazing. A mix of her perfume and the fresh raindrops. "There's protection in my bedroom. We can go there—"

"I'm clean, too," she panted as she arched against him. "I'm on the pill."

Nothing else needed to be said at that point. He was way beyond words, anyway. With one easy thrust, he joined their bodies. Jax stilled, torn between wanting to make this hard and fast to give in to his need or taking just a moment to relish in the fact Livie was wrapped all around him. She panted, threading her fingers through his hair as she captured his lips.

Her urgency had him jerking his hips as he gripped a handful of her soaking wet hair and tipped her head to the side. Jax broke the kiss to slide his lips down her neck and back up to that sensitive spot behind her ear.

"Jax."

The way she groaned his name only added to his desire

for her. She pumped her hips faster, matching his own urgency. Jax slid his hand up over the swell of the side of her breasts, causing her to cry out even more.

Livie's fingernails bit into his shoulders as she jerked faster. Her entire body tightened around his and Jax watched her; he couldn't tear his eyes away even if he tried. Livie's mouth opened wide, her eyes squeezed shut, and the random rain droplets on her skin were absolutely breathtaking.

Olivia Daniels in total abandon was the sexiest sight he'd ever seen in his life. And soon he'd take her upstairs, lay her out on his bed, and do this all over again.

The more she jerked, the more difficult it was for him to hold back. The moment her body started to settle, he let himself go. Jax dropped his head to the crook in her neck, tightened his grip on her hair, and held her body firmly in place with his own as he let every bit of passion overtake him.

In the distance, her cell starting ringing, but Jax completely ignored it, as did she. He kept his head down even when his body stopped trembling. The last thing he wanted to do was look up and have her witness exactly what was in his eyes. He knew this was more than sex and if she saw him right now, she'd know it too.

Jax didn't want to freak her out, he wanted to just enjoy their time together . . . because the clock was ticking.

Her cell started ringing again.

"If that's your coworker again, I'll kill him myself and you won't have to worry about him getting the promotion."

Livie laughed as she untangled her legs. "I can't imagine that's him, but someone apparently needs me."

He eased away, instantly feeling the damp chill to his skin. Having Livie draped all over him was all he'd wanted, and having her in his life was becoming all too comfortable.

Wearing nothing but those delicious curves, Livie raced through his house toward her phone. Jax gathered up all the clothes and tossed them into the dryer. He'd let her borrow one of his shirts—after they made use of the warm shower and his bed. Hell, did she even need clothes? It was such a shame to cover up such perfection.

Jax locked the back door just as another rumble of thunder nearly shook his house. A pop-up storm, perfect for what he had in mind. If she loved the rain, then he'd open his bedroom windows and let the sound of the storm surround them.

Just as he stepped out of the utility room, Livie came back down the hall. She'd draped the throw from the couch around her shoulders, clutching it between her breasts as if modesty had a place here now.

"That was Jade."

Jax froze. "What's wrong?"

"Nothing's wrong," she reassured him. "But the storm is a little scary for Piper so Jade wanted to know if she could bring her home."

"Yes," he said without thinking twice. "I can go get her so Jade doesn't have to come out. Call her back."

Livie's soft smile warmed him. With her hair in utter disarray, her face void of most makeup, and her wearing nothing but a grin and a blanket, he felt himself falling and there wasn't a damn thing he could do to stop it.

"I already told her to bring Piper."

Yeah, there he went slipping down that slope again. He was quickly stumbling headfirst in love with this woman. The fact she didn't ask him, but put Piper's needs ahead of their plans spoke volumes for the type of woman she was . . . perhaps the type of mother she would be one day.

No. He wasn't thinking along those lines. He'd gotten tangled up once with a woman who wanted something bigger out of life than what Haven, or a family, had to offer. Jax's eyes were wide open this time around . . . unfortunately, so was his heart.

"Come to my bedroom."

"We don't have time for another quickie," Livie grumbled as she shook her head.

Jax snaked an arm around her waist and jerked her against his chest. "When I get you in my bed again, it sure as hell won't be quick."

He smacked a quick kiss on her lips before releasing her. "We're getting clothes before my daughter arrives and wonders what the hell kind of sleepover I was having."

As he circled around her to head out of the room, he gave her a swat on her butt. She yelped, then laughed.

"Go get me a shirt and pants," she scolded, following him. "I'm drawing the line at wearing your underwear."

A visual of her wearing nothing but his clothes against her skin had his body stirring to life all over again. He stopped at the base of the steps and turned to face her.

Without any warning, he bent and put his shoulder into her midsection to lift her into a fireman's hold. "If you keep talking dirty to me, your friends and my daughter are going to have to wait for us to finish."

The electricity flashed as she smacked him. "Put me down before you drop me. If the lights go off, I don't want to tumble naked down these steps."

Jax tightened his hold. "I'd never let you get hurt, Livie."

There was so much more to that statement, so much he could continue on about, but right now they had to get dressed because the storm was raging and he knew Piper was going to be scared when she got here. His night had been cut short with Livie, but he knew for certain that her feelings were just as strong as his. The question was, who was going to cave first and admit it?

"I can give you a ride back home."

Olivia glanced from a trembling Piper being held in her father's arms back to Jade, who stood in the doorway. "I think I'll stay."

Jade raised her brows. "You know what you're doing?"

"Not at all." And that's what terrified her the most, but she had to figure it out. "You okay to drive in this?"

Jade nodded. "It's not that far. Melanie is pulling out all the candles and flashlights. She already made snacks in case we lose power."

Olivia laughed. "Food is important. I'll see you guys in the morning."

Jade looked as if she wanted to say something else, but she merely nodded and stepped out into the storm. Olivia watched as her friend pulled her hood up over her head and took off running toward her car.

Olivia carefully closed the door and flicked the lock. When she turned, she met Jax's questioning gaze and instantly felt like a fool. She hadn't once asked if she could stay. Maybe now that they'd had sex he didn't want her here—not that she got that vibe from him, but it was rude of her to just assume.

"I hope this is okay?" she asked, her hand still on the door.

"More than okay." His smile instantly relaxed her. "When it storms we make a blanket fort in the living room. You up for it?"

"I've never made a blanket fort."

Piper jerked her head from her father's chest. "Never? That's sad. Daddy gets all the blankets and cushions. It's a mess."

Jax laughed and hugged Piper tighter. "Why don't you start taking the cushions off and I'll grab blankets. Olivia will stay in the room with you in case the lights go off. Okay?"

Piper nodded and jumped to start her job. Jax crossed the room and stood directly in front of her.

"You look like you're about ready to run out that door." He pried her hand away and gripped both of hers between his own. "What are you afraid of?"

The truth slammed into her. She'd seen it dangling in the back of her mind before, but right now it was front and center. They'd just been intimate—for a second time—and now she was going to stay over and have a slumber party with the man she was falling for and his daughter. Things didn't get much more serious than that . . . at least not for her.

"This all seems so . . ." She couldn't say the words. Didn't know how to verbalize her thoughts without sounding utterly terrified. "I don't know how to do the family thing."

Jax lifted her hands to his lips and kissed her knuckles. "Right now we're going to build a fort and have shadow puppets on the wall because I can just about bet the electric will go. We're going to comfort Piper and laugh and tell stupid jokes until she falls asleep. That's all you need to focus on."

But when he touched her like that, so caring and so gentle, and when he looked into her eyes like she was special, precious, she had to worry about so much more. Like her heart, her mind . . . her life. She was getting too cozy here, she saw it happening. Little by little each day something happened that made her fall more for her hometown, for the people in it. For Jax.

"Daddy," Piper cried. "Hurry."

He shot Olivia a wink and darted up the stairs to retrieve

blankets. Piper had all the pillows spread all over the floor. Throw pillows, sofa pillows, the pillows from the oversize chair.

"Can you move the foot thing?" Piper asked.

Olivia glanced around the room. "Foot thing?"

Piper pointed to the ottoman. "Daddy puts that here." She pointed to the open area in front of the fireplace. "Then we put blankets over that and he sets the big pillows up. I crawl in the fort first."

Olivia bent down to slide the ottoman across the hardwood floor. Conscience of the fact Jax's shirt was huge on her, she didn't bend at the waist because she would totally flash a toddler.

Trying to keep her breasts concealed by the shirt, Olivia carefully scooted it to the spot Piper still pointed to. Apparently, there was a system she and her father had down pat and Olivia didn't want to screw it up.

"Why are you wearing my daddy's shirt?"

Piper glanced down to the oversize tee that he'd apparently had from his air force days. "We were outside roasting marshmallows when it started storming and we got soaked. My clothes are in the dryer."

There, that was vague, but honest.

"Okay. I have all the usual blankets." Jax came down the stairs carrying an armload of comforters and blankets. "We'll have to see about making this a bit larger since we have a guest tonight."

Piper slid her hand in Olivia's. "I'm glad you stayed so I can still have my first sleepover."

Olivia couldn't pull her eyes away from the delicate hand inside of hers. There was such innocence with Piper. She was sweet and honest and everything about her was Jax's doing. He'd raised this precious girl from just a few weeks old and he'd done so single-handedly. Well, she was sure he had help from Tanner and Cash.

Everything about Jax was becoming more and more difficult to resist.

Jax dropped the blankets in front of her, pulling her from the moment. When she looked over and met his eyes, she saw that same look she'd seen earlier. It went beyond desire, beyond lust . . . and it ventured into a territory she wasn't sure she could accept. Because if she let these emotions in, if she let them overtake her, someone was going to get hurt.

"I'm glad I could stay for your first sleepover too," she told Piper as she turned her attention back down to the smiling toddler.

The lights flickered once again as a rumble of thunder boomed. Piper's hand tightened around Olivia's.

"It's all right," Olivia assured her. "You've got two adults here now and we won't let anything happen to you. I'm excited to see shadow puppets. I don't know that I've done that since I was a little girl."

Jax worked on shifting pillows and spreading out the blankets. Olivia picked up Piper and held on to her as the lights flickered once more.

"Let's get that flashlight and you can show me your best shadow puppet."

Piper nodded. "But hold me until Daddy gets the fort ready."

Her little arms wrapped around Olivia's neck and something in her heart turned over—almost as if something clicked into place. Never once had she thought about a family of her own. Never once did she dream of having children or a husband. No, Olivia had been too busy building her corporate world exactly the way she'd envisioned. She'd had a plan and she was well on track to the biggest success she'd ever known.

Getting sidetracked by her hometown and diving into

renovations at her father's airport was one thing, but falling headfirst in love with Jax—

Damn it. She'd let that word slip into her mind. She'd tried so hard to avoid it. She knew once that dreaded "L" word entered the scene, she would be screwed.

"The flashlight is over there," Piper said, pointing to the end table.

Olivia turned her head and Piper ran her little fingertip over the side of Olivia's neck.

"You have a birthmark?"

Confused, Olivia glanced back to Piper, whose eyes were still focused on her neck. "Birthmark?"

"This red mark. I have a birthmark, too. It's on my shoulder, but Daddy says it's shaped like a strawberry."

Red? On her neck?

Olivia jerked her attention to Jax, who had the nerve to start whistling. As if that weren't frustrating enough, he shot her a quick glance and winked. If Piper weren't in her arms, Olivia would be all too happy to explain to him she'd never had a hickey and at the age of thirty-four she sure as hell didn't intend to start getting them now.

"I must've burned myself with the curling iron and not realized it." The excuse was lame, but it was all she could think of on the spur of the moment.

The electric flashed once, twice, and finally went. Tiny arms tightened around Olivia's neck.

"It's all good," Olivia assured Piper. "I've got the flashlight."

She clicked it on and shone it against the far wall. Piper lifted her head. Instantly she started with her puppets and before long she was giggling.

"Let me see yours," Piper exclaimed, clearly having more faith in Olivia's talents than she should.

"I can't hold the flashlight and you and do a puppet."

Piper took the flashlight. "Now."

Jax's soft chuckle from the other side of the room mocked her. Oh, so he thought she couldn't do them?

Olivia held up her hand in some obscure angle and watched on the far wall. Yeah, she was terrible at this. But there hadn't been a need to learn such social skills. Drawing up spreadsheets and attending forced cocktail parties for clients was pretty much as social as she got.

"What animal is that?" Piper asked.

Olivia put one of her fingers down until it looked somewhat like . . . a dog?

"Dog," she quickly said. "Roof, roof, roof."

She bounced her hand around in the circle of light and kept barking.

"That's not a dog," Jax stated, coming to stand beside her. "This is a dog."

He was all too eager to show her, not with his own hand, but he reached around her from behind and adjusted her fingers. The warmth from his back, the weight of his daughter, it was all so much. Too much. Was he doing this to torture her? Did he want to shove her deeper into this rabbit hole? Because at this point she was having a difficult time recalling why she wanted in and out of Haven so fast.

Yes, she had to get back to her job, to the potential promotion, but part of her was growing more and more content here. When did that happen? *How* did that happen?

"That's a dog," Jax stated once he got her hand in position.

Light briefly flashed in the room as the thunder boomed and lightning streaked across the sky.

"Okay, squirt. You climb into the fort first." Jax lifted Piper from Olivia's arms. "Keep the flashlight you have with you. We have others."

Piper crawled into the mound of pillows and blankets. "This is huge. We need this size all the time."

"What were you thinking giving me a hickey?" Olivia gritted between her teeth in a low whisper. "Do I look like someone who wants to be marked?"

Jax curled his fingers around her neck and stroked his thumb over where the mark was. "You didn't seem to mind anything I did earlier. In fact, you were beg—"

"All right." She batted his hand away. "Let's get in the fort where I know you'll be on your best behavior."

He aligned their torsos and nipped at her lips. "You've already seen my best behavior."

The next second he released her and disappeared inside the fort. Piper's giggles started instantly while Olivia remained standing in the dark trying to figure out how her life had gone from trying to dodge this small town to suddenly finding herself falling for it.

But it wasn't Haven she worried about missing when she left.

Chapter Seventeen

"Dude, that was so awesome. When can we go again?"

Jax rounded the Cessna and met Brock's wide grin. "I'm here every day. You tell me what your schedule is."

"I'm free Thursday," he replied.

With a nod, Jax started heading from the hangar toward his office in the main building next door. "Follow me and let me look over my flight schedule."

After the storm last night, Jax had barely gotten up in enough time to fix Piper breakfast and run her over to the sitter. Thankfully, the sitter was just next door to their house, which was handy on days he had to come in and she couldn't fly with him. There was no school for her today and he was going to be here until at least six.

Jax wasn't even going to entertain the flashbacks of this morning and when Olivia hurried out the door like she was being chased.

Because that's what she did. She ran, and he wasn't going to be the one chasing her anymore. Her own insecurities and demons did that. But, damn it, he thought they were getting somewhere last night. He thought when she'd opted to stay after they'd been intimate that she was finally coming to the realization they were so much more.

Apparently not, because she'd freaked out this morning and left wearing his clothes with an awkward wave and quick smile . . . all directed to Piper. She'd completely ignored him.

The wind kicked up just a little and the sound of metal scraping against metal had Jax stopping between buildings. Both he and Brock turned toward the clanging.

"Up there," Brock pointed.

Sure enough on top of the hangar was a piece of the metal roofing blowing in the breeze. The wind wasn't even strong, or he never would've taken Brock up in the sky, but obviously, the storm last night had done something to the hangar. Of course it did. Because they needed more issues with this place.

"I'll look at it in a bit," Jax stated. "Let's get you on the schedule so you can get those hours in."

"Macy said she would work around my schedule for this and school." Brock stepped into the office behind Jax. "My family has been pretty awesome in their support. I think they just want me to fly in guests for the resort."

"Not a bad idea," Jax agreed. "Especially if this renovation goes through."

Brock rested his knuckles on the edge of the scarred wood desk. "You think you're going to renovate this whole place?"

Jax stared down at his schedule for the next few weeks and mentally calculated how to get in more hours.

"I think it's going to take quite a bit of work before we could actually begin the labor part," he replied honestly as he glanced up. "But Livie is confident it will happen and she and her friends know more about these dealings than I do."

"Do you want the expansion?"

Jax considered Brock's genuine question. Did he actually want to grow the airport? Whenever the thought or question crossed his mind, Jax immediately considered what Paul would've wanted. Ultimately, as long as the doors were open, they had paying customers, and Livie wasn't gearing up to sell the property, Jax figured this was the most logical step.

"I want this airport to stay open and I want to serve the needs of this town. So, yeah. I want it to grow."

Brock stood straight up and crossed his arms over his chest. "You think there's something to all those shows and movies being filmed down here?"

"I sure as hell hope so," Jax laughed. "If this expansion goes off as planned, we'll be able to add another plane to the fleet in order to bring in some elite clientele."

"Zach mentioned something about the runway may need to be lengthened."

Jax nodded. "If we're going to grow and allow certain size planes to land here, we need to expand the runway to accommodate that."

He glanced back down to the schedule and rattled off various days and times. Once they had the next few sessions in, Jax closed his book and took a seat.

"If you have free time any other days, just text me. We'll get those hours in before you know it."

Brock's grin widened. "I think I like being in the sky more than I like being on land."

Jax rocked back in the creaky old chair. "You've got all the makings of a good pilot."

The cell on his desk vibrated and an unknown number lit up the text. He glanced to it and quickly saw it was Jade with some information on the grants.

Anger and a sense of emptiness filled him. Jade would've had to have gotten his number from Livie, who obviously had reached a new level of running away.

"I'll let you get back to work," Brock stated. "Thanks for everything, man."

Jax gave a clipped nod. "No problem. I'll see you Thursday."

Once Brock left, Jax grabbed his phone and read the text. Apparently, Zach had given them the final costs and she had passed that on to the committee to review for the grants. At least they were keeping him in the loop, but he'd rather hear from the woman he'd spent the night with. He'd rather be in contact with his legal partner in this entire process.

Jax shot off a quick thanks and pulled in a deep breath. Gritting his teeth, he pulled up Livie's name and sent her a message as well.

**Wear old clothes and come to the airport.
No excuses.**

There were some minor repairs from the storm that needed his attention and this would be the perfect time for Livie to get her hands a little dirty and learn that he didn't do games. He didn't appreciate her racing from his house, he didn't appreciate her pawning off the latest info onto her friend, and he sure as hell didn't appreciate how he was so torn up over her. She'd been in Haven such a short time and had this hold over him he wasn't used to.

Whatever was going on between them wasn't like what he'd had with his ex-wife. Their relationship had been fiery passion and built on sex. They'd married on a whim and he'd gone overseas. When he'd come home, they'd pick up their affair where they'd left off. One time on leave had produced Piper and that's when Carly decided family wasn't for her at all.

Hell, he hadn't thought it had been for him, either, but there was no way he was going to just walk away from responsibilities . . . especially an innocent child.

His cell vibrated in his hand and he assumed it was

Livie coming up with some excuse as to why she couldn't meet him. But he instantly smiled when he glanced to the screen. He opened the picture that had come in from the sitter. Piper was sitting on the kitchen island at the sitter's house and she had her hands in some dough and the biggest grin.

Making biscuits from scratch.

Yeah. This child of his was his entire world and he'd give up his military career again in a heartbeat. While he'd always wanted to continue on in the air force, some things were just not meant to be. He'd had several good years with them, but he had even better years being Piper's father.

Jax spun the chair around to the desk along the wall behind him. The invoices spread across the space hadn't disappeared like he'd hoped. There was so much behind the scenes that most people never considered for this small-town airport. But he was doing the best he could to keep everything running just as smoothly as when Paul was alive.

Jax reached over to fire up the computer just as the office door slammed open. Throwing a look over his shoulder it was all he could do not to burst out laughing.

"You really take old clothes to heart," he stated, glancing over Livie in her mussed state.

"You told me to get over here, so here I am." She slammed the door at her back. "What do you want?"

Oh, that timeless loaded question. For now, though, he opted to remain serious.

He motioned to her neck. "You have paint on your hickey."

Obviously, that serious state didn't last long. But he couldn't help himself. She had a pale gray slash on her neck, covering his mark—he was sure there was some metaphor about trying to mask their intimacy to the world, but he was too emotionally drained to try to figure it all out.

She also sported some hairstyle that he'd never seen on her and he sure as hell wasn't about to comment on that . . . whatever that pile of blond was on top of her head. Random pieces framed her face, and the matching shade covering her hickey was splattered all over her shirt and shorts.

"What. Do. You. Want." Each word came through gritted teeth and Jax circled his desk, slow as he pleased. Apparently, she wasn't in the mood. Ironically, he was.

"What are you painting?" he asked as he propped a hip on the edge of his desk.

"My bedroom. I need to get these projects done before Friday."

Intrigued, he tipped his head. "What's Friday?"

"I have to head back to Atlanta for work that morning. I just want some sense of accomplishment and moving forward with Dad's house." She let out a sigh and dropped her arms to her sides. "There's an important meeting Friday. I can't miss it, and if the CEO decides to go ahead and announce the promotion, I want to know that I am one step closer to putting my house on the market."

She was going back to work in a few days, a fact she hadn't mentioned one time to him before or after their intimacy. The pushing toward putting her childhood home on the market didn't sit any better with him. Even though they'd been intimate, and they'd spent time together and gotten to know each other on a level deeper than he'd thought possible, she still kept him at a distance. That personal life of hers remained just that and she never once offered a glimpse into her future.

Clearly, he knew where he fell in her life.

Whatever Jax thought they might be developing . . . well, it was completely one-sided. He'd do well to remember the original vow he'd made to himself about getting emotionally involved with a woman who never intended to stick. He'd more than learned his lesson . . . or so he'd thought.

Something about Livie had seemed so different, though. Even when she spouted over and over how she was leaving, he always got the sense she was reminding herself and not actually talking to him. Their intimacy was so much more than he'd ever had before . . . how could his feelings be so strong when she didn't share them?

Or maybe she did and that's what had her running scared. She was most likely terrified because she hadn't expected all of this between them, but neither had he and he'd be damned if he was going to ignore it. He wanted to know her full feelings before she left town. If she wasn't going to volunteer the information, he would get it from her one way or another.

"We've got some damage on the roof of the hangar from the storm," he told her, pushing his thoughts aside. If she could ignore her true emotions, then he'd damn well do the same . . . for now. "We're going to fix it."

She let out an unladylike snort. "You sent me an emergency text for that? You're dreaming if you think I can climb up on a roof and fix anything. Call Zach. He'll fix it."

Livie spun around, obviously ready to head out the door, but he was faster. Jax jumped up and in front of her, blocking her escape. Her eyes widened as she stared up at him.

"Get out of my way so I can get back to painting. I left Melanie and Jade arguing over the way the tape was being applied around the crown molding in the dining room."

Without thinking twice, he reached out and raked the pad of his thumb over her neck. "You put paint here on purpose."

She swatted him away. "I'm a messy painter."

"You didn't want anyone to see." He muttered the words as he placed both hands on her shoulders and stepped into her. "If you're that ashamed of what we have, why did you stay last night?"

Her eyes darted away. "It was storming."

"That's a lame excuse. Do you need more time to come up with another?"

She shot him the side-eye glare. "I need to get back to my dad's house."

"Your house," he corrected. "Paul is gone and the place is yours."

"Legally, but that hasn't been my home since I left at eighteen."

Something was bothering her, something beyond them and beyond the painting and rush to return. There was a sadness in her eyes and now that he looked closer, there was a little bit of redness to them as well.

"You've been crying."

Livie drew her brows in. "Don't be ridiculous."

"Why do you lie to me?" he demanded, dropping his hands and taking a step back. "You think I can't tell you're terrified of your feelings when it comes to me, to my daughter? You weren't expecting us, were you? Now you're in a rush to get back to work, to get that precious promotion, but you're getting too involved here and you don't want to admit it."

She said nothing as she kept her gaze averted to the floor between them. Jax raked a hand over his stubbled jawline and willed himself to be patient toward this most frustrating woman. She was hurting and obviously didn't know how to deal with the pain. He knew a thing or two about wounds, but even if he didn't, he wasn't about to let her feel alone.

"What happened today, Livie?"

She shook her head, still not meeting his eyes.

"What happened?" he pressed.

With tears filling her eyes, she lifted her head. "Tell me how sick my dad was when we left."

The topic was bound to be brought up and he wasn't about to lie. "He wasn't terminal, but he did have cancer. He beat it and lived years in remission."

Livie blinked away the moisture. "Did you know he kept a journal? I found it with pictures in a decorative box under his nightstand."

"No, I wasn't aware of a journal."

That didn't surprise Jax. Paul was big on not keeping feelings bottled up. Perhaps if Livie had stayed, being more open would've been a trait she would've continued to learn from her father.

"He had so much planned for this place, for you." She glanced away again and whispered, "For me."

It was a wonder she got any painting done at all if she'd spent the morning reading her father's thoughts. Jax would love to see this journal, and he believed he had the right, but now was not the time to ask.

"More than once he mentioned what he'd do if he had the money." Livie toyed with the frayed hem of her old T-shirt. "He wanted to repair everything and add in a little restaurant. He didn't want anything grand or over-the-top. He just wanted to continue to serve the community."

Livie pulled in a shaky breath and scratched her cheek, resting her open palm on the side of her face as she continued to stare aimlessly. "Jade came into the room as I was reading and told me about Zach's quote for the renovations so I just gave her your number. I didn't want to talk to you or anyone else, really. I just wanted to read."

And now he felt like an ass for being so angry with her earlier. She hadn't been running, at least not that time. She'd been reading and reconnecting with her father in the only way possible now. She'd most likely been feeling guilt for not being here and for losing him suddenly.

"Then I got your text and came right over."

Jax leaned back against the door and shoved his hands in his pockets. This tiny office seemed to be closing in on them and all of these feelings. Too many feelings that neither of them knew what the hell to do with. They'd both steamrolled right into unchartered territory and they were floundering through it together.

Well, he was floundering around. Livie had a pretty clear picture of what she wanted for her future . . . and he wasn't in it.

The thought squeezed at his chest like a vise and he hated that he'd lost control over his plans and his life. There was so much he wanted, so much that seemed within reach, but in reality all of this was totally temporary.

Clearing his throat, Jax pushed aside those emotions. She wasn't ready to face them and he wasn't going to press her. He had to remind himself she was dealing with much more than just him. She was going through Paul's things, trying to get her house on the market, vying for a top spot at her firm . . . and he was purposely trying to make her realize what she had here.

But this wasn't her home. Haven hadn't been hers for some time now. Just because he loved it here, because he wanted to keep his roots firmly planted, didn't mean she did.

"Listen, I do need your help."

He held his hands up, palms out, when she opened her mouth. No doubt she was about to protest, but he wasn't having it and he wasn't letting her leave so soon.

"You can hold the ladder and the tools if you want, but I

am not calling someone in when I'm sure it's something I can do myself," he explained.

Livie pursed her lips together and finally nodded. "Fine. But I do have to get back to paint."

Jax smiled. "You give me an hour and I'll come help you paint."

"Where's Piper today?"

"She's at the sitter's. I'll get her later and then we'll come over. Surely one of you ladies can keep her entertained while I work."

Livie rubbed her hands over her damp cheeks, then glanced to the paint splotches on her hands. "I'm such a disaster," she groaned. "I don't even recognize myself. I don't know how to paint without making a mess."

"Honestly, I'm impressed you were painting at all. Figured you would try to hire that out."

With a swat across his chest, Livie let out a slight laugh. "I'm offended. Just because I appreciate nice things and I prefer to wear heels instead of tennis shoes doesn't mean I don't know how to do manual labor. I'm still Paul Daniels's daughter."

Which was both a curse and a blessing at the moment. If she were anyone else, he may not have had that initial physical reaction to her. But, if she were anyone else, she wouldn't be here.

Paul Daniels's daughter. The woman who had sparked his interest since he was too young to even know what to do with a woman. But he knew now. He knew exactly what to do with Livie and she knew exactly what to do with him to drive him out of his ever-loving mind.

He couldn't start down that path or he'd make use of this empty office and clear that desk with one swipe of his arm.

"Let's get this over with." Jax turned and opened the office door, gesturing for her to go on ahead. "I have a guy coming in this afternoon to set up some flights for work. He has several over the next couple of months, so I hope we are still up and running during renovations . . . if that even happens."

"Oh, it will happen," she stated as she marched by him. Those little shorts did nothing to keep his mind in the professional territory and had him seriously reconsidering cleaning off that desk. "We're a step closer every day and Melanie is determined. She's one sharp attorney and between her and Jade, they won't let us down."

"Is there an us?"

Damn it. Did that question seriously just pop out of his mouth? What was he thinking? He didn't need her to affirm or deny anything. Unfortunately, the words were out and from Livie's rigid stance, she was just as shocked at his question.

"Jax—"

"Forget it." He cut her off. Why make this even more uncomfortable than he'd already made it? "We'll get this metal roofing back in place and then you can be on your way."

Livie glanced over her shoulder, her eyes swirling with both desire and pain. "I don't want to hurt you."

Jax shrugged. "I'm not going to get hurt, Livie. Besides, I've been through quite a bit before you came to town. I can handle being roughed up."

She turned fully to face him. "Which is why I don't want to lead you on or pretend this is some happily-ever-after we're going to have. I'm not staying. I'm here for the airport and I'm here to get the house sold. I mean, I'll come back every now and then since this is my investment, too, but it won't be often."

"Are you telling yourself that or are you trying to convince me? Because, baby, that wasn't very convincing."

Her eyes narrowed. Obviously, he'd hit a nerve. Good. She'd hit all of his for some time now.

"I'm well aware of my goals," she countered. "You just need to remember what we're doing. We're going to renovate Dad's airport so you can keep it running. But on a personal level, we should probably keep things light from here on out to avoid a messy ending."

Jax stared at her for a half second before he closed the gap between them and curled his fingers around her shoulders. "You are delusional if you think this ending won't be messy. You can lie to me, you can even sidetrack me for a bit, but don't fool yourself."

She attempted to step back, but he tightened his hold. "You cannot brush me off that quick. Last night clearly scared you to death, but don't think for one second that it didn't affect me. I've never let anyone in my life since my wife left me. But you're here and Piper is over the moon about you."

No need to state his own feelings. They were too complex, especially compared to that of a toddler.

"So if you don't want a messy ending, then you sure as hell better go back to Atlanta now and leave this up to me," he warned. "Because I'm not done with you and I'm not letting you just casually throw out that little speech about being the end of the road."

Jax released her and headed to the storage area with his tools and ladders. He wasn't going to say any more on the subject. He'd said enough. At this point, Livie could decide what to do, what to say, and how to approach their personal relationship.

Legally, they were bound, so she couldn't run too far, but he wanted more. Damn it all. He wanted her and having her spend the night and play shadow puppets with his daughter to get through the storm had been the final piece linking his heart to hers.

Frustrated with himself for allowing these feelings to creep up again, Jax jerked on the storage room door, sending it clanging back against the wall. There was no one to be angry with other than himself. But the relationship he'd had with his wife was nothing like this.

Jax knew Livie. He knew her well, even though time and an age gap stood between them. He still got her, something he never truly had with his ex.

Perhaps that was the crux of the whole situation. This was new territory and he didn't like it. He didn't know how to handle it and he didn't have a game plan.

"Do you want me to go?"

As he stood in the doorway staring at the various tools, Livie's soft, questioning tone came from right behind him.

That he could answer with one hundred percent certainty. "I don't want you to go."

Propping his hands on his hips, he dropped his head between his shoulders and blew out a sigh. "I want to get this roof fixed, finish my day, and get your painting done. Other than that, I don't have the emotional energy for much else."

"You're hurting," she whispered.

When he turned around all he saw was those red-rimmed eyes and a vulnerable woman staring back at him. He closed the distance between them, framed her face, and tilted her head back.

"So are you," he whispered as he rested his forehead against hers.

Now what? They were at an impasse. She wasn't about to let him heal her, but Jax refused to let her go through this alone. She'd been alone for far too long. Whether she liked it or not, he was going to make sure she knew how much he cared.

And if that meant putting it all on the line, then so be it.

Chapter Eighteen

Olivia pulled her car behind the trucks currently occupying her driveway. What were all these people doing here? More importantly, who were they?

Jax's truck she recognized, but who were the others?

"Yay." Piper squealed from the back seat. "Cash and Tanner are here!"

Melanie and Jade both let out a groan. Once Jax had come by with Piper, he'd immediately jumped into painting. Since Olivia wasn't quite ready to face him, even with her friends around as chaperones, she, Jade, and Melanie took Piper to get some ice cream.

The ice cream trip turned into a walk in the park, literally, followed up by a quick run by the pet store. Piper seriously knew how to wrap adults around her adorable little finger.

Not only had Olivia's heart taken a drastic turn since coming to Haven, her diet had gone all to hell. The run this morning was replaced with prepping walls for painting, so she doubted that burned the calories she'd just inhaled with a double chocolate mocha chip in a waffle cone. A waffle cone dipped in chocolate.

If going through your late father's belongings and

falling for a sexy pilot who gave you hickeys as a sign of endearment weren't cause for calorie overload, she didn't know what was.

"I didn't know they were coming over," Piper announced as she unfastened her belt and hopped out of her booster seat. "We should've brought them ice cream."

"They aren't staying long," Melanie mumbled as she got out of the car.

Olivia laughed. Melanie was still a tad bitter over the whole ticket situation. For a woman who'd been through what she had, Melanie deserved a break. Instead, she'd caught the eye of the small-town officer. If only Tanner knew he was seriously wasting his time in his warped way of flirting with Mel.

As they all headed toward the back door, Piper ran ahead and went on inside. The entire house was a bit of a wreck. Boxes were stacked in rooms not being painted that moment, drop cloths covered the old hardwood floors. Blankets and plastic wrap draped over furniture that had been shoved to the middle of rooms. It would all be worth it once she got it done and sold.

But a piece of her had a pang of guilt over taking her father's home and completely changing it.

"They're upstairs."

Piper's anxious yell came from the staircase. Olivia followed her to make sure she didn't step her foot in a tray of paint or trip over the mayhem.

The fumes weren't too overpowering with all the second-story windows open allowing a breeze to pass through. Fans were stationed around as well to help with ventilation and drying time. Olivia reached the top landing and came in direct eye contact with Cash's backside.

"Well, good evening," she laughed.

He glanced over his shoulder and down from his perch

on the stepladder. "Hey, Livie. I'm on ceiling duty. Jax said they needed to be done."

Did he now? Because she hadn't said anything about ceilings. And where had that paint come from? She didn't have ceiling paint.

"Thanks, Cash." No need to gripe at him. "Where's Jax?"

"Guest bedroom." He flashed a quick wink to Jade. "Yours, if the little pink sports bras are any indication."

Jade let out an unladylike snort. "I better not be missing any of my unmentionables or I'm coming after you."

"I sure as hell hope so," he muttered as he focused back on the ceiling. "You should swing by my gym and we could spot each other."

"I'm good. Thanks."

Livie didn't have time to get into whatever verbal sparring match those two had going on. She headed down the hall and found Jax in the bedroom, pulling off tape from the trim around the windows. Piper sat in the middle of the floor playing on her father's phone.

"Did you completely overtake this project?"

Without turning to face her, he replied, "You seemed in a hurry to get this place ready to put on the market. Tanner, Cash, and I all had a few free hours so I coordinated a team."

Something about the way he seemed so matter-of-fact about her leaving didn't set well with her. It wasn't that she was eager to put the house on the market, but . . . okay, fine. She was ready to sell it and have one less headache, but she didn't like how this entire situation made her feel.

How could she be so torn when she'd had the perfect detailed plan all lined up before she ever stepped foot back in Haven? And now she was all a mess. Between sleeping with Jax, and loving every delicious moment of it, and his pulling in his cousins to help, she wasn't sure what to think or how to feel.

Livie examined the room, which had gone from a pale purple to a homey shade of slate gray. With the old hardwood floors, this place would catch the eye of some young couple who was just starting out. It was perfect with the extra bedrooms and close to the park.

A niggle of guilt slithered through her at the thought of never coming here again. Once it sold she'd have no reason to. Granted, she hadn't been back since she'd graduated, but the place had been here and in the back of her mind she knew she could've.

Maybe that's what helped her keep distant for so long. She always knew she could come back on her own time if she was ready . . . and now she'd run out of time. That old life, the good and the bad, were gone. The little girl who ran through these halls, the rebellious teen who pushed her father away at her mother's coaxing . . . all gone.

Seeing the fresh coats of paint cut through the defensive shield and pierced her heart. There was no other way to say it because it was almost as if she were erasing every memory from every room. That's what she wanted, though, right? She wanted to be done in Haven.

Well, except for the airport she jointly owned and the hunky man moving about the room. Would she ever be done with him? Not on a business level, but personal? Would they ever be able to just go their separate ways after they'd been intimate?

Sleeping with someone wasn't something Livie took lightly. She had to care about someone before giving herself to him. And as much as she didn't want to, she deeply cared for Jackson Morgan. Damn that man for making her want things and confuse her even more.

Raised voices came from out in the hall and Jax finally

shot a glance to Livie. He quirked a brow and she merely shrugged.

"Sounds like Uncle Tanner isn't happy," Piper stated as she continued her game on the floor without a care in the world.

Livie stepped out into the hall and saw Tanner's back in the doorway of the bedroom at the end of the hall . . . Melanie's bedroom.

"I'll get my stuff out of the way later," Mel told him. "I wasn't aware this room was going to be painted so soon."

"I can help you move it and we'll be done here."

Did her friends simply not mesh at all with Jax's cousins?

"I'll handle it later," Melanie insisted. "Besides, this is Livie's call and she didn't tell me to remove anything. We don't even have paint for this room."

"We bought the same shade for all the bedrooms," he replied, then crossed his arms over his chest. "Are you still angry over the ticket I gave you? You really should be more—"

"I'm not angry about that," she growled. "Would you get out of my personal space? I can't breathe."

"Sounds like a lovers' spat," Jax whispered in her ear, making her jump.

Livie glanced over her shoulder, finding her mouth so close to his. So, so close. She turned back to the entertainment at the end of the hall.

"Melanie won't be pushed around by men, no matter how minor the situation is."

"Want to share that backstory?" he asked.

Needing to get away from his touch, which muddled her mind, Livie turned and went back into the room. She squatted down and picked at the edge of the blue tape running along the baseboard.

"Not my story to tell."

"I love stories," Piper chimed in. "Daddy tells the best ones at bedtime."

Yes, Jax was the epitome of fantastic father. He rocked that job just like he did everything else. The man was too damn perfect and she was having difficulty finding fault with him.

Oh, wait. He drove her out of her ever-loving mind and made her question her sanity and her future. So apparently, he did have some epic flaws.

"Thank you," she told him without turning to face him. "You didn't have to do all of this and I don't even know where you got all this paint, but I'll pay you back."

"You're not paying me back," he demanded. "Paul was like a father to me, a grandfather to Piper. This was nothing in comparison."

Of course her father had been close with Piper. It only made sense that if he and Jax were so tight, Piper would spend quite a bit of time around Olivia's father.

And why wouldn't he surround himself with Jax and Piper? The rest of his family had left. Guilt of her past actions settled in deep. What would've happened if she'd taken him up on one of his offers to come back? Just once in all those years . . . what could've happened between them without her mother's interference?

The thought that she'd been a pawn for her mother to use in the marriage left a burning hole inside Olivia. She'd been young and impressionable, but that was no excuse. She'd made the mistake in thinking that her father was invincible and she could come back when she was ready. Unfortunately, the time she came back was for the funeral of the one man she could've counted on but didn't.

Olivia glanced over her shoulder to Piper playing on the floor on her father's phone. Jealousy settled heavy on Olivia's heart knowing this sweet girl possibly knew Paul better than Olivia in the past few years. Why had Olivia let her mother persuade her to move? Why had Olivia believed her father loved the airport more than his family?

Because the longer Olivia stayed in Haven and learned about her father, the more she read in his journal, the more she was coming to realize he loved his family with his whole heart. He was seriously trying to hang on to his dream and provide the best way he knew how and her mother simply wanted more.

More raised voices came from the hall—this time Jade and Cash seemed to be going at it. Jax laughed and continued working.

Olivia figured they all were rubbing one another the wrong way and the sooner she and her girls left town, the better off they'd all be. Of course, there was that whole airport project they'd be working on, so they wouldn't just cut all ties when they left.

And Olivia worried it was those ties that would keep pulling her back in whether she wanted it or not.

"When are you going to tell her you're in love with her?"

Jax didn't even try to dodge the question, because it was valid. He'd fallen for Olivia Daniels and his cousins were calling him on it. Bastards.

Cash rested his arm over the bar and swiped at his forehead with his other hand. They'd been spotting each other for the past thirty minutes and Cash wasn't even winded. Clearly, Jax needed to get here more often.

"Pretty sure he's not telling her," Tanner chimed in as he replaced his weights on the rack.

Jax sank to the bench to gather his thoughts and to catch his breath. Cash's workouts were brutal, not that he'd ever admit that.

"Why would I?" Jax asked. "She's leaving, she's got a life in Atlanta and my life is here."

"Maybe if you told her, then she'd stay."

Jax stared at Tanner, who clearly didn't know women as well as he thought. "I'm not asking her to stay or playing some game where I hint at such a thing. If she wanted to be here, then she would. She's already called Sophie Monroe to put her house on the market and she's in Atlanta today for some damn meeting for her promotion."

Not that he wasn't thrilled for her. She'd worked hard in her career and should be praised and granted this promotion she so desperately wanted. But that selfish side of him kept rearing its ugly head and he wanted her to see just what she was throwing away.

There had been a change in her since coming here. She was a different person and she seemed happier. Oh, she was definitely frustrated, but overall, she'd relaxed, she'd gotten comfortable with the town, with him. Did she not see that he'd do anything for her? That he'd completely fallen for her?

"So is that why you called this session?" Cash asked with a knowing grin. "You needed to work out some frustrations."

"Pretty much."

Jax wasn't going to lie. The three of them had been through too much together, but they'd always been honest.

Weights clanged across the room as another trainer assisted his client. Cash's gym was the best in the area, but it was still rather early. The place seemed to really pick up when locals got off work.

"Is she coming back?" Cash asked.

"She never really said. I assume she was just going for the meeting."

Plus, Melanie and Jade were still at the house. He knew this because he'd seen them running when he'd been on his way to the gym. He had no idea when Livie was coming back, perhaps tonight, tomorrow . . . next week.

She never told him and he didn't ask. He hoped like hell she was thinking of him and just as mentally frustrated as he was.

Part of him wanted her to get that promotion, to move up where she belonged, but the other part of him wanted her to come back and proclaim she'd had some epiphany while she'd been in Atlanta and she never wanted to return. Doubtful, but a guy could hope, right?

For someone who swore never to get emotionally invested again, he was a complete failure. Honestly, though, he didn't care. Livie did something to him and he wouldn't trade it. Even when she left for good, he'd carry her in his heart. As ridiculous as that sounded, the times he spent with her, frustrating as they were, were so much more than he'd ever had in his marriage.

But his heart literally ached at the thought of not having her in his life. Piper loved Livie as well, so he'd have to figure out a way to make sure those two stayed in contact. Would Livie take the time to text or call Piper? Knowing Livie, she absolutely would. There was complete adoration whenever she looked at his daughter and the way she interacted with her.

"Your turn," Cash stated, pulling Jax from his thoughts. "Ready to do some squats? Can't just work on the arms, have to sculpt those chicken legs."

"I don't have chicken legs," Jax growled, coming to his feet.

Cash nodded to Tanner. "He sure as hell does. Good thing he has to wear pants for his uniform."

"You wish your legs looked half as good as mine," Tanner retorted with a snort. "I run daily."

"But you don't build muscle." Cash slid weights onto the bar and patted the middle. "Who's up first, ladies?"

Jax shot Tanner a look and shook his head. "I'm done here. I have Brock coming in for flight lessons shortly."

"I don't have an excuse," Tanner stated. "I just don't want to."

Cash laughed. "Let me know when you two think you can keep up. I'll be here."

Jax headed out and welcomed the fresh air. He needed to grab a shower and get to the airport. Brock wasn't coming for about three hours, but Jax was done at the gym. He needed to be alone with his thoughts, he wanted to figure out what the hell he was going to do when Livie came back. At some point he was going to have to be up front and honest with her about where he stood.

And he was going to have to shore up enough strength to handle it when she walked away for good.

Chapter Nineteen

Finally. Fi-nal-ly.

Olivia had cinched the promotion. Her boss was all too anxious to announce the new shift in authority and then he'd taken her and several coworkers—including Steve— out for drinks. She'd gotten out way too late and ended up staying in her condo for the night.

Now the early morning sun was shining as she headed back into Haven. She passed the sign, announcing the miniscule population; she passed the hill with Bella Vous resting proudly on top, she traveled down the main part of town passing Knobs and Knockers, then the roundabout with the tall, antique clock.

Haven was a beautiful place full of charm, but it wasn't Atlanta. Atlanta thrived with nightlife, theaters, her coworkers, and friends.

As she drove farther through town and stopped at lights, people would wave. She'd been here too long. People all around loved her father and the fact she was back in town seemed to get them gossiping and speculating. Hopefully, they could be given facts fairly soon about the renovations. All they needed was the green light on the grants and then Zach's proposed plans to be approved by the city engineers.

There were careful steps to take, but Olivia was confident when she went back to Atlanta, the airport would be in good hands.

Jax's hands.

Swallowing the lump of emotion, she turned down the road that led straight to the airport. She owed him the courtesy of explaining what happened in Atlanta. The entire drive home she rehearsed what she'd say, how she'd finally end their intimate relationship. From here on out, they had to be business partners only, not bed partners.

In two weeks she'd be back to her big city, back to her condo and her new corner office with two walls of windows offering her a beautiful city view. She couldn't wait to take a seat behind her new desk in her new space.

As she pulled into the lot, she noticed only Jax's truck was there. It was still early and she hoped he wasn't out on a flight. She wanted to talk to him before her excitement from the promotion wore off. If she sat in his office too long waiting on him, she wasn't sure where her thoughts would go and what doubts would creep in.

Being in her hometown had a way of skewing her thoughts, but she'd just been handed the top position she'd been vying for and nothing was going to take that from her—not nostalgia and not a fling.

Olivia shut off her car and pulled in a deep breath as she tugged on the door. As she stood beside her car, she glanced to the main building while smoothing a hand through her hair. She'd grabbed her favorite yellow sundress from her closet and a little kitten heel, strappy sandal, and opted to leave her hair down.

Why she went to great lengths to look good for this talk was beyond her, but she had to. She needed to feel back in control of her life and for the first time in the past several weeks, she finally could say she was back on top.

She made her way across the gravelly lot and headed straight to the side door that would lead into Jax's office. If he wasn't in there, his flight pattern would be listed so she'd know how long he'd be gone.

The old door squeaked open, and her heels clicked on the concrete floor as she made her way down the hall. His office door was closed, but she kept going. Nerves curled deep within her, but Olivia knew she was out of time. They both knew this was coming, they just needed to talk about . . . well, everything.

Olivia slid her hand over the cool knob and turned. Easing the door open, she peeked inside and was instantly met with that piercing blue stare she'd become so familiar with.

His eyes locked with hers as she let herself in. "Bad time?" she asked, not sure where to start.

"Just got in."

Olivia remained in the doorway. "Do you have a flight or lessons this morning?"

Jax stared at her another minute before he came to his feet, never once taking his eyes from her. Olivia swallowed as he circled the desk and came around to stand directly in front of her.

Without a word, he grabbed her shoulders and pulled her farther into the tiny space. He closed the door, again never taking those striking eyes from her. Jax then backed her against the door and with an expert flick, he slid the lock into place. The click seemed to echo and every part of Olivia started humming.

There wasn't just passion in those eyes, there was pure fire.

His hands slid down over her hips and to the hem of her dress. "I missed you."

The featherlight touch of his fingertips slid along her bare thighs and her entire body went on alert. Mercy, she'd missed him, his touch, the way he looked at her as if she were the air for his lungs.

He continued pulling the dress up. "Did you wear this for me?" he asked, gliding his lips along the sensitive spot just below her ear. "Because you look hot."

Yeah, she had worn it for him, but she didn't know he'd be all over her when she arrived. Not that she was complaining. But she did need to talk to him.

His hands palmed her backside and jerked her toward his hips. Whatever words had formed in her head vanished. She'd try to recollect those thoughts later.

"What are you doing?" she whispered.

Jax eased his head back just enough to flash her that naughty grin. "Baby, you know what I'm doing."

When he called her "baby" in that low, whisky-smooth voice, she couldn't suppress the tremble. When the man spoke to her like that, she couldn't help but think of promises. Olivia's body arched up from the door and into his.

"You missed me, too," he told her as his lips traveled down the column of her throat. "I wondered."

Well, she could say whatever she wanted, but her body betrayed her and always told the truth. Olivia thrust her hands into his hair and pulled him up. She caught sight of that devilish grin once more before she pulled his lips to hers.

They would talk later. Right now her body was too revved up and she needed him.

Jax lifted her up, her legs instantly went around his waist. He turned and took two steps, then she heard a crash and realized he'd cleared the desk. Nobody had cleared a desk for her before. The fact that he was that anxious only made him that much sexier . . . as if he needed help.

He sat her on the cool top and stepped between her spread knees.

"What if someone stops by?" she asked.

Jax reached behind his head and yanked his shirt off, then he went to work on his worn jeans. "I've locked my office door. So long as you're quiet and don't moan like you do, we should be fine."

They should be fine. But what if someone just dropped in? She would be mortified.

Jax's hand slid up and under her dress, sliding beneath the edge of her panties and Olivia decided she didn't care if someone stopped by. They could wait.

She flattened her palms on the desk behind her and shifted to give him better access. As she stared at that toned chest sprinkled with dark hair and that familiar tattoo, she bit down on her lip to keep from crying out.

"You can make noise if you want," he told her, smiling as he leaned down to glide his mouth over the vee in her dress. "I'm not expecting anybody and I'd hate to be deprived of those sweet sounds you make."

He slid one finger in and Olivia couldn't suppress the groan. He felt too good and she'd missed him. Her hips jerked of their own accord and her head fell back. Jax used his other hand and slid the straps of her dress down her shoulders.

That mouth traveled all over her heated skin and Olivia literally ached for more. She was done being tortured. It had been a few days since she'd experienced his touch and she hadn't even realized how much she missed it until he got his hands on her . . . and his lips.

Pushing off her hands, she eased up and scooted forward on the edge of the desk. She reached for the opening in his jeans and trembled as her fingers brushed against a hard abdomen. His muscles tightened beneath her touch and he batted her hands away.

Jax reached for protection from his wallet and in no time had shed his clothes. He reached for her once again, only this time when he reached beneath her skirt, it was to jerk on her panties . . . which came apart with a snap.

Olivia didn't care about her torn underwear, she cared about the ache that only Jax could cure.

She wrapped her legs around his waist and let out a low moan when he joined their bodies. He covered her mouth with his as he flattened his palm against her back and eased her torso flush with his. It was almost as if he couldn't get close enough.

Olivia jerked her hips, held on to his shoulders, and opened for his kiss. Jax knew exactly how to make her feel desirable—now was no exception. She hadn't expected this when she arrived today, but she couldn't deny how fabulous it felt to be with him again.

For the last time.

"Livie," he muttered against her lips.

Her body tightened at her name. He seemed to know exactly the moment she started to break because he slammed his mouth over hers again and arched her back onto the desk. Olivia locked her heels behind him and clenched her knees against his waist. Waves of pleasure crashed over her and as she dug her nails into his bare back, Jax's body tightened. Muscles beneath her hands bunched as he rested his head next to hers.

When his body stopped trembling, Olivia held on. She didn't want him to rise up and look at her. She didn't want to break this moment because she knew the second they released each other, they would never be back to anything like this again.

Was it so wrong for her to want to make this last?

* * *

Jax pulled away, instantly missing Olivia wrapped all around him. She lay half dressed, sprawled across the desk, and he knew he'd never be able to sit there and work again—not without seeing this exact image of her with her dress bunched around her waist and the top scooping so low he was awarded the view of a very sexy, lacy strapless bra.

When she threw her arm over her face as if to block out the world, Jax wasn't sure what to say. He quickly got dressed because if someone did come by, at least he could step out and give her privacy.

But something was wrong. He could feel the tension from the moment she'd stepped into the room. Perhaps that's what spawned this morning's quickie, but he'd known when he saw her again that he'd want her. Their attraction clearly wasn't the problem. But he hadn't expected the need to be so all-consuming. He'd allowed her to become just as important as everything else he loved in his life.

Wait. Love? No, he couldn't . . . could he?

Jax glanced back to Olivia and realized she was either having regrets or she was gearing up for a battle. Either way, this did not bode well for him . . . or them.

"Care to tell me what's got you so silent?" he asked, fastening his jeans.

He pulled on his boots and shirt before Olivia replied. Without unlocking the door, Jax leaned against it. She wasn't going anywhere until he knew what the hell was going on . . . though he had a feeling he wouldn't like whatever she had to say.

Still lying on her back, arm thrown across her face, and dress all askew, she said, "I got the promotion."

Jax cringed. Who knew four words could be so life-altering and so depressing? But he knew she'd get the job.

Anyone who knew her had to realize her worth and he wasn't the least bit surprised.

Then again, she didn't seem overly joyed about it. So, that was a point in his favor . . . wasn't it?

"Congratulations."

What else was there to say? Please don't leave me? He'd never begged in his life and he sure as hell wasn't about to start now. It was obvious she was fighting her own internal battle without him gearing up to fight, too. She either wanted him or she didn't.

Olivia sat up and smoothed all that mass of hair away from her face. Without looking at him, she slid her arms back into the straps and adjusted the top of her dress. She jerked the hem down over her legs and let out a sigh as she finally met his gaze from across the room.

"Do you mean that?"

Jax shrugged. "Of course. Why wouldn't I?"

"Because we obviously have a complicated relationship and I wasn't sure how you'd react."

Even though his heart literally ached, Jax let out a laugh. "I'm a big boy, Livie. I knew you weren't staying whether you got the promotion or not."

Her brows drew in. "You don't seem upset."

Jax threw his arms out wide. "Do you want me to be upset? I don't do games, Livie. You either want to stay and see these renovations through or you don't. I can't tell you what to do."

She hopped down off the desk and adjusted her dress. "I didn't ask you to tell me what to do, but I thought maybe you'd give me some hint as to what you're feeling. And the renovations aren't the issue, we both know that."

Admitting more would give her all the power here and he was barely hanging on as it was. She wanted to be excited about her job, so he needed to be genuinely happy for her.

"Want to open up and share feelings?" he asked, pushing off the door. "I'm glad you got the promotion because you clearly deserve it. I'm excited and nervous to see how these renovations work out and how that will affect my business."

Silence settled between them and she crossed her arms over her chest as she continued to stare at him. "That's it? That's all you feel? We just had sex on your desk and all you feel is . . ."

"What?" he asked.

"Nothing. Forget it. This makes things easier, doesn't it?" She attempted a smile, but failed miserably. "So, what was this? Just one last hurrah before I leave town for good?"

Her harsh words were like a slap to his face. That's exactly what this looked like, but damn it, everything between them was so much more. If they'd had sex on the desk or a bed, his emotions would still be just as deep and just as strong.

"If you're leaving town, then I guess this was it."

Her lips thinned as she continued to stare at him. He wanted to tell her exactly how he felt, but that would border on begging and he refused to go there. She had to make the decision for herself and, clearly, she'd made it. All this time they'd been nothing but physical and he'd been so naïve in thinking they were more.

He'd been played for a fool again.

When she continued to stare without saying a word, Jax reached behind him and flicked the lock on the door. Keeping his eyes on her, he stepped aside and silently gave her the out she clearly wanted.

Jax hooked his thumbs through the loops of his jeans

and leaned back against the wall. Though his heart was breaking, he couldn't let her see just how she'd destroyed him.

Livie bit down on her bottom lip and blinked as if trying to fight back her emotions. If she'd just tell him what she was feeling, what she wanted, maybe they could work this out.

The second she started for the door, Jax knew there would be no working it out. She'd gotten what she wanted—the job and the sex.

As she opened the door, her arm brushed against his and his entire body tightened. That sweet jasmine scent mocked him when she passed through and the soft click of her heels on the concrete floors out in the hangar echoed.

Unable to take the pain anymore, he slammed the door and didn't give a damn that she'd heard. He was done. They were done. And he was utterly and completely shattered.

Chapter Twenty

Olivia jerked the laces on her running shoes and cursed the tear that fell onto the back of her hand. Why had she gone to the airport to begin with? She could've texted or called.

But no. She thought Jax deserved to be told in person exactly what was going on. The second he'd touched her, though, that had been it. The man knew how to light her up like nobody else ever had and the whole alpha swipe of the things off his desk had been the biggest turn-on of her life.

Unfortunately, their personal relationship was over— the slamming of his office door was like one giant exclamation point. She could still hear that echo through the hangar. She'd managed to hold it together until she'd pulled out of the lot. Then she'd had to park on the side of the road until she could manage the drive home.

What was she so upset about? She'd gotten the job. She'd found a solution to the airport and had placed her childhood home on the market. Wasn't that all what she'd set out to do only a short time ago?

She'd vowed not to leave Haven until everything was resolved . . . and now it was.

Olivia pushed off her bed and adjusted the waistband of her running shorts. Jade and Melanie were out already, which was a blessing because she wasn't quite ready to answer questions or dive too far into why she couldn't stop the tears.

She'd hurt Jax. There, she admitted it. She'd seen the pain in his eyes though he tried so hard to mask his emotions. The last thing she ever wanted to do was hurt him, but she'd warned him once before that someone was going to end up on the wrong side of a broken heart. Unfortunately, they both had.

Olivia bounded down the back steps leading to the kitchen. She swiped at her damp cheeks just as the back door opened and Melanie and Jade stepped in.

Both friends glanced at her and that was all it took for the damn to burst again. Melanie stepped forward.

"No," Olivia stated, holding her hands out. "Don't touch me, hug me, or ask me about my day. I just . . . I need to go for a run and clear my head."

"I have to assume you're not upset over the promotion," Jade stated, still holding on to the doorknob.

Olivia shook her head. "No. I got the job. I'll start in two weeks."

"Congratulations?" Melanie asked in that unsure tone. "I mean, I guess you're happy about that since you've worked so hard, but—"

"Oh, there's a but," Olivia confirmed with a sniff. She rubbed her eyes and wondered if she should put on her sunglasses to head out so the neighborhood didn't see her puffy red eyes. "The but has Jax written all over it. Right now, though, I can't talk about it."

"Go on," Jade stated, stepping aside so Olivia could get out. "When you get back we'll make a nice lunch and talk. Someone is coming to look at the house tonight at seven, by the way. Sophie texted me this morning because she wasn't sure when you'd be back."

Olivia nodded. "Okay. We'll do lunch, I'll explain everything, and then we'll make sure the place is picked up for the showing."

"Want us to come with you?" Jade asked, her brows drawn in.

Olivia shook her head and grabbed her phone and earbuds from the counter. "No, but thanks. I need some time alone."

Alone. She was definitely feeling that at the moment now that she and Jax had pretty much ended. No, *alone* wasn't the right term. Empty, shattered, broken.

Olivia started with a jog around the corner of her house and set off down the street. With earbuds in and music blaring, she attempted to focus on the future. She had a new job waiting for her, the new office was being re-designed to her liking, and she was going to have her own team. Her very own team of employees to assist her on projects. It was absolutely her dream come true.

So why did she still have that vise-like grip around her chest? Why was she still blinking back tears?

Someone honked and waved as they passed. She wasn't sure, but it looked like Mrs. Kinard. The people of this town were so friendly whether you lived here your whole life or were completely new.

Olivia had a really great feeling about the airport and the direction they'd decided to go. If all of Zach's designs were approved, she knew it would be a big job, but the end result would be amazing. Part of her wished her father was here to see this come to fruition. What would he think of her having a hand in all the changes? No doubt he'd be thrilled she was back and had decided not to sell.

Between reading in his journal and the emotional mess

with Jax, was it any wonder she was a walking tissue commercial?

Before she knew it she was heading by Cash's gym. A familiar black truck sat in the parking lot and Olivia's heart lurched. Most likely Jax was inside taking out his frustrations as well.

Olivia tried to keep her gaze away from the windows as she focused on the next block up ahead. Unfortunately, her foot landed on a crack in the sidewalk and she felt her ankle give. Olivia hit the concrete hard and cried out as she landed.

Damn it. Her ankle throbbed, her palms and knees were skinned up . . . and all right in front of Cash's gym. She didn't dare look up to see if anyone witnessed her wipeout.

With careful movements, she pushed herself up and attempted to put weight on her ankle. Sharp, piercing pain shot up her leg. Olivia sat back down on the sidewalk with a groan. This was not happening to her. Could this day get any worse?

A car door slammed and she closed her eyes and sighed. Apparently, it could because now someone was approaching her.

Please don't be Jax. Please don't be Jax.

"Hey, Livie. You hurt?"

Not Jax, but that familiar voice was the next worst thing.

She turned to see Tanner striding toward her in all his uniformed glory. He was definitely hot, but he did nothing for her . . . not like Jax.

"Nope. I just thought I'd stop here to rest."

Tanner squatted next to her. "I'll let your snarky comment slide since that was a stupid question." He glanced up, then back down to her. "Jax is inside. I can go—"

"No," she all but shouted. She'd rather crawl back home

than for Jax to see her now or offer help. "I just, can you help me up?"

"Is it your ankle?" He put his arm around her waist and held her up. When she leaned against his side, he gripped her tighter. "Okay. I'm not even going to ask why you don't want me to get Jax, but how about a lift home?"

Olivia glanced to the patrol car and laughed. "Can I sit in the back and you'll turn your lights on?"

Tanner led her toward his car. "You can sit in the back, but I can't turn on the siren."

"You're no fun."

Olivia actually climbed into the front seat next to Tanner and gritted her teeth as her toes banged against the door panel.

"Hurts that bad, huh?" he asked, leaning down into the car.

"I just need to get home and ice it," she assured him with a smile. "Not a big deal."

"Want an X-ray?"

Olivia gave him a side eye. "What do you think?"

With a chuckle, he closed the door. Olivia just wanted to get out of here before Jax spotted her. She wasn't ready to face him, didn't know if she'd ever be ready, but definitely not after having hot sex in his office and then severing their personal relationship only an hour ago.

He drove her the few miles back to her house. Melanie was out front on her hands and knees fluffing the mulch. She still wore her sports bra, tank, and shorts, but was barefoot. When she spotted the cruiser, she came to her feet and swiped her forearm across her head.

Olivia opened her door, but Tanner was already out and assisting her. He wrapped his arm around her waist and lifted her from the car.

"What on earth happened?" Melanie asked, running across the lawn.

"I fell, it was stupid," Olivia muttered, still embarrassed over the fact. "Tanner happened to be there so he gave me a lift."

Melanie's gaze darted to his. "You do something other than write tickets?"

"I was in the process of chasing old ladies and giving them reckless op tickets, but decided to stop and help Olivia," he tossed back.

Olivia rolled her eyes. "If you two are done, can I get inside for some ice? I'm swelling around my shoe."

Melanie reached out. "I've got her from here, Officer."

He gently released her and steadied her until Melanie had her arm secure around Olivia's waist. This was so ridiculous to have to lean on someone just to stand. But she really didn't think anything was broken.

Jade ran out of the house. "What in the world?" she cried as she crossed through the front yard. "We leave you alone and you come back in a cop car?"

"Not my first choice, but since only one ankle is cooperating, Tanner came to my rescue."

Jade flanked Olivia's other side. "This is just like when Mel hurt herself in that marathon. Really, ladies. Watch yourselves."

"Yes, because we love to just get hurt on purpose," Melanie stated.

"I'll get her inside," Jade stated. "Why don't you thank Tanner and finish the mulching?"

Melanie laughed and called over her shoulder. "Thanks, Tanner."

"Anytime, ma'am."

Olivia may have been in some pain, but she didn't miss the way Melanie bit her lip and shuddered. Tanner was quite an attractive guy and even Melanie couldn't deny that. Apparently, she couldn't deny her attraction, either, but Olivia wasn't about to call her on that . . . not when Olivia's own personal life was off-limits for now.

By the time they got inside the house, her ankle was throbbing something fierce.

"I'll get a bag of ice and some pain reliever," Melanie offered.

Jade eased Olivia down onto the leather sofa and pushed the ottoman over. After propping her leg up, Melanie reached down to unlace her shoe.

"Let me." Jade sat on the edge of the ottoman and carefully tugged at the laces. "So you just fell?"

"I stepped wrong on the sidewalk."

No way was she going to admit she'd been eyeing the gym and Jax's truck.

"You've got some serious swelling," Jade stated. "You sure you don't want to get an X-ray?"

That was the last thing she wanted. "I'll be fine after some ice and pain meds, though you all might have to make that lunch you promised and feed me right here."

"Happy to do so," Melanie said as she came back in. She placed the ice bag gently on the side of Olivia's ankle. "Sorry, but I just want to get it on there good."

"I'm fine." Olivia reached for the bottled water and the pain meds. "Thanks."

Her earbuds still dangled around her neck and her phone was still tucked in her armband. She quickly took the pills and started pulling off her accessories.

"Well, this day has gone all to hell," she muttered, dropping her head back against the cushions. "I'll give you both the run-down, but please hold off questions until the pills kick in."

Olivia closed her eyes as she felt the sofa dip beside her. Melanie no doubt wanted to be close to offer support. How much comforting was she going to need? Olivia had no clue because right now she felt utterly helpless. Oh, sure, her career was at the greatest point of her life, but on the personal side, Olivia had never felt more confused and empty.

"I was offered the promotion, there was fanfare and drinks until late last night so I stayed at my condo. Then I drove in early this morning and went straight to the airport to see Jax. We had sex, we broke things off, I kept my feelings bottled up, he slammed the door."

Wow, even this abbreviated version hurt to discuss. Who knew what would happen once she started delivering details?

"That's when I came home and opted for a run. Saw you guys, headed out, ran past Cash's gym where I saw Jax's truck and where I face-planted on the sidewalk."

Her life was just one big ball of awkward lately.

"Tanner happened to be coming by, stopped and rescued me." Olivia took in a deep breath and opened her eyes. "That brings us up to date."

Silence settled into the room as two sets of eyes continued to just stare at her.

"Say something," Olivia demanded.

"Have the pain meds kicked in yet?" Jade asked. "Because I only have one question."

"Only one?" Melanie asked. "I have at least ten."

Olivia held her hand up. "Your ten can wait. I'll start with Jade's one."

Jade patted Olivia's knee and leaned forward. "Did you tell him you love him?"

All the air vanished from her lungs. Love? She didn't love Jax. What in the world did she know about love? How could such a whirlwind affair and arguing over business translate to love? It just wasn't possible.

"I don't love him," Olivia stated. "So of course I didn't say the words. There's no reason to mess things up by pulling that word in."

Melanie took her hand and squeezed. "If any man ever looks at me the way I've seen Jax eye you, I would be one lucky woman. My ex only looked at me with disgust and anger most of the time. I would love for someone to look at me like I was his only reason for breathing."

Jax didn't do that . . . did he? Olivia glanced back to Jade, who was all serious. Normally she was the friend Olivia could go to for snarky, honest advice, but apparently, she was on board with Melanie.

"I'm pretty sure Jax doesn't love me." Olivia sat up a little higher, causing her ice bag to shift. Jade quickly adjusted it. "I mean, he's never said so, he's never asked me to stay. We have sex, we argue."

"You went to a party with his daughter," Jade reminded her. "You had a sleepover with them—that screams family. You took her shopping."

"*We* took her shopping," Olivia corrected. "I can be friends with Piper, she's adorable."

"She's in love with you just as much as Jax is," Melanie murmured.

Damn it. Olivia hadn't thought of the repercussions that this would all create for Piper. There was no way Olivia could just cut things off with her. She had to continue that relationship and explain that her life was in Atlanta, but she'd always be part of the airport and Piper could call any time. The girl needed another woman in her life and Olivia could fill in temporarily . . . until Jax found someone permanently.

Pain sliced deep into her heart. The thought of another woman coming into Jax's life was crushing. The idea that someone else would make shadow puppets with them during a storm or have movie night or do birthday parties . . . it was all too much to consume right now.

"There's no love," Olivia repeated, mainly to make herself feel better or at least give herself some reassurance she was doing the right thing. "Besides, Jax doesn't need a woman in his life. He's told me before how awful his marriage was and how he won't do that again. He's definitely only upset because I'm the one who ended things and I'll be leaving town soon."

She refused to believe anything more than that because if she thought he was having deeper feelings, then that would put a whole slew of issues in her path and she simply didn't have the energy to jump them.

Chapter Twenty-One

Jax had just finished his preflight check when his cell vibrated in his pocket. Since his lessons were canceled for the day, he was restless and needed to get up in the sky where he could think. Piper was already getting picked up from preschool by the sitter since Jax had planned to be gone anyway. He'd still make a short day of it and get her earlier than planned, but first he needed to clear his head.

Hitting the hell out of that punching bag earlier hadn't helped. The only thing he knew to do was get back to the way his life was pre-Olivia. So flying and spending time with Piper was his best bet to try to find some sense of normalcy in his life.

Jax pulled his cell from his pocket and read the text twice. He didn't respond. What the hell should he do now? Didn't he promise himself not to get tangled up with Olivia? Didn't he preach to himself just how wrong it would be to give in to those desires that started when he'd been too young to know what to do with such emotions?

Propping a hand on the side of the plane, Jax drew in a deep breath. Some guidance from Paul would be really useful right now. Paul always had the right attitude and knew what to do in every situation.

Jax used to think he was prepared for anything after serving overseas in the air force for so long, but nothing had prepared him for life with Olivia . . . or without her.

Resigned to the fact he wasn't going anywhere—at least not by plane—Jax cursed himself for being all kinds of a fool. He jerked his keys from his pocket and headed out. After making sure the hangar and his office were locked up for the day, he hopped into his truck and headed to the one place he didn't think he'd be again.

When he pulled into Olivia's drive, she was sitting on the porch on an old rocker with her foot propped up. She immediately glanced his way, her eyes widening.

Was he really doing this? Was he really going to put himself in this path again?

Yes and yes. Because he was a damn fool.

He stepped from the truck and rounded the hood. Whistling as he headed up the sidewalk, he quickly rehearsed in his head what he wanted to say.

"Who told you?" she demanded. "Jade? Melanie? No, it was Tanner, wasn't it? Took him longer than I thought."

Jax stopped at the base of the steps and met her fiery gaze. "You didn't want me to know you were injured?"

"It's a twisted ankle. It's nothing major."

"If you're hurt, that's major."

She shrugged and glanced out toward the street. "Now you've seen me. You can go, unless you needed to discuss the airport."

So, she was going to be difficult. Fine. He didn't need her to apologize for earlier or tell him she'd changed her mind and was staying. They could be civil and business partners and anything else that he'd hoped would just have to fade into the background.

"I actually do want to discuss the airport."

Her eyes whipped back to him. That's right. He'd thrown her off because she hadn't expected him to say that. He wanted to continue to keep her world tilted because his sure as hell was.

"Fine. Have a seat."

Oh, she wasn't running this show. "I actually have something to show you at the airport. I'll give you a lift and bring you back."

Her eyes narrowed as she eased her foot off the railing.

The screen door screeched open and Jade stepped out. "Oh, hey, Jax."

He gave her a nod in greeting. "Livie and I are heading to the airport to discuss some things."

"No, we're not."

His eyes held hers. "We. Are."

Jade laughed. "Go right ahead, Olivia. Melanie and I will finish here. We only need to run the sweeper, so it's not like you could do that anyway."

Jax raised his brows.

"There's a showing for the house later," Jade explained.

Things were moving too damn fast. Was she that eager to leave? Damn it. He was going to put himself out there one more time and then he'd be done. He called himself every kind of moron and masochist, but the truth was he loved this frustrating woman. He loved her and he damn well knew she loved him. She loved being here, so why the hell was she so determined to leave?

He had to get her back to her roots. Just once more, he had to try. Then, if she truly wanted to go, he wouldn't stand in her way.

Without a word, he mounted the steps. He shot Jade a wink as he bent down and lifted Livie up and over his shoulder. She draped over him like a sack of potatoes.

"Put me down, you Neanderthal."

"I love when you talk dirty, but we don't have time for that."

He shot a glance to Jade. "Don't worry about her. I'll

have her the rest of the evening. We'll be back well after the showing."

Jade merely offered a grin and headed back inside the house. Livie continued to smack at his ass while he walked toward the truck. She could throw all the temper tantrums she wanted, but until she could walk on two feet, she was at his mercy. Just where he wanted her.

He plopped her in the passenger seat of his truck and reached to fasten her seat belt. She swatted his hands away.

"I can get my own damn belt," she grumbled.

Good. She was just as irritated as he was. This would make for an explosive chat. Maybe they could keep their clothes on this time.

As he drove to the airport, Livie remained silent, but her anger radiated off her in waves. So he started whistling.

"Why are you doing this?"

Jax shrugged as he turned onto the road leading up to the airport. "I enjoy the tune, plus—"

"Why are you doing this?" she repeated. "Why are you taking me anywhere? We talked earlier."

"We had sex on my desk and you walked out," he reminded her. "I still have plenty to say and you're going to listen."

"I don't want to."

Too damn bad. This relationship, crazy and screwed up as it was, needed to be dealt with. Not her storming out and him slamming doors.

He parked right next to the hangar and killed the engine. Shifting in his seat, he rested his arm on the steering wheel and stared at her profile. She continued to stare straight ahead as if she had no clue why she was here.

"What are you thinking right now?" he asked.

Livie blinked, but didn't even look his way. "You don't want to know."

Probably not, but call him a glutton.

"Then I'll tell you what I think." He reached out, sliding his finger beneath her chin to turn her gaze toward his. "I think you're looking for a reason to leave, you're looking for that out you so desperately want so you don't have to form any type of emotional commitment."

Her mouth dropped open, then snapped shut. "If you brought me here to analyze me, you wasted your time. I'm not looking for anything other than moving my career forward."

Ah, yes. That damn career that she was married to.

He stared another second before he jerked on his door handle and hopped out. The sun stretched across the horizon, showing off brilliant shades of orange and yellow. The perfect evening.

Being a parent, Jax had learned early on that actions spoke louder than words. He rounded the hood and opened Livie's door. She unfastened her seat belt and started to get out.

As soon as he reached for her, she shot him a glare. "Don't even think about throwing me over your shoulder again."

"No problem." He shoved one hand behind her back and another beneath her knees and lifted her out. "Shut the door, would ya?"

She did as he asked, but let out the most unladylike growl in the process. He headed to the hangar and eased her down beside him, keeping an arm firmly around her waist.

"I'm not flying with you."

He pulled the keys from his pocket and shoved one into the padlock. "Of course you are. It's the only place I can guarantee you'll listen. We'll keep our clothes on, and you won't storm out."

As soon as he had the door unlocked, he pulled it open

and lifted her back into his arms. Damn it. This felt too right. Could she seriously keep denying this? Was she going to insist that what they had was nothing more than a heated affair? Because he knew there was much more and if she were honest with herself, so did she.

Even though he'd done a preflight check before he left, Jax still sat Livie in a chair and went about going through the routine again. Safety always trumped rush, especially when it came to flying.

By the time he was done with the check, had pulled the plane from the hangar, and went around it once more, he still had no clue what he was going to say to her.

Jax assisted her, carefully and a bit awkwardly, into the passenger seat of the plane. She seemed to still be just as angry. "It's good that you're quiet," he told her as he put his headphones on. "Makes it easier for me to get everything out."

There were two ways he could approach her and he honestly didn't know which one would be the most effective. Livie was all business, all the time. Perhaps that's the side he needed to appeal to. But, on the other hand, they were so much more than legal documents. They'd been intimate, just this morning in fact, and they knew each other's hopes for the future.

He picked up her headset and extended it to her, smiling when she yanked it from his hands.

Jax started the plane and slowly circled around to the end of the runway. Once they were beyond the crucial period of takeoff, he'd get his thoughts all out.

"Can I do it?"

Her abrupt question caught him off guard and he turned to her.

She met his gaze. "If I'm going to be leaving, I'd like to fly once more before I go."

Oh, of course. She was leaving. Because she hadn't thrown that around enough since she arrived. Jax gave a clipped nod and watched as she checked her gauges, the wings, and pulled in a deep breath. She gripped the controls and started them forward.

Jax didn't know the last time he'd been in a plane piloted by someone else, but he had to admit, seeing Livie at the controls was a hell of a turn-on . . . which was the last thing he needed.

She took off with the ease of a seasoned professional. Jax couldn't help but think Paul was smiling down on his prodigal daughter.

"I'll fly, you talk," she told him once they'd reached the desired altitude.

He had to admit, he loved hearing her voice come through the headset. He wanted to get used to this, but he also had to be realistic.

"I want a timeline of when you're leaving and a projected time of when things will get started on the airport."

Livie's grip tightened on the controls, her knuckles turned white, and he had to bite the inside of his lip to keep from smiling. He'd purposely thrown her off. She expected him to discuss their rocky relationship. Not going to happen. The second she took those controls he knew how to make her think, make her want. She hadn't lost the love of flying. The temptation had been too great for her to avoid.

"Well, um, I'm leaving in two weeks and the outline Jade had drawn up indicated that the process should take about a year to fully develop."

A year. Sweet mercy, that seemed like a lifetime. He couldn't even imagine how his tiny piece of real estate would grow. But he honestly didn't want to go through this process without her. They were a team whether she wanted to admit it or not.

"I'm going to need to give my renters some information," he went on. "Is their rent staying the same? Will there be a time the hangars are out of commission while the renovations are going on? My customers are going to have to be—"

"I get it," she demanded. "I know. There's a lot to take in."

"We're partners in this," he reminded her.

She eased the plane a little to the west and headed farther away from Haven. Surprisingly, he figured she'd get uncomfortable with the topic and take them back to the airport. That would so be a Livie move.

"Are Jade and Melanie leaving when you do?" he asked.

"I'm not sure. We haven't really discussed that. I'm sure they'd rather stay behind. They're facing their own issues in Atlanta, so they're not as eager to get back. Jade quit her job and Melanie can technically work from anywhere since she has a successful online business."

As if she needed to twist that knife deeper.

"You think things are going to be neat and tidy, Livie?"

She glanced his way for the briefest of moments before she focused her attention back to the darkening sky. The timing of this flight couldn't be any better. Livie loved being in the sky at night and he wanted to drive home the fact that all of this could be hers—*was hers*—if she would just reach out and take it.

For years he wondered what would happen if she ever came back and now she was here . . . but her temporary status had hung over their heads the entire time. He wasn't nearly finished with her. She'd have to come back at some point and each time he had to deal with her whether by phone or in person, he'd be reminding her exactly what she was missing.

Was that fair? Not at all, considering she'd worked damn hard to get that promotion. And if he thought she was stoked about starting, he'd leave her be. But his Livie was torn, she was confused, and he knew if she listened to her heart she'd have the right answer.

They flew in silence and Jax was perfectly fine with that. He wanted her to be thinking, and he needed to do some evaluating himself. Even though his heart was crushed, he had to remain strong because he would live. He'd go on and do what he loved, which was flying and raising Piper.

"Will you see Piper before you go?"

"I'm not leaving for two weeks."

"Will you see her?" he repeated. "Because I don't want you just disappearing. She's grown pretty fond of you."

Livie's deep sigh resonated through the headphones and had his entire body tightening. No, he'd never have enough of Livie Daniels. Not if they lived for another hundred years. She was it for him and he hoped like hell she'd come to some quick conclusion.

Since when did he become so desperate? Since when did he let control of his emotions slip away?

The moment Livie stepped out of her little sports car and he put his greasy hands on her ass . . . pretty much since then. And then again when she obviously fell in love with Piper. There was no denying that Livie adored Piper and that was a huge part of why Jax wanted Livie in his life. He and Piper were a package deal and they were both head over heels for Livie.

"I wouldn't just leave without talking to her," Livie stated. She eased the plan a little more, circling back to the airport. "I hope she calls and texts me so I can stay up-to-date on her birthday parties, school work, her new friends. Though I'm not a fan of that one little girl, Megan, I think? She seemed too snotty for Piper so watch out for that one."

Jax was not going to have this discussion. She was either going to be in their personal lives, or she wasn't.

"I don't want Piper becoming too attached," he stated, as if it weren't already too late. "I think if we just explain that you're going back to your job and your life, then she'll understand. She knew you were from Atlanta and were only here for the airport, but she'll miss you regardless."

"So you don't want me to text or call?" Livie asked as they began their descent.

"It would be best if you didn't."

Livie let out a humorless laugh. "We're not talking about Piper anymore, are we?"

"No."

As much as the pain continued to slice deep, he knew if he wanted her to ache like he did, he was going to have to sever all ties. Well, except for the obvious with the airport. But, she wanted all business, so that's what he planned on giving her.

"So cutting me out permanently, huh?"

Jax didn't reply as Livie checked the gauges and lined up with the bright blue lights of the runway. The plane bounced a bit when they hit the pavement and any other time he'd call her on her rustiness, but that wasn't the best idea right now.

"I'm not the one doing the cutting," he told her as she slowed the plane. He should've kept that thought to himself, but the words had just slipped out.

"So we're at the fighting stage?" She took the curve at the end of the runway and circled back toward the hangar, letting the engines cool before she came to a complete stop. "Because that's not how I want to leave things."

Jax jerked the buckle on his seat belt and snorted. "No,

you just want to leave and pretend you never got involved with me."

"That's not true."

"You're a liar."

The plane came to a stop and she twisted in her seat to stare at him. She yanked the headset off and clutched it in her lap.

"I don't ever want to forget we got involved," she claimed. "Is that honestly what you think of me? That I regret what we did?"

"I doubt you regret it, but you're done and want to pretend like it didn't affect your life when I can tell you"—he leaned forward and came within a breath of her—"it did."

Her swift intake of breath had him cursing himself. He was teetering on a dangerous line, crossing back into the territory he'd told himself to steer clear of until he knew what the hell was going to happen between them.

The lights from the control panel lit up her face, making her vibrant eyes sparkle even more as she held his gaze. The floral lotion or perfume or whatever she used to drive him insane enveloped him. He wanted nothing more than to forget every single ounce of heartache and kiss the hell out of her until she came to her senses.

"Fine," she muttered. "You win, Jax. Is that what you want to hear? You're right. What we had is more than I've ever found with anyone."

Had. Out of everything she'd just said, that one word completely summed up everything. She may have feelings for him, but she was already pushing everything into her past . . . because she didn't want him in her future.

There was no use in continuing down this path because he was wasting his time and she . . . well, she was mentally already gone.

Jax shut the plane off and got out. The fresh air didn't

help, but he took a minute to just breathe. He needed to calm down. Unfortunately, he was going to have to carry Livie where they needed to go because of that damn ankle. He'd asked for this. All of it. He'd insisted on going to her house after they'd clearly ended things earlier.

But hell. She was going to be here for two more weeks? How would they survive?

By the time he circled the plane, she'd opened her door and was attempting to climb down on one good ankle. Stubborn woman.

He gripped her around the waist and eased her down until she stood before him, but leaning completely against his chest. She was hurt more than she wanted to let on because Livie never wanted to lean on anyone, literally or figuratively.

Her palms flattened against his chest and she stared up at him. "I told you one of us would get hurt," she murmured. "I didn't want this to happen."

"The hurt or the intimacy?"

Jax couldn't help himself. He brushed a strand of hair over her shoulder and slid his fingertips over her collarbone before dropping his hand. She shuddered beneath his touch and only solidified what he already knew.

"I didn't want any of it," she admitted. "I knew how this would end and it's not good and here we are both miserable. But I have to go, Jax. I can't stay here. Haven isn't my life and if I stayed, I'd always wonder if I'd given up my dream. How can I trust what we have would be permanent?"

"So you'd rather play it safe?" he countered. "You'd rather just let your fear guide your life? That's not how I work, Livie, so if that's how you want to live, then it's best you go."

As much as those words hurt to say, they were one hundred percent accurate. He wouldn't want to be with a woman who was afraid to take risks. Life was all about risks and he'd wanted to take the ultimate one with her.

Her fingers curled into his shirt and she bit down on her bottom lip. He'd slay any demons for her, but right now, she was on her own.

"I have to go," she whispered.

Jax knew in that moment, he'd lost her. She'd made up her mind and just like his ex-wife, he and his daughter were not a top priority. He was done fighting for this, for them.

He reached down and picked her up, carefully settling her against his chest. When her arms looped around his neck and her head rested on his shoulder, he said nothing as he carried her to his truck.

Call him a glutton, but he was going to relish these last few moments of her in his arms. Even though she wasn't leaving for two weeks, he knew in his broken heart there would be no more times of intimacy. Once he took her back home, they would be done on every personal level. They would only be professional partners and that would break him.

"I'm sorry," she whispered, her breath tickling the side of his neck.

"Me too."

For so much, but mostly because she didn't trust him enough to ensure she wouldn't get hurt by staying.

Chapter Twenty-Two

"You can take the documents on your way out of town."

Jade stood with said documents extended to Olivia. She glared at them, then back up at her so-called friend. "Can't you just drop them off?"

Shaking her head, Jade replied, "You can. It's on your way out of town and you can't avoid him forever."

Olivia had done a stellar job of dodging Jax for the past two weeks since he romantically carried her to his truck after she'd flown her father's plane. She had called and talked to Piper on the phone to explain that she had to leave and go back to her job and home in Atlanta.

Piper understood, and no doubt Jax had already had a discussion with his toddler. Kids were resilient. Too bad adult emotions couldn't bounce back that fast.

Jade merely raised her brow and Olivia jerked the documents from her hand. "I hate you."

"Of course you do, but since Mel and I are staying behind to help sell this place, you'll love me again."

In theory, the plan sounded utterly flawless. Jade and Melanie were going to hang back for a bit since Atlanta was a whole host of issues for them right now. That would keep the worry of setting up showings off Olivia, and then when it sold she would come back and sign the papers.

The airport papers in her hand, though, was a whole other host of issues. But this would be simple, right? Go in, drop off the packet, leave. Maybe Jax would be out on a flight. It was a gorgeous Sunday afternoon, surely someone wanted to go somewhere. Oh, maybe he was giving lessons. This would be an ideal time.

"Are you standing there trying to find another excuse not to go?" Jade asked.

Olivia opened her handbag and slid the documents inside. "Not at all. I'm not afraid to stop by on my way out of town."

More like terrified. She wanted . . . everything. She wanted the job and the man, but that wasn't possible and she'd made her decision.

And guilt had spawned her to set something into motion that would probably upset Jax, but she had to do something. She knew what the airport meant to him and she knew he'd been saving for a new-to-him plane. Maybe once the surprise came through, he wouldn't hate her so much. She hoped. The thought of him hating her was more than she could take. She'd already hurt him, hurt herself, but there was no way to have it all. There just wasn't.

"You sure you're going?" Jade asked, her tone sincere and concerning. She crossed her arms over her chest and tipped her head to the side. "No one would think less of you if you decided to stay and turn down that promotion."

"I need to do this. I have to at least try."

Jade reached out and pulled Olivia into her arms. "You realize you're not near as excited now that you're leaving as you were when we first got here?" She eased back and looked Olivia in the eye. "When we first got here you were counting down to when we could leave and you could get back to work. You've been dragging your feet the past several days like maybe you're having second thoughts."

Second thoughts? More like third, fourth, fifth . . .

Olivia gave her friend a gentle squeeze. "I know what I'm doing. I'll text you when I get home and I'll be sure to send you a selfie from my new office in the morning."

"Do you need help to your car?"

Shaking her head, Olivia adjusted her handbag and reached for the handle on her luggage. "Nope. This is all I have."

Because she hadn't planned on staying so she hadn't packed much. With a deep breath, she headed out the back door and eased her suitcase down the steps.

Once she was packed up and backing out of her drive, she took a moment to stare at the house that she'd grown up in. Memories flooded her mind, stirring her heart and procuring tears she hadn't expected. This was all she'd wanted, and she was finally getting everything she'd asked for.

Blinking the moisture away, Olivia pulled out of the drive and headed toward the airport. She knew she'd better calm her emotions for the next little bit. Once she left Jax, she could have all the pity parties and emotional meltdowns she wanted. For now, though, she needed to be strong.

Her heart clenched when she spotted his truck. With fake confidence, she pulled right up beside his truck and grabbed her handbag. She adjusted her sunglasses and stepped from the car, tugging her skirt down in place.

She glanced inside her bag, making sure everything she wanted to hand over was inside and to take another minute to get herself together.

"Livie."

That familiar voice washed over her. She lifted her head to see Jax standing in the doorway to the hangar. Déjà vu of her first day back into town rushed over her. So much had happened since then. She'd made memories, and dare she say, fed some of her roots she'd established as a teen.

"Thought you'd be gone by now."

Squaring her shoulders, she crossed the grassy area. "I'm on my way out, but I needed to drop some things off to you."

She had no idea what he was thinking because he hid his eyes behind that sexy pair of aviators he always wore. After a moment, he turned toward the main building.

"Come into my office. I have something for you, too."

Fantastic. The last time she'd gone into his office he'd given her something . . . and she was still tingling from the memories.

Olivia followed him inside, instantly feeling relief from the heat when the cool air hit her. As soon as she stepped in the tiny office, the coffee mug on his desk caught her attention. MY COCKPIT IS BIGGER was in bold white letters on the black mug and Olivia truly didn't even want to think about what happened on that desk or about Jax's cockpit.

Okay, she seriously needed to drop this stuff off and get out. "I have the plans from Jade regarding the timeline, the funding, and the breakdown as to where the money will be spent in various areas. She said some of the areas are negotiable and can fluctuate, but that will be up to you and me to decide."

Jax took off his glasses and tossed them onto the desk before leaning back against it. Crossing his arms over his broad chest, he continued to stare at her. This tension was too much and threatened to take over if she didn't hurry up.

She reached into her bag and pulled out the file. "This is what she wanted you to have. I have a copy too."

He took the file and sat it beside him, that gaze still unwavering. "Jade could've brought this. Is there something else you wanted?"

Swallowing the lump of remorse, she reached back into her bag. Why did he sound so cold? So distant? This wasn't the Jax she'd gotten to know on every level. He seemed . . . hard, like he'd put up a steel barrier between them or like she was some stranger.

Pulling out the journal, she handed it over. "I want you to have this."

He stared a moment before taking it. He didn't open it, but he didn't toss it onto the desk with the files, either. Apparently, her father's journal meant more to him than the renovation plans.

"Okay, well, that's all I wanted to give you." She attempted a smile, which probably looked ridiculous because he was still frowning and wasn't making this the least bit easy. "Actually, there is one more thing."

She wasn't going to tell him this, but she figured she should leave with him having some nice thought about her . . . she hoped.

"I, um, I sold some stock with my company." She gripped the strap on her purse and wished he'd stop starring at her so intently. "There was an '87 Skyhawk that went up for auction. Similar to the one you'd been looking at but a couple years newer. It holds the same number of passengers and, um . . ."

He shifted, his brows raising. Apparently, airplane talk got his attention.

"Anyway, I bid on it and it's mine. Well, I'm gifting it to you."

Again, he said nothing. Olivia stared at him for another second before turning on her kitten heel, more than ready to retreat.

"Stop."

That demand had her stilling in the doorway, but she didn't turn back around.

"You bought me a damn airplane? Why?"

His questions caught her off guard. "Excuse me?" she asked easing back around. "Why did I get the plane? Because you'd been saving and we're expanding. Call it a good investment, but I figured you'd be a little more excited."

Was she out of her ever-loving mind? Excited? It took all of Jax's control not to snap and go off on this frustrating, beautiful, sexy-as-hell woman. She drove him out of his mind and made him want to silence her with his lips and strangle her at the same time.

"You honestly think I want you to buy my affection or use this present as some type of payment for what . . . a broken heart?" Jax laughed and pushed off his desk. "You're ridiculous."

He closed the space between them and watched as her eyes widened. But he reached beyond her and just behind the door to the bag hanging on the hook. When he pulled it out, her eyes darted to the clear sack protecting the pink suit.

"I picked this up last night from the cleaners and was going to run it to Jade or Melanie today so they could get it to you." He held it out to her, careful not to touch her in the process. "I have your shoes in my car."

She draped the sack over her arm. "My shoes?"

Keeping his eyes on hers, and trying like hell to remain impassive to everything swirling around inside him, he shoved his hands in his pockets. "You left them . . . that first night."

When her eyes widened, he knew she recalled sneaking out of his bed and out the door with no shoes. "Oh, um. Thank you."

He was close enough to touch her, breathe in her familiar floral scent, yet he continued to guard himself. And the fact she thought she could drop off business, leave the journal, and casually announce she'd bought a damn plane and he would be all right with everything was absolutely insane. Who the hell did she think he was? Had he ever struck her as someone who cared about material things? He'd been saving for his own plane and he didn't want her thinking this smoothed things over.

"Would you have bought the plane had we not gotten involved?"

Livie jerked slightly. "Excuse me?"

Shifting his stance, he gripped the doorframe right beside her head and leaned in closer. "If we hadn't slept together, if we hadn't formed a relationship outside of business, would you still have bought the Skyhawk?"

She blinked, glanced away, then looked back. "I have no idea. What does it matter?"

She still didn't get it. Jax turned and paced through the office. "Forget it," he commanded. "I'll pay you for the plane. I don't want your pity gift."

"Pity gift?" she repeated. Livie stepped back into his office and flung her suit onto his desk, then dropped her purse to the floor with a thud. "I bought this plane for *our* business and I bought it because you need it. Believe it or not, I care about what happens after I'm gone."

Jax widened his stance and crossed his arms. "Is that so? Because you've dodged me for two weeks, so you don't care too much, because I've been here. You never bothered to stop and check on the place."

"I've been busy," she insisted.

"Getting on with your life, I'm well aware. But this is my life, Livie, and I'm done with you flittering in and out as you damn well please. If you're done here, get your stuff and go. You're not the only one with a busy job."

Livie threw her arms wide, which only pulled her little

pink tank across her chest and had it lifting just slightly to show the creamy skin around her waist.

"What the hell do you want from me, Jax?" she yelled. "I'm doing all I can to try to keep all these balls in the air. I've fixed up Dad's house, I've jumped through hoops to get this partnership moving in the right direction, and now I have to get back to my job. I thought I was helping."

"Helping what?" He took a step forward, then another. "Helping ease your conscience?"

"Why are you doing this?" she cried. "Do you want me gone so badly that you're fighting and refusing to accept this gift?"

"I don't want your damn gifts and I don't want you gone," he yelled, looming over her. "I want you to stay, I want you to be part of every step of this journey to your father's airport. I wanted you in Piper's life, in my life. I want too much, Livie, and all you want is to be done here."

He stared down into her wide eyes and realized he'd opened a piece of himself he hadn't meant to reveal. Raking a hand through his hair, Jax took a step back and cursed beneath his breath. Only a fool would show his true feelings at this point. But, hey, what did he have to lose?

"I would've given you anything," he went on, calming himself down. If she was leaving, then he wanted her to be fully aware of what she was leaving behind. "I've never opened my heart or my life to another woman after my wife left. I swore it wasn't worth the heartache and Piper needed stability. Then you came back and I couldn't stop myself even if I wanted to. You stirred something so deep within me. It had nothing to do with the crush I had on you when I'd been younger; it had nothing to do with you being Paul's daughter."

Jax took a deep breath and closed the space between them, finally reaching for her because he wanted to touch her, just once more. He slid his hands over her face, his fingertips sliding into her hair. "My feelings had everything to do with the fact I'd fallen in love with you."

Livie's mouth dropped open. "What?"

"Believe me, I didn't want to love you. I even tried to deny it. There's nothing I can do to make you stay and I don't want you here when your heart is so obviously in Atlanta."

He leaned in, brushing his lips against hers before stepping back and releasing her. "Even though you're leaving, I still love you. I probably always will, but I can keep my personal feelings out of this business."

Livie's shaky hands came up to her lips. "Is that true?"

"What?"

Her hand dropped to her side. "Will you keep everything separate?"

With a shrug, he answered honestly. "I have to. I won't make things more complicated for you."

Livie stood there for a moment, then busted out laughing. "Complicated? Do you want to know what's complicated? I wanted the COO position for years. I'd worked on nothing else but gaining the attention of my superiors. I busted my ass and turned down dates, missed social events with my friends, and lost sleep over that damn promotion. But nothing was as complicated as when I came into town and you put your greasy hands all over my ass."

He wasn't going to apologize for that, either.

"Complicated is knowing that when I get back to Atlanta and walk into my condo, it will feel empty. I'll be alone and I'll be wondering what you're doing here. I'll want to know if you and Piper are having movie night, I'll wonder how she is the next time a storm comes through. And I'll get that urge to fly again with nowhere to turn."

Jax fisted his hands at his sides because he wanted so badly to reach for her again. But he waited, listened, as she seemed to be working out her internal battle.

"Complicated is also right this moment," she went on, looking up at him. "I need to leave, but when I'm with you, I realize there's nowhere else I'd rather be. Not in my condo, not in the big city, and not even in my brand-new cushy office."

For the first time since she'd declared she was really leaving, a sliver of hope slid through him. But he remained silent and still.

"I'm scared," she whispered as she reached for him. Her fingers curled in his and she brought their joined hands between them. "What if I go and I'm miserable without you? What if I stay and wonder what it would've been like in the job I've always wanted?"

"The answer is simple," he told her. "Only you can know which one you want more. You'll have a career either place, but your lifestyle will be vastly different."

She glanced to the suit she'd tossed onto his desk. The feel of her delicate hands in his had him wanting to continue to hold tight and never let go.

"I've worked so hard to be a COO."

"I understand that," he replied, urging her closer until she fell against his chest. He disengaged their hands and wrapped his arms around her. "But know this: If you stay, you'll be the only COO here because I hate numbers and I don't want that title."

A slight smile formed on her lips.

"I told myself I wasn't going to ask you to stay because I wanted you to make up your own mind. But, damn it, Livie. I need you. I don't want to run this place without you. I don't want to do anything without you.

But if you need to go to Atlanta and figure things out, I won't stop you."

Her bright eyes brimming with unshed tears stared back at him. "I'm not sure leaving would make things more clear. I love you, Jax. Whether I'm here or there, that won't change."

Crushing her against his chest, he closed his eyes and inhaled her. "Finally," he murmured against her ear.

Her arms wrapped around him. "Will you still take the plane? Because it's kind of legally done and I don't have anywhere else to store it."

Jax laughed and eased back, framing her face between his hands. "I'll only take the plane if you're here to fly it."

"Are you sure about this?" she asked, worry lacing her voice. "You want me? You want us?"

He nipped at her lips. "Have I ever given you the impression I don't want you? I want the hell out of you and I don't just mean on this desk. I want you, I want us, I want a family."

Livie's eyes widened. "What will Piper say?"

"Considering she's been hinting again about a mommy, I'd say she'll be just fine with you staying in our lives."

"Is that what you want me to be? Piper's mommy?"

Happiness consumed him and he slid his mouth across hers, lifting her up off her feet. With his arms banded around her, Jax feathered off the kiss, but didn't put her back down.

"I want you as my wife first."

Livie smacked her lips to his. "If that's a proposal, then yes."

She kissed him again, then kissed across his jawline and up to his ear. "Are you going to clean off the desk or should I?" she whispered in his ear.

Jax's body stirred. "I think for this celebration, we need to go home."

"Which home?"

He eased her down and looked her in the eye. "Mine, ours."

"Take me home, Jax. And love me."

Lacing his fingers through hers, he tugged her toward the door. "Always."

Connect with Us

Visit us online at
KensingtonBooks.com
to read more from your favorite authors, see books
by series, view reading group guides, and more.

for sneak peeks, chances to win books and prize packs,
and to share your thoughts with other readers.

facebook.com/kensingtonpublishing
twitter.com/kensingtonbooks

Tell us what you think!

To share your thoughts, submit a review,
or sign up for our eNewsletters, please visit:
KensingtonBooks.com/TellUs.